
★

Detective Inspector Mott was confronted by a strangely familiar face. Grotesquely so, because when he had seen it before it had been vitally young, unheeding, eager for experience. And he had so nearly provided a part of that.

Sight of the dead girl was like an accusation. He knew he must declare involvement in the case, but surely not such great involvement that he'd need to be taken off it?

"Yes," he agreed somberly. "As it happens, I can put a name to her." No, to *it,* he thought, because this wasn't any longer the girl he'd touched, kissed, laughed with, coming home crushed together in the back seat of the red Porsche Cabriolet.

"Vroom. She called herself Anneke Vroom."

★

"(Curzon's) Thames Valley coppers are always interesting."

—*Kirkus Reviews*

"Nothing satisfies a mystery fan more than discovering a writer who can turn out a thoroughly entertaining puzzler...
Clare Curzon could be just such a discovery."

Also available from Worldwide Mystery by
CLARE CURZON

CAT'S CRADLE

Forthcoming from Worldwide Mystery by
CLARE CURZON

DEATH PRONE

CLARE CURZON

FIRST WIFE, TWICE REMOVED

WORLDWIDE®

TORONTO • NEW YORK • LONDON
AMSTERDAM • PARIS • SYDNEY • HAMBURG
STOCKHOLM • ATHENS • TOKYO • MILAN
MADRID • WARSAW • BUDAPEST • AUCKLAND

FIRST WIFE, TWICE REMOVED

A Worldwide Mystery/May 1995

First published by St. Martin's Press, Incorporated.

ISBN 0-373-26168-3

Printed in U.S.A.

FIRST WIFE,
TWICE REMOVED

ONE

DEATH VERY MUCH in the midst of life. The emergency call at 08.45 hours caught Superintendent Mike Yeadings in a plight uncommon to detectives of his maturity, young Sally's pick-up having failed to arrive, Nan sleeping late, pole-axed by a night of tending to baby Luke still howling with an ear infection.

Almost literally holding the baby, Yeadings noted the details sourly: body of a young woman found at her home in High Wycombe; DS Beaumont notified, but DI Mott on one day's leave, so should DCI Atkinson be called in?

'No,' he snapped. 'I'll go myself. Better send a car.' He pushed the phone back on the wall-bracket beside the bathroom door and returned to the cot, measured out a fresh 5ml dose of paracetamol syrup, dipped in a fingertip and popped it in the howling mouth.

There was a slight reduction in decibels and the toddler's lips puckered, moving against each other. 'Your favourite glop,' promised Yeadings and pushed in the plastic spoon before the next roar started.

With a more quietly sobbing baby on one shoulder, and holding Sally—in blazer crossed by packed satchel—with his other hand, he went downstairs. The minibus arrived as he was about to take the little girl next door.

'Sorry we're late, Mr Yeadings,' called the elderly woman driver. 'Jimmy had unhappy returns of his breakfast. Had to stop for some mopping-up.'

He handed Sally in to an overpowering smell of disinfectant and waved the busload off.

In the long mirror of the hall he glimpsed his paternal figure shambling past, diminished by domestic crises. 'Villains, tremble!' he commanded and grinned ruefully. But, for all that, he felt the professional stirring within him.

The complex reaction was alerted: a profound inborn distaste for all aspects of violence, and at the same time an exciting of the senses at the promise of a puzzle, an animal keenness on scenting the prey. Softy and predator: so many men inside us, he thought, not for the first time. Part of the human condition: to become something different, from one moment to the next.

On the job he wasn't a total rationalist. A genetic echo of his old Welsh granny, supposedly the last of a long line of Wise Women, made him oscillate in the presence of mysteries. A moonlit moor, with the bulky silhouettes of his experts dark against the floodlights; the rites of Scenes-of-Crime; it linked him with dark and ancient practices.

A quite separate part of him reached for a carton of orange juice in the fridge and filled Luke's favourite beaker with the perforated spout. The child's hot hands closed round the plastic and it went into his mouth with a moist plop, stifling a sob. Sobs now, not screams, but if Mike attempted to lay the child down ...

And then mercifully Nan was in the doorway, pushing back tangled hair from her eyes. 'I'll take him now. Was that the phone I heard through my dreams? Sorry, love. I was fathoms deep.'

Which was the moment the car arrived, saving him time as he hadn't to get out the Rover, allowing him to sit back, draw breath, get his tie from under one ear and orange juice off his cuff, make the final transition from Jekyll to Hyde. Or, perhaps, in his case from Hyde I to Hyde II: demon father to necrophiliac.

The morning streets rolled steadily past. Don't be so bloody fanciful, he told himself. Come down to earth. Yours is a job like any other.

AND AGAIN DEATH in the midst of life; this time at the end house of a dowdy Victorian terrace. One built round a staircase with two fair-sized rooms to each landing and, at the rear, a mezzanine bathroom above a jutting semi-basement kitchen. The front ground-floor windows were boarded up. Old, defaced posters showed it had once been local party headquarters for one of those minor-nuisance political movements. Provocative enough for someone to have thrown a brick through the glass, but now those tenants had moved on, to reform the world elsewhere.

He nodded at the uniformed constable guarding the front door and went through. The steep staircase facing him had brown vinyl strips tacked over the treads. Yeadings wondered if the people living here were tenants or part of a squat.

The body—before well-intentioned interference from a neighbour—had been lying head downwards on the short flight above the bathroom, and a rough chalk outline showed its presumed position. A dark pool of vomit had been partially cleared from the steps below. A recurrent theme of that morning, it seemed.

'Where—?'

'Through here, sir.' Detective-Sergeant Beaumont, sharp nose perkily jutting from flat, Pinocchio face, indicated the bathroom behind him. Inside, there wasn't enough space for two healthy men, with the dead woman spread out along-side the bath. This last was a genuine old iron one with lion's claw feet, free-standing, no integral soap-dish, no surrounding tiles. Yeadings itemized the room: bath, basic, white; green loo and basin of more recent vintage; walls of pitted ochre distemper with childish crayon scribblings; sash window with frosted glass and a sunburst crack in the lower right-hand pane. It had been opened wide in a vain attempt to remove the stench on the stairs.

Lastly, the body itself: ah yes—female, quite young; now turned face upwards; grubby nightdress partly covered by tatty nylon wrapper; feet bare; wedding ring on left hand. The woman's face, made grotesque by the manner of her death, would otherwise have had the cute rodent look of the sharp-featured young. Now the lips were drawn back to reveal two long central incisors slightly overlapping. Between them, near the gum, was a fleck of bright red that might be lipstick or blood. The eyes were closed. Ivor Venner, the police surgeon on call, had officially confirmed death and gone on his way to serve the living, leaving a verbal complaint that the body had been moved before his arrival.

'There are two kids,' complained Beaumont. 'A neighbour's got them next door. The older one, aged four, found her mother and ran out into the street. Nearly went under a car. WDC Zyczynski's with them now.'

'Then I'll join them. The SOCOs will be cramped enough in here without me. They'll need to fix up more light.'

A second salute from the uniformed man as Yeadings stepped over a low wall to reach the neighbour's door. Stairs led upwards as in the first house, but to the right a stretch of patterned orange Vynoleum and the smell of frying bacon pointed him towards a rear kitchen. There a plump black woman stood at a table buttering sliced baps to fill as burgers. On the carpet behind her two white children sat cross-legged beside an almost spherical black baby nursed on the lap of Rosemary Zyczynski, DS Beaumont's partner.

'Hello there,' said Yeadings in general.

'Morning, sir,' Rosemary answered for the others who merely stared. 'This is my boss, Mr Yeadings.'

The black woman nodded. ''Mornin' sir, I'm Sister Barbour. Goin' to see they get somethun good and nourishun inside them before I go off to work. Come on, kids. Up to table or have it down there, it's all the same to me, but don't gobble or it don't do you any good.'

She had to leave in half an hour to relieve duty sister at a nearby home for old folks. 'Eight-hour shifts, and I'm on eight till four,' she announced. 'Only I rang in, and Nancy'll stay put till ten, just so's I can see the kids through here till a social worker comes.'

'That's very kind of you. And when did you know something was wrong next door?'

'Jest as I was leavun. Lordy, that child came out like the devil was after her. Don't ever again want to see anythun as near an accident as that. So I sat her down on the wall and she starts yellun that her Ma's sick and fallen on the stairs. Well, me bein' a nurse, even though the lady's not what you'd call a close friend of mine—'

'You went straight in to see what could be done.'

'Well, saw at once it wasn't any use. All the same, you gotta try's what I say. Collected the kids' clothes and brought the little one out.' She threw a significant toss of the head in the children's direction, meant to caution him to discretion.

'How about me giving you a lift to work when you're ready?' Yeadings suggested. 'Would you let our policewoman here see to locking up after the children are collected?'

'Why not? Little enough here for any burglar to take, Lord knows. Have to drop off Marigold at the crèche first, if that's OK? Hey, you, Ginny there, why're you not eatun your lovely burger? Come on, now, your little sister's gonna be done before you're started.'

And so on and so forth, Yeadings thought, with the cheerful generous woman overriding the ugly drama of death such a little time and space away, so that the youngsters might, even briefly, forget a horror printed on their inner minds forever.

She sat with him in the back of the car jigging on her knee the contented baby, huge-eyed in a hideous pink bonnet, and confided everything she knew about Ms Penny Winter, deceased, her late next-door neighbour.

'Sure she has a husband, only I never seen him close. They only come here coupla weeks back and it's my belief the gennleman has another roof to live under. Anyway some man helped them move in and then he was off like hornets were after him. Brought her bits and pieces in a plain van. Must've hired it, I guess, because he sure wasn't any mover's man.'

'Did you ever speak to Mrs Winter?'

'Very next day, over the back fence. She was shiftun some junk in the yard there to make room for the kids to play. Offered to help her lift the stuff. She coulda hurt her back, reachun down and not bendun her knees like we're taught to. You'da thought I'd called her a bad name or somethun. Well, I told myself, someday she'll need me and I sure can wait for that. But I seen her times enough from our upstairs window. Joe an' me we rent the two bottom floors. Attics belong to the old fella owns the place.'

'If you don't speak with your neighbour, how did you know she had a husband?'

'Because the health visitor came about the kids and she wouldn't let her in. Stood at the door and shouted that she should go and have it out with her husband, if she could find him.'

'The health visitor should find the husband?'

'That's what the lady said. Then she slammed the door and later I heard her cryun. Mebbe I shoulda gone in then, only who asks for trouble?'

'There's certainly enough without. So how did you know what her name was?'

'Got some post delivered through the wrong door. Jes' the one letter, for Ms Penny Winter, number 28. We're 26. So I put it through her letter-box. And I've heard her calling the kids in from the garden. Ginny and Miranda. That's all I know for sure, Mr Yeadings.'

For sure: there was almost an invitation there. She had observed more and had opinions on it, but she wasn't going to gossip unless he asked for it. Well, he could wait. He'd seen the dead woman from close at hand and he'd taken a look at the place where she'd lived for two weeks. He could guess this Sister Barbour had picked up much the same impressions as himself.

'Well, thank you for your help,' he said as, having delivered the baby, she prepared to alight herself. 'By the way, are you a qualified nursing sister?'

Mrs Barbour stood very straight. 'I'm a qualified nurse, sir. But I'm also a sister of the Glorious Mission of The Risen Lord Christ, in Desborough Lane. *Halleluiah!*'

We all have our little deceptions, Yeadings admitted to himself, smiling. He watched the woman march righteously away, a little heavy on the heels, and he guessed the old folks she looked after would be allowed few airs and graces, but they'd be fond of her and with reason. She needn't feel any guilt at having failed her neighbour. The dead woman had made it clear that her affairs were no concern of Sister Barbour's.

'Nor possibly of mine,' he conceded. The death looked accidental; fatal fall aggravated by food poisoning. Whether of chemical or bacterial origin, the post mortem would later reveal. The children were lucky to have escaped eating whatever had killed their mother. All moves now lay with the Public Health Department and whichever agency was delegated to trace the missing husband. Yeadings hoped this case wasn't the first of a major outbreak of illness from contaminated shop food.

THERE WAS PAPERWORK stacked waiting in the superintendent's office, then he was due at Kidlington for a statistics session with the ACC Operations, the hour chosen to allow an informal discussion first over lunch in the mess. There was plenty of material to work on and it was after five that he cleared the contra-flow rush-hour traffic to park again behind his office. News of his return produced WDC Rosemary Zyczynski, entrusted with Beaumont's typed notes on the morning's sudden death.

Yeadings shed his jacket. 'Let's get some coffee perking first, eh? Is Beaumont at the post mortem?'

'No, sir. PM's not until tomorrow morning, so that will be DI Mott's treat. DS Beaumont has to attend court then for the Townsend committal.'

'So where is he now?'

'Chasing up the dead woman's husband through Social Services.'

Yeadings looked ostentatiously at his watch. 'Not unless civil servants have changed their working habits. Give him a bell at home. Say I'll see him here tomorrow at eight-thirty.'

'Ring now, sir?'

'Right now.'

He waited while the woman DC phoned through and woodenly withstood the inevitable banter, wordlessly putting across the fact that Authority was within earshot.

'And you can tell him that I just this minute got back,' Beaumont concluded righteously.

'Any success?' Yeadings asked over his shoulder, then started to fill two coffee cups.

'Mrs Winter was divorced, having a bit of trouble over arrears of maintenance. The husband seems to have gone to earth.'

'Then he'll have to be dug out, if only because of the children. We've nothing new there. I take it you have some follow-up on the death. What are the chances of it not being accidental?'

Rosemary accepted the cup and found a space for it beside her notes. 'It's complicated. Unofficially the cause of death could be one of two things. Some kind of poisoning, or a broken neck.'

'Broken neck?' Yeadings stared at the policewoman. 'Who says she had a broken neck? Beaumont didn't quote Dr Venner to me on that.'

'I don't know what Dr Venner confided. I was next door.'

'So what are you going on? Ah, a diagnosis volunteered by "Sister" Barbour, I take it? Was she the one who moved the body?'

'She said it felt cool, but not cold. When she turned the shoulders the head rolled back. The eyes were open. She saw then that the woman was dead.'

'Only a doctor can actually state death has occurred, Z.'

'Yessir. But Mrs Barbour observed there was no pulse, and breathing had ceased. Since she had to get the younger child down the stairs and out of the house she removed the woman's body to the nearby bathroom.'

'I see. So, pre-empting the official findings, we need to know what the woman ate to upset her, and then who, if anyone, was with her when she fell/was pushed on the stairs.'

'Only six stairs to the half-landing,' Rosemary said thoughtfully, 'If I'd meant to kill her that way I'd have sent her down the lower flight.'

'But she was vomiting, heading for the bathroom, not running out of the house. Or was she? Being chased and fell, broke her neck, *then* vomited?'

'Running to or running from,' Rosemary appreciated. 'It must have happened in the early hours, with the little girls still asleep. They never mentioned any visitor that evening, but then they hardly said anything, except for Ginny going on about Mummy being sick on the stairs.'

'You'll need to talk to her tomorrow. I take it they've been taken into care?'

'Yes, together. I have the address.'

'That older girl, Ginny. She's only four, but apparently she ran out into the street in her night clothes. So how did she get the front door open? Wasn't it kept locked?'

'Mrs Barbour found it open when she went in. There was a kitchen stool lying on its side in the hall. She thought Ginny must have dragged it downstairs, then used it to climb up and pull back the lock.'

'Struggling over her mother's body on the way. Poor little scrap.'

'Kept her head. It was afterwards she went to pieces.'

'A wretched business. Let's hope it's a straightforward accident—a fall while weakened by some form of bacterial food poisoning. No doubt the Public Health people will be quick looking into the samples taken.'

'In case it wasn't an accident, the SOCO team have covered everything.'

'Good, and tomorrow Angus will be back, so he'll take over.'

TWO

EVEN WITHOUT the frosting effect of the refrigerated drawers which reached out for the marrow of the living, the whole atmosphere of the place with its white lights, pallid slabs and gleaming chrome—not to mention the gruesomely functional guttering and drainage—so chilled Angus Mott that he was disinclined to part with his raincoat.

Littlejohn on the other hand was stripped for action, shirtsleeves rolled up, head in a white cotton cap, front covered with a stiff green plastic apron. He held his latex-gloved hands hygienically at shoulder level, as though he were a surgeon about to go for living tissue. Well, there must be parts of the body that were clinically still alive: hair and nails went on growing in the grave.

The mortuary attendant, a hyper-dignified old-young man, had previously taken blood for analysis. Now he stepped forward and at a nod from the pathologist made the long, clean incision from throat to pubic bone. As if he had completed conducting a concert overture he stood back, seemed to bow, reached out to activate the tape recorder and gave way to the solo instrumentalist.

There was a slight shuffling sound from the other two policemen present as each settled to his own way of coping with the need to be present. The Coroner's Officer, his eyes distantly fixed on the porthole windows of the swing doors, was sucking persistently at some meaty thread caught between his front teeth. His face had assumed the expression of a choirboy at sermon-time who wishes it known he has no truck with all this rubbish and is only here for the money.

Every few minutes he would glance dutifully at the corpse to ensure it was still the one he'd first viewed *in situ*.

The beat policeman, originally called in by Sister Barbour—a green-neck who seemed barely old enough to have left school—looked stiff and startlingly pale under his freckles and ginger hair. If the odds hadn't been so high on this being an accidental death, Mott reflected, Division would have pulled in half a dozen more poor buggers to toughen their stomach muscles.

Right, Mott told himself; think of something else until there are hard facts to be made use of. Concentrate, perhaps, on Paula's performance yesterday at the Old Bailey. She'd looked nervously sick herself when he'd first glimpsed her from the public benches, but once the case was under way she became aware only of the evidence as it was presented, the challenge of the job itself.

It was an unfamiliar facet to the girl he loved, somehow daunting. Then he'd begun to feel the case forming up, started responding to it as if he were personally involved, but from habit on the opposing side. Accustomed to grinding his teeth as he saw the defence deviously parrying the main thrust of the prosecution, he found himself now pulled in both directions.

Unable to take more than one day off, he'd been deprived of the sequel. Paula would eventually tell him which way the verdict went. But that wasn't enough. He needed to see her every move, and watch each blow delivered by the opposing barrister, a smug, squat fellow Mott had wanted to grind underfoot.

'Aha!' trumpeted Littlejohn, deep in heaving bloody squelch.

'Something interesting?' Mott managed to sound casually curious. He watched without relish as the pathologist slopped crimson offal into a waiting steel bowl.

'Stomach, etcetera.' He sounded delighted, as if such a presence in the corpse had been an unexpected bonus. 'Not entirely empty either. Well, press on, shall we?'

Angus Mott drew in a generous breath, slowly, lest he should be thought suffering from nausea. Back to considering Paula's career: scope enough there for distraction. He'd have to examine it from her viewpoint, not his own.

It was a fortnight ago that they'd spent that weekend at Chardleigh Place, a weekend of which he'd expected so much, and which had turned into a near-disaster. Because—to be fair to himself—he wasn't prepared for what was coming and he'd had little practice at turning the other cheek. And mad at her as he'd been, he was no woman-beater, so he'd taken it out on her by acting awkward and subsequently wasn't all that proud of his behaviour.

His presence yesterday in court had been partly an act of penance, partly a sop to her vanity, the bunch of roses after the row. Only, having seen her in the throes, he knew now there was a dimension to their relationship he hadn't taken full account of: she was as fully committed to her work as he was to his own. It looked as though he'd some book-balancing still to do in his own mind.

So recap, seeing with her eyes how things went wrong. Not easy, that. Paula is a woman: it makes her different.

IT WAS LESS A QUESTION of how than of when, Paula had told herself. The manner of approach must be direct: she and Angus had never been devious. There would be no point in it, since their times together were so rare and so brief. Deviousness was a necessary spice only for lovers with jaded palates.

So, when to tell him? In the car on their way? At the end of dinner when both were at their most relaxed? Never in bed. But if too soon, would they even reach that desirable stage? Because Angus wasn't going to like it. Under his sunny exterior lurked a load of male pride due to take a considerable wallop.

He must have sensed her dilemma, because at the traffic lights he glanced sideways and put a hand over her own. 'Something wrong?'

'Not wrong, no.' She allowed him to rejoin the moving line of cars before adding, 'A complication, that's all.'

'Forget it. We've two whole days to enjoy simple things. Monday comes all too soon.'

Only it wasn't a workaday complication but a question of choosing the moment, and there just wasn't going to be a right one. Whenever she spoke out, it would spoil what must come after. But if she delayed too long she'd feel that much more in the wrong. Guilty over keeping him cheerfully in ignorance, not over what she had to say. The essential was that they should find a moment alone together, without interruption.

Once they'd been shown to their room, the two cases set down side by side, Angus couldn't ignore that something was off-key. Paula should have been blissfully bouncing to test the bed springs, flinging the windows wide and waltzing him across the floor. Instead she started to unpack; serious, bending over the folded clothes with her lovely face anonymously hidden by the trailing wings of dark hair.

He stood behind her and challenged ruefully, 'Hadn't you better break it to me?'

She straightened, crumpling a silk dressing-robe between her hands. 'I'm afraid of spoiling everything.'

'*Everything?* God, is it that bad?'

She turned to face him. 'Spoiling our weekend, I mean. You aren't going to like this, Angus. Old Wheatman has asked me to stay on as his junior. I've said I'll give him my answer on Monday.'

'I see.' She could recognize that he did, and it hurt her to be hurting him.

'And you've already decided on it.'

'It's a great compliment that he asked me. Another two years working mainly at the Bailey, sometimes handling my own cases. I may never get such a chance again. And I do like defence work.'

'I thought you'd opted for the Crown Prosecution Service. I thought—in a few months—you'd be finalizing it.'

'And joining you in Thames Valley, so we'd both be working from the same side. Yes, all of that. I thought so too. But this is something unexpected, a chance I just can't turn down if I take my work seriously.'

'You'd turn me down instead. Is that it?'

'You know it's not like that.' Her voice went low, 'Unless you ever want it that way.'

'What I want hasn't come into it yet.'

'Look, I know you're hating the idea. I'm sorry too that we shan't be together as soon as we'd hoped—'

'Shan't be married by Christmas. Simply put it on ice, eh? Just like that?'

'Angus, I love you.'

'Love the Law a bit more, though. God, passed over for the Old Bailey, that's rich!'

She waited for him to laugh, even bitterly, then take her in his arms, but when he didn't, standing there beleaguered, hands thrust deep in pockets as though he willed them not to respond to her need, she pulled her toilet bag from the case and moved away across the room.

'I'd better wash my hair. Shan't be long.'

When she emerged from the bathroom she saw only his back. His case was still packed and he was leaning from the open window with his hands on the outer sill. As she came close he stood up and looked solemnly at her, then deliber-

ately took her in his arms and kissed her. She clung almost
desperately but, as if he was doing it by numbers, he disen-
gaged himself and held her at arms' length, studying her
face.

She endured it humbly. 'I haven't changed,' she said. 'I'm
still the same me.'

'Well, something's changed.'

'I haven't given Wheatman my answer yet.'

At last he was angry. 'You want me to beg you to change
your mind? That's smart! Shift the onus, then never let me
forget that I ruined your career?'

'No! If we were already married it would be different,
Angus, but just two years more—before we give the rest of
our lives to each other. Is that too much to ask? If it's really me you want, can't you wait? If it's just marriage—and
in the meantime you find someone else—well, I wouldn't
hold you to our engagement. It wouldn't be fair. It's a risk
I hate taking, but don't you see, I have a hard choice to
make, and that one would be yours.'

He faced her grimly, resenting that she called all the
moves. God, he had thought Paula was above this battle of
the sexes stupidity, but here she was doling out the old cli-
ché conflicts—lib v. love, career before home, management
versus man—like any cheap women's magazine. And how
did she expect him to take it? Snarl and storm off into the
night? Or start in right now saying 'Yes, dear,' and making
a career of that for himself? But one thing was sure: he'd be
damned if he'd allow her to turn it into grand opera.

He switched on his deadpan policeman's face. 'Well, we'll
just have to see, won't we?' he told her. 'Is the water hot
enough for a bath, would you say?'

FROM THE TERRACE below she waved to him as, dressed
again, he leaned from the bedroom window. He pointed

downwards, but inside the hotel, not towards the gardens. She rearranged the lacy shawl about her bare shoulders and walked on towards the lake, exchanging a comment or two with the ducks before coming in. Denied more palatable tidbits, they tired of it before she did.

She found Angus perched on a bar stool alongside a man in a pale grey suit, pink shirt, cyclamen tie. In the barman's absence they were being served by a tall blonde in a yellow cellular sports shirt unbuttoned to reveal a generous cleavage.

Give them a break, Paula warned herself, recognizing her own symptoms of frustration. The girl had probably come from a brisk game of squash and was lending a hand before showering off. The man's outfit had possibly been wedding-guest gear and now had to stand in for country club weekends. She glanced at the face above it. Thirtyish, fine pinky complexion a trifle wind-burnt; large, pale blue eyes with liquid appeal; high, slightly bulbous forehead with thin light brown hair starting to recede; small, quite ridiculous moustache; childish mouth; insignificant chin. Queen Victoria's Albert scaled down with a Julius Caesar haircut.

He was smiling at her winningly. Or that was the intention. She looked up at Angus and left her own smile to explain she wasn't available.

'I didn't order your drink,' Angus said. 'I thought you might want something different for a change.' Wryly challenging. Well, yes, she did get the point.

'White wine would suit me, thanks. Dry or medium.'

'Just arrived?' asked the man in the pale grey suit. 'Thought I hadn't spotted you both among our lot.'

'Our lot?'

'Sorry, thought you'd know. They must have taken the notices down. Joint training and conference session, Cosmos Assurance. An intensive five-day Communication

and Selection course, ending up with the trainees inter-
viewing mock applicants for jobs. Outsiders, the last-
mentioned—and a right rum crowd in some respects.'

'Instructive experience all round,' Angus assumed.

The other man showed an expanse of white teeth.

'They have lecture hall facilities here, then?' Paula inquired.

'VDUs, film projectors, fax, intercom, everything it
takes,' the blonde interrupted, spilling herself happily over
the counter. She might have been more revealing had not the
barman come marching back then and nodded her off-
scene. He did some smart cloth-flicking along the counter-
top and whisked two small dishes of salted nuts between his
three customers. He knew better than to ask questions,
busying himself polishing glasses, stationed where he'd have
access to whatever conversation ensued.

'Another of the same for me,' said Angus, pushing his
tankard along the bar. 'Not ready yet, Paula? How about
you, er—?'

'Coleman,' said the other quickly. 'Arnold Coleman.' He
seemed torn by the invitation. 'Got to make a call,' he regretted. 'Another time, maybe? I'll be around. Staying on
a couple more days.'

The two men nodded to each other and Coleman slid
from his stool, smiled brightly at Paula and went out.

'Like the place?' Angus asked Paula, his upper lip wet
with foam from his fresh beer.

'As far as I've seen. The gardens are lovely, and there's
even a lake and a little putting green. Everything inside looks
brand new. How did you get to hear of it?'

'Oh, the subject came up at work.' His voice was so casual that she glanced at him quickly. Chardleigh Place an
object of police interest? Did that mean that their precious
weekend had an ulterior purpose, *Detective-Inspector* An-

gus Mott of Thames Valley CID here undercover, with herself thrown in as unclaimable expenses?

She caught the brief gleam of amusement that broke through his hitherto wooden expression and was reassured.

'It only opened in March, so they've yet to make their reputation, one way or the other. Combined country club, hotel and conference centre within twenty miles of Heathrow. If the catering's good it should do well. I thought we both deserved a really relaxed few days, overworked as we are,' he explained. 'More or less on our doorstep, too. Mine, anyway. And a rural retreat from your Temple Chambers.'

That should settle the barman's curiosity, Paula noted. Now he could write them off as a couple of legal eaglets on an amorous adventure. She wondered casually who their fellow guests would be and how anxiously the management probed backgrounds with an eye to recommendation.

'Cosmos Assurance were quick off their marks,' she commented, sipping her wine. She turned towards the barman's corner. 'Have you had many companies interested in conference facilities?'

'Yes, miss. Erskine's Bank was the first, then a couple of airlines for training sessions. Getting nicely booked up, I understand. There's a suite of offices along with the two lecture rooms, all modern equipment. Mr Long'd be glad to show you round if you ask him. Our sales manager, that is.'

'So what was it before?' Angus asked. 'The main wing's eighteenth century, I'd say.'

'Well, a family home first, up till after the First World War, then a private nursing home, but it was empty for some ten years before this company took it over. The redevelopment's still not finished. There's a covered pool to come and a bistro in what's left of the stables. That's when the big advertising campaign starts. Until then we're only half-staffed.'

'Let's go and look round before the light goes,' Angus suggested and, as they strolled out on the terrace, mused, 'Erskine's Bank and Cosmos Assurance among their first commercial customers; not difficult to guess who actually owns the place, is it? Still, if it's well run they can't miss.'

They explored the nearer grounds, thought better of launching an ancient punt moored among the reeds, and circled the lake on foot for only a quarter of its circumference before dusk and wild undergrowth made the going too hard for Paula's shoes. They returned by way of a walled vegetable and fruit garden which promised well for fresh produce for the table. Back in the cobbled stable yard which did duty for a car park Angus unlocked his MG and took a flashlight from under the dashboard.

As they moved away a car turned in and drew up alongside. While the young detective-inspector's eyes took in the sleek lines of the scarlet Porsche Cabriolet its driver's door opened and Arnold Coleman stepped out.

'Admiring the bus? Nice little job, isn't she? 2990cc. The blurb claims she'll do 149mph, but maybe that's just teasing, to make you squeeze that final mile and get even figures. Thought I'd better bring her round from the front. Don't want to excite any envious natives. Friday night, so there'll probably be quite a crowd in for dinner.'

In the powder room off the galleried hall Paula found a group of women busy at the mirrors. As a cubicle became free behind them she stepped forward.

'Hey, that's mine!' Her way was barred by the tall blonde who had served their drinks, still in the skimpy black waitress's skirt but topped now by a pink silk blouse.

She turned back with a slow smile for Paula. 'I've become much more assertive since I've come here,' she said proudly.

There seemed no fit reply to this except to observe that yes, you could get that way if you weren't careful. Paula, however, wasn't one to spat with strangers. She raised an eyebrow and nodded her forward. 'After you, then.'

Outside, the two men were still talking cars. Somehow, without any invitation being made or accepted, they found themselves ushered into the restaurant as a threesome to a good window position. Not until he was seated did Arnold Coleman look up round-eyed and exclaim, 'I say, maybe you two would rather be on your own?'

Without attempting to rise he gazed from one to the other until Paula allowed, 'Not at all. Nice to have you join us.'

With a quizzical glance Angus handed her the menu and leaned back expansively. 'Extra diversions always welcome.'

And in the event the man came up to scratch, covering up for any awkward silences, and entertaining them with anecdotes from his experiences in insurance adjustment—clients' cons, and tricks of the trade he'd acquired in foiling the same.

Despite her earlier prejudice against the man Paula found herself smiling at his patter and seconded his suggestion that his 'friend Anneke' should join them for coffee.

This just had to be the pushy blonde from the powder room, and by the time she had caught his signal, slid into the vacant fourth chair and accepted a filter coffee, Paula recognized why the voice had seemed unusual.

Anneke was from the Netherlands; near Hilversum, she told them. It was the slightly singsong melody that was so distinctive rather than the accent, which was near-perfect. Angus complimented her on having almost passed for a native product.

'You British never learn languages properly,' she complained, 'because you expect us others to do all the work.

We Dutch are very hard-working, which is also why I am happy to help out here. I am not regular hotel staff, you know.' She threw up her bare arms, passing the long-fingered hands under her mane of Pre-Raphaelite frizz to toss it forward over her shoulders. Having ascertained that all attention was properly focused she panned a wide, dazzling smile.

If she wasn't hotel staff, she didn't, Paula noted, specify exactly what she was. Believably good at it, whatever; but demure she clearly was not. However, as Angus had said, diversions were welcome, this evening if never before. Perhaps by the end of it he would be in a more amenable mood, at least used to the idea of her own changed plans if not actually approving them.

From coffee they progressed, still in a foursome, to the billiards room where they found one of the two tables free and set up for snooker. 'Gals against boys?' Coleman queried. 'Or toss for partners?'

'Why don't we swap ladies?' Angus suggested, adding with mock innocence, 'Just for a change.'

The men were above average players, Coleman possibly with a slight edge on Angus who built up steady breaks but missed out on the wizard shots. Arnold played flashily, had clearly had more practice but lacked concentration. Paula's own game had only developed since she'd been occasionally included in groups at the local club favoured by her Chambers.

Anneke, swearing she'd never handled a cue before, needed arms held round her to guide her aim. This involved a certain amount of tickling and whinnying, after which badly muffled shots were declared null and void while the ball was replaced to 'get it right this time'.

Unsurprisingly the Coleman-Paula's side won by three frames to one, qualifying to pay for the final round of drinks. Since Arnold was demonstrating triple-cushion potting when these arrived, Paula signed the chit with her shared room number. It struck her that if Angus had finally to settle, it was only true to a form already established for the evening. Drinks had indeed flowed like water, and now Anneke, who had stuck to fruit juice, suddenly declared a preference for champagne.

'Oh, I say,' Coleman protested at last over his winking brim, 'shouldn't this have been my round? Tell you what, chaps, I'll take you all out tomorrow. Picnic's on me, bubbly, the lot. Run you all down to Portland. Got to see a man about a boat beached at Chesil. What d'you say?'

'What kind of boat?' Angus demanded, already half-hooked on recalling the Porsche Cabriolet.

'Thirty-foot sailing vessel with auxiliary engine. There's a claim been raised on it after a fire in the galley. Query a spot of arson.'

Since their sailing holiday of a year ago, anything that had a hull, mast and sails exercised a magnetic pull on Angus. He looked up now like a puppy promised walkies. 'Paula?'

'If you'd really like to go.'

'Great,' said Angus. 'Something to look forward to.' For the moment he seemed convincingly restored, as if she'd never done anything to spoil their weekend together. It was just a pity that she hadn't restored his good humour herself. It had taken two strangers, a high-tech car and the promise of a trip to sea. And a hell of a lot more booze than either of them normally took on, she conceded.

But he was stifling a yawn now and had muzzily put around her the arm he'd previously been hooking under Anneke's bust to steady her cue. Time at last for bed. And she did love him anyway.

THREE

THE CONSTANT FLOW of commentary from Littlejohn into the mike clipped to his apron front was full of highly technical jargon. Many of the terms had become familiar to Mott over the years as he stood by at such undelectable proceedings, but he knew that the final summary would be couched in language a policeman with only a modicum of anatomical knowledge might be expected to understand. Until this was available he merely noted that what the next-door neighbour had confided to Rosemary Zyczynski seemed borne out. There was a broken neck, there had been severe vomiting. The newcomer to the list of ills was vagal inhibition—and that was probably the actual killer.

Littlejohn had by now emptied the dead woman's chest, abdominal and cranial cavities. The neck flesh had been peeled back to reveal something like the intricacies laid bare when British Telecom open up a complicated commercial switchboard. Except that BT are spared the gore.

The pathologist waved his assistant in to take over, plodded to the sluice where he ran water over his arms and finally removed the gloves with a pair of stretchy *plops*. 'Right, we can let the lady rest for the moment. As to the cause of vomiting, it's a question of waiting for chemical analysis and seeing what further cultures can be grown from specimens taken. Maybe you'd just sign the book, Angus. Let Authority know we opened the right body, eh? What's the personal history behind this one, then?'

Mott moved his weight from one stiffening leg to the other and back. 'Not a lot known yet. A recent divorcée.

Two small children, both girls. The husband seems to have done a runner and there's maintenance owing.'

'Say no more,' said the pathologist with a grimace. 'That sort of thing upsets my stomach.'

Mott followed him into the ante-room, unsure whether the man was being ironic or saving the policemen's faces by pretending kindred squeamishness. By the door Littlejohn turned and paddled with both hands, palms down. 'Tell Mike Yeadings there's still no more than a fifty-fifty chance it's a job for him. Time alone will tell.'

'I have to ask *how* long,' Mott reminded him.

'Same question, same answer every time.' The pathologist shrugged, turned away. 'As soon as we're ready you'll know. You can't hustle petri dishes.'

Because he mustn't overlook the possibility of a genuine case of bacterial food poisoning. Meanwhile, Mott thought, we go on digging into background, just in case. Maybe Beaumont's had better luck with Social Services and turned up the husband's whereabouts. Eight out of ten solved murder cases were domestics, and this set-up had a number of the required ingredients.

DS BEAUMONT HAD BEEN kept hanging around at the Magistrates' Court, the Townsend committal hearing having been shoved down the list because the defence lawyer had mislaid his papers. It was only a charge of demanding money with menaces, but they'd been a long time getting anything on the man which would stick sufficiently to reach Crown Court, and there'd be hell to pay if he wriggled out of this.

The brief sent in by the Crown Prosecution Service looked still wet behind the ears. There were three magistrates on the bench this morning, but one was a trusting old bat who seemed to think that any defendant on oath must be telling the truth. She'd already worked on the other two to bind over a dairyman proved guilty of adulterating milk, and now she was cooing sympathetically towards a case of common assault.

In disgust Beaumont slid out into the corridor and made for his car where he'd stashed some cans of cola. He radioed back a no-progress report, swallowed some drink, stowed the can, took a leak and returned to find the usher clucking over his late appearance as arresting officer.

Mrs Busby wasn't as sympathetic to guardians of the peace as she was to law-breakers, and he had to endure a few sour words on the standards expected of him. Fortunately the defence brief's delays had equally needled the two men on the bench (or they'd had their fill for that morning of Mrs B) and they promptly found that there was a case to answer. Townsend was to be released on bail pending presentation of his case at Crown Court.

At least that one thing was achieved, Beaumont reflected, and he'd managed to avoid the post mortem on the Winter woman, but DI Mott would expect him to have caught up with the missing husband by now.

He tried to reach Wycombe Social Services by phone but, as ever, the lines were engaged, so he ended by going in person and struggling to cut through the waiting crowds. When eventually he reached someone senior enough to accept that a warrant card didn't damn him out of hand he learned that the late Ms Winter had, in fact, been a Mrs Gardner who reverted to her maiden name after the divorce. She'd been transferred from her previous address at Colchester but some papers were missing, so details weren't available.

Well, unless the Essex constabulary had succumbed to the general clerical slackness of the day, Beaumont hoped to get something from that end. He'd return to base, grab some food, have a word with Mott and then settle down to a chit-chat session with his counterpart in Colchester.

From there he learned that the Gardners had no criminal record, but a patrol car had visitcd the house some five weeks back, the call initiated by a neighbour complaining of a brawl. A routine domestic, and no charges made. On receiving a warning the divorced man left and drove off.

He had been making an unexpected visit after an absence of months. The argument had started over money, what else? Her wastefulness; his tardy payments; bills accumulating; mortgage arrears; plus the tatty state of the house which was due to be repossessed. There had been no cause to breathalyse the man; purely a case of spleen, whether justified or not.

Despite the beginnings of a black eye, the woman wouldn't file a complaint; the little girls were weepy at being noisily roused from their beds. The beat policeman had stated that all remained quiet for the remainder of that week. He hadn't reported that they'd moved from the area because he hadn't known. No change of address had been notified.

'I'd like him to ring me,' Beaumont requested, but the man was off duty so it would mean a wait for further information. The only new details were the ex-husband's full name and occupation: Ronald Walter Gardner, car salesman. The house had been a semi-detached on a post-war private housing estate where disturbances were relatively uncommon.

The lack of background meant that someone would have to look up records of the divorce to discover the woman's solicitor, a chore he could pass to Zyczynski. The maiden name of Winter might also ring a bell with Colchester police and help turn up any family in the locality. It still looked more like a job for Social Services than CID, but Beau-

mont couldn't get out of his mind the two blank-faced little
girls and the helpless way they had looked towards WDC
Zyczynski when the Children's Officer arrived to take them
away. The sooner they were back in family care instead of
entered as statistics, the happier everyone would be.

'WHAT DO YOU THINK?' DI Angus Mott demanded when he
reported. 'Anything sinister in that domestic fracas?'

Beaumont shrugged. 'Happens all the time. Tempers flare
up. Neighbours a bit too keen to jump the gun probably.
Then she moves to Thames Valley when the house is repossessed. Husband again fades into the mist. I'll go and have
another look at the flat. If there's nothing there suggesting
suspicious circumstances we can scrub this one, I think.
Somebody else's worry.'

'Interview Gardner when he does turn up, just in case the
lab finds something fishy. Now, to more urgent matters, this
reported cache of firearms at Datchet. It's very vague, and
Special Branch have been tasked, but we'd better put a couple of men in there to help, see what they can sniff out. It's
a decent little place on the surface, but a damn sight too near
Windsor for us to take any risks with terrorists.'

'How about the informant?'

'Anonymous, so it could be a hoax, a troublemaker or an
involved party chickening out. The call's on tape. You'd
better listen to it. Deliberately disguised mature voice,
sounds rough and countrified, but the grammar's too perfect. I want you and Rosemary Z to visit the pubs, maybe
park around in quiet spots tonight. Eyes and ears open.'

'Courting couple?' Beaumont asked gloomily. 'My son's
just waiting to catch me at that, silly kid.'

'If I were Z, I wouldn't be too enchanted either,' Mott
told him, grinning. 'Still, we all have to take the rough with
the smooth.'

Beaumont went in search of his partner and found her finishing her coffee in the canteen. 'Had any lunch?' he demanded.

'Sort of.'

'Bloody silly. You'll fade to nothing. Crumple up when I need you to throw a fifteen-stoner. You don't need to cut calories.'

Rosemary grimaced. 'It's not slimming. I just don't feel up to eating.'

He looked at her assessingly, mouth puckered. 'Still camping out at Auntie's? How's the old feller?'

'Yes, I am. And much the same, thanks. Look, I don't want to discuss it.'

'Well, I hope you're not daft enough to make the arrangement permanent. They should manage with a district nurse coming in daily. You can't do this job with hassle at home. God, I ought to know. Peace on earth since Cathy left me, even if the place looks a pigsty.'

'I thought young Stuart had staked a claim on the housework.'

'Some prospector! That was a thin vein, fast exhausted. He was new-brooming so that I'd let him stay on after the school holidays. Anyway, it's you and your eating habits we were discussing.'

'We weren't. And we aren't going to. What's on the programme for this afternoon?'

'Not a lot. See what the kids have to say about the night their mother fell downstairs. Check over the flat again, then knock off until a pub crawl and some officially sanctioned snogging tonight. Locality Datchet.'

'The arms cache?'

'The *reported* arms cache. I've a feeling we're into the silly season, so don't expect too much.'

Rosemary rose and slipped the strap of her bag over one shoulder. 'I'm not expecting anything, DS Beaumont. And you'd better not either.' From the sound of her voice she was half smiling as she walked out ahead of him, leaving him the rear view of a very trim figure topped with a cap of dark-brown curls.

It hadn't been possible to find a foster-mother overnight for the Winter/Gardner girls, so the Children's Officer had had recourse, as so often before, to Saint Nick's, usually referred to informally in this manner to avoid the word 'Home'. 'Small aitch and never the capital,' briskly explained Ma (definitely not Matron) Sellers.

Neither Beaumont nor Z had seen the charity in action until now, although its aims and successes were well advertised in the local press. 'A real family of never regularly more than eight children, both sexes, a permanent Ma, a cat, a dog, and numerous outside volunteers supplying DIY maintenance, companionship and outings in their spare time,' they were told.

Ma eyed them both speculatively. 'Why don't you two pop in sometimes now that you've met us, maybe give Roddy and Meg a bit of help with their homework? Algebra's beyond me, so's French. It's always open house Friday evenings when friends bring along something to eat.'

'Spare time,' Beaumont said tersely, 'we don't get.' He had responsibilities enough with a quirky teenage son and a semi-detached wife, without taking on extra family.

Rosemary Zyczynski gave her warm smile. 'That's truer than you'd think, but thanks for the invitation. I might take it up sometime.'

'Still, it's Ginny and Miranda you've come to see, isn't it? Have you managed to reach their father?'

'He's been lying low,' admitted Beaumont, 'but he should get to hear what's happened in the next day or so.'

'How are the little girls?' Rosemary asked.

'Subdued, though the younger one's opening up to the other children. Ginny—well, she's had a terrible shock. Must have been very brave at the time, but it's catching up with her now. She's old enough to understand her mother isn't coming back. Had her in my room for the last part of the night. Nasty dreams, she said.'

The woman had spoken almost casually. Not indifferent, but able to reduce tragedies by implying they were commonplace. As doubtless they were in her experience. An *oh-dear-the-pudding's-hit-the-floor-so-let's-clear-it-up-and-open-a-tin-of-rice* attitude. A pity that hadn't been her own emotional background as a child, Rosemary regretted.

They waded through a scattering of toys in a large, square living-room where a toddler staggered around inside a play-pen and Miranda—Beaumont recognized the younger Winter child—lay on her stomach turning the cardboard pages of a *Spot the Dog* book. Through open patio doors they could see a black boy of eight or nine digging in a flower bed with a shiny trowel.

'That's Desmond,' said Ma Sellers. 'Kept him home from school this morning with a rash, but seems it's just an allergy. He's mad keen on gardening. I think it must be some plant he's touched, then scratched at his chest.'

She turned and addressed a row of raspberry canes towards the garden's end. 'Ginny, love, here's a lady and gentleman come to see us. Will you look after them while I get some biscuits and lemonade?'

The woman disappeared into the house without waiting for a reply. There was a moment of silence, then a slight scrabbling movement at soil level behind the canes. Another pause and reluctantly a small girl in a pink check dress sidled out, her arms held stiffly behind her out of sight. On her cheeks whiter tracks of tears ran through muddy streaks.

Her mousy hair stood out in two stiff pigtails with tufts hanging down where she had pulled it free. She put up a hand nervously to smooth it straight now and her bare arms and hands were ingrained with earth.

Rosemary sat on her heels, resisting the urge to reach out for the child. 'Hullo,' she said. 'It looks as though Desmond's not the only gardener round here.'

The child shook her head. It could mean anything.

'Desmond's got a rash, did you know?' Rosemary asked, smiling. No answer. 'It meant he couldn't go to school today. Have you started school yet?'

'Um.' She was looking past the two visitors to where her little sister came wobbling out on to the terrace. The younger child held out her hands to be lifted. There was a distinct odour of soiled nappy.

'You *pooh*!' her sister accused.

Assuming that um meant yes, Rosemary left Beaumont to deal with Miranda and turned back to Ginny. 'Was that a nursery school in Colchester?'

'Um.'

'Cotchta,' echoed little Miranda rapturously. Then, quite distinctly, 'Jumbo!' And sat down as her legs suddenly buckled.

'Whoops, dearie. Up you get then,' said Ma Sellers firmly, appearing behind them with a laden tray which Beaumont took off her. 'Yes, apparently Ginny hasn't joined a school here yet. Well, there really hasn't been time. Lucky we're nearly at the long holidays. Gives us a chance to find somewhere really nice.' She started distributing plastic beakers of pale yellow liquid. When they were all, except Ginny, seated on the grass, she held out the plate of biscuits. They were assorted, some iced, some chocolate. Slowly the little girl came closer.

'When you're sitting nicely, dear. That's right. Just one at a time, or they get sticky in your hand. The plate isn't going away.'

And eventually, corrupted by custard creams and Garibaldis, Ginny told them what they needed to know: that she and Miranda had eaten baked beans on toast the last evening at the flat; Mummy always had her supper later and she hadn't opened her new box of chocolates before the girls went to bed; no visitors had come to see them that day; she hadn't seen Mummy being sick or falling downstairs but she thought she'd heard it all. Then it had gone quiet and she'd slept again.

There was no need to take her any further in the grim recollection. 'Chocolate box,' Beaumont said to Z when they had left St Nick's. 'Always a popular way to introduce poison. Let's have another look at the flat. There could be some wrappings.'

The contents of the pedal bin in the Winters' kitchen had already been removed for examination by the forensic scientists. Depending on what was found in the food remains, the case could pass to the Public Health authority. Beaumont found nothing but tissues with make-up stains in the waste-basket of the woman's bedroom.

'Dustbin?' Rosemary suggested. There was just a chance it might have been overlooked.

They went downstairs and out by a dark passage to a double-bolted door. Beyond it was a narrow, concrete yard between scullery and garden wall. Among stacks of empty plant pots and bottles, a broken rocking-chair, an antiquated gas cooker and other discarded junk was a metal dustbin with the edge of a black plastic sack showing under its lid. And the sack was empty, never used.

'So the bin was cleared out for examination too,' Beaumont observed.

'No. Scenes-of-Crime wouldn't bother to reline it. Penny Winter must have done that herself when the full bag was put out for collection. She died early on Wednesday morning. The bin men probably came Tuesday. Not much chance of chasing up that garbage once it's been dumped at the pit.'

'Maybe she hoarded old carrier bags and such. We might find out where she shopped if we go through the cupboards.'

They returned to the dead woman's cramped little kitchen. There they found only a pile of tabloid newspapers thrown in among the cleaning materials under her kitchen sink. Beaumont was staring glumly out of the window when Rosemary came in carrying a blue handbag. 'I knew she must have one somewhere, apart from the empty white one in her wardrobe.'

'A bit small for a mum's, isn't it?'

'Quite dinky. She kept just money, the Children's and Supplementary Allowance books and personal things in it. But no credit cards or bank book. Used to sleep with it under her pillow. I expect any bulky things which she took around—feeder bottles, spare nappies and such—went into the big bag strapped on the toddler's buggy. Aha, an itemized checkout bill from Tesco! Would you like to look at that while I go through her purse?'

Beaumont ran a finger down the list and almost simultaneously they struck pay dirt. 'Choc mints,' said the DS. 'As soon as we know what the poison was, the store and the manufacturer will have to be warned. Just in case it was in the chocs. Let's hope we haven't another loony running loose like the one who put ground glass in baby foods.'

Rosemary was smoothing a small triangle of stiff brown paper. Affixed to one side were two postage stamps. She frowned over the postmark. 'She must have been saving these for someone who collects stamps. The postmark is pretty indistinct but the date's the twenty-first. That was Monday. As it must have reached here Tuesday the package would have come by first-class mail. From which we could work out its maximum weight. What do you make of the place of origin?'

Beaumont peered. 'Nantwich, I'd say.'

'Or Norwich. Not Ipswich. We could get the postmark enhanced, but does it matter now that we know where she bought the chocolates? The package was probably some toy for the children or something she'd ordered.'

Beaumont blew out his cheeks and considered this. 'She could have been sent poison through the post just as easily as buying it. It's about the only alternative we've got, so it's worth following up. I'll go along to the Post Office, have them hunt out the delivery man.'

FOUR

THE PUB CRAWL at Datchet was unproductive, just ran up legitimate expenses but happily no headaches since both Beaumont and Z changed to non-alcoholic beer after their first stop. Between calls the DS aired his opinion that the rumour of an arms cache was dreamed up by the publicans to increase custom. Certainly for a Thursday night there must have been noticeably more new faces in the pleasant little town, given the Intelligence Support Team alone.

After closing-time they parked at a total of three secluded points where they had command of roads leading to Eton, Old Windsor or Slough. Until 3.15 a.m. they kept up a desultory pretence of being a courting couple, aided by a half-pound of butterscotch and a selection of smooth-music cassettes, taking turns at cat naps until a promising suspect walking a mongrel dog approached the driver's window and muttered, 'OK, that's it for tonight. Dead zero. See Mr Mott at ten-thirty at the Copper Kettle.'

'He could've made it lunch-time,' Beaumont complained. He hoped young Stuart hadn't taken advantage of his absence to promote some entertaining of his own. This wasn't the right job for a lone-parent father. In one sense the boy might do better with his mother. Not that she'd scored highly with him lately. Usually women were naturals with kids. Look at that Ma Sellers at St Nick's, and Sister Barbour who'd weighed in on finding the dead woman. Even Z had a sort of way with her. Trouble was kids grew too big, then for mothered read smothered.

'Ten-thirty,' Rosemary considered. 'DI Mott expects the Winter pathology printout by ten. It gives him time to read through and plan the tasking. Lord, I'm tired. I think I'll sneak back to my old digs for the rest of the night. You can drop me off at the end of my road.'

BEAUMONT HAD GIVEN his home number to his Colchester counterpart and groaned when wakened at 7.53 a.m. by a call with details of the dead woman's connections.

There were three sets of Winters in the Colchester directory, but none of them was in any way related to the woman in the mortuary. There was also a scarcity of Gardners, but an older sister of Penny Winter's divorced husband had been traced, assistant at the central library. She lived at home with her mother and stepfather. Since the telephone was registered in his name it hadn't been possible to contact the family instantly. The mother was now a Mrs Bertie Boulter, forename Doris.

A policewoman had called on them and broken the news of Penny Winter's death. The ex-mother-in-law appeared to be in very poor health and there was no question of her coming to identify the body. In Ronald Gardner's absence—and no one seemed quite certain where he was living at present (his mother said, 'London somewhere')—his sister, Freda Gardner, had reluctantly volunteered and would arrive by train at Wycombe station at 11.49.

Beaumont made a note on the pad beside his bed, buried the receiver under his pillow, applied his mental switch-off technique and returned to sleep. He barely made it to pick up Z from her digs and get them both to the Copper Kettle on time for Mott's briefing.

'I hear the Datchet was a washout,' the DI greeted them.

'Nothing happened out our way,' Beaumont agreed. 'Except that Z had a bad case of hiccups just when we were meant to look most convincing.'

Mott hid a grin and bit back the comment that it confirmed admirable initiative on her part. 'I've looked through the path, report on the Winter woman,' he told them. 'Alimentary contents showed a meal eaten ten to twelve hours before death. A considerable presence of biscuit, processed meat such as rough Ardennes pâté, peppermint cream, chocolate and cheese. She could well have stuffed herself sick with that lot alone, but it seems there was a bug present that made it a dead cert. Our old friend *Salmonella typhinirium* in an advanced state in the pâté. Littlejohn was certainly giving a strong hint when he mentioned petri dishes.'

'So that's one we can strike off the case list,' Beaumont appreciated.

'It looks like it. Uniform branch will assist Public Health in warning the press and consumers and isolating the source once it's identified.'

'Penny Winter's shopping list,' Rosemary said. 'I've got it here. Hang on a minute.' She opened out the length of till roll and ran a finger down the items. Once, then a second time.

'No pâté here. She must have bought it some time before and been keeping it in the fridge.'

'But not cool enough. When will people learn?' Beaumont grunted. 'We'll get the source from labelling on the container—if it was in the pedal bin garbage and not carted off the day before. But not our concern any more, thank God. At least the silly cow didn't include the little girls in her gourmet binge.'

'Right,' said Mott, mentally closing that file and opening another, 'back to on-going situations. While we're on

Wycombe patch I'd like Z to meet a group of young Asian
women who're complaining of harassment. Get the background first from PC Patel. I think it's outside racial prejudice. There could be trouble at home. The generation gap's
particularly dodgy for them with their mixed-culture
schooling. The Boss wants that given priority.'

'I'm meeting Miss Gardner's train in half an hour,'
Rosemary reminded him. 'She's coming to identify Penny
Winter's body. She may need me for a while afterwards.
And I thought she should visit the children.'

'A sister-in-law? Were they that close? Well, see Patel
right after you've put her back on a train.

'Beaumont, there's that break-in at Widmer End. It could
be an insurance fiddle. Put them through the whole thing
again. Take it easy, let them sweat a little, and see if you
flush any birds out. If so, where do they fly? I'm giving you
DC Silver for that. You and Z can send urgent messages for
me to Datchet. It looks as though I'll be in that area for the
next day or two. Meanwhile take your instructions direct
from the Boss.'

FREDA GARDNER WAS a drab-looking woman, possibly not
more than thirty-five, but if ever she had set out to enjoy life
she seemed to have given up trying. A square, rather flat
face sat uneasily on a square, almost neckless body. A bis-
cuit-coloured complexion was hung about by short, sandy
hair. Her coat-dress, of much the same colour, was merely
worn to cover her.

She seemed ill at ease when Rosemary tried to make conversation, as though communication was not her way. The
only time the ends of her discontented mouth turned up was
when the policewoman noticed the paperback protruding
from the corner of her duffel bag and exclaimed, 'Oh,
you're reading *A Share of the Spoils*. Isn't it good?'

But when her relationship to the dead woman and the little girls was raised Freda Gardner displayed a marked flaccidity. She had had little contact with her brother or his family. He had been several years younger, so she was already at school when he was born. He had been delicate and their mother had been over-preoccupied taking care of him. Z recognized covert resentment there, rancour at exclusion which was so long established as to be acceptable, almost cherished.

At the mortuary, after the first shock of encountering the dead face, Freda was transformed. Instant repugnance slowly faded to leave her fascinated. Her eyes lingered over every stilled feature of the younger woman. She was smiling as she nodded. Yes, this was—had been—her sister-in-law, lost once through divorce, now again by death. The detached, almost literary comment—sister-in-law twice removed, Rosemary paraphrased—had a certain heartless irony. She realized that, for the first time, the woman had volunteered speech without it being dragged from her. There was a slight flushing of the sallow cheeks. Her eyes had a quite new vitality.

It was macabre, but Z had witnessed it before, a phenomenon of some funerals, which could turn wakes into half-shamed celebrations. The energizing recognition of 'that is death there, but here am I still alive'. An unfamiliar and wonderful elation. She felt a brief pity for the colourless woman, but couldn't like her.

They had a pot of tea together in the town and then walked up the steep hill to the station. Freda had declined to visit the little girls, giving too many excuses to be convincing: she must get back for an evening lecture at the library; she was no good with children; if Ronald got to know he might think she was interfering; and anyway the girls probably wouldn't remember her.

At the last Rosemary felt she should supply the details the woman had neglected to ask for. 'We think it was some cooked meat she ate. Luckily the little girls didn't have any.'

'Contaminated, was it? She should have thrown it away. Fancy taking risks when the fridge was broken. But that was like her. Mother said she had all the makings of a slut.'

It was stated with smug satisfaction but—more than the tone—it was the information that startled Z. 'She'd had trouble with the fridge. You knew that?'

'Yes. Some part got broken in the move and the fluid ran out. She rang to complain to Ronald, but of course he wasn't with us. Mother was in bed and I couldn't do anything. I told her to get it mended wherever she was and not make more trouble.'

'But it was working when we checked the flat.'

'Well, this was a fortnight back that she phoned. So she must have done what I said, had it mended.' Freda Gardner dismissed the incident as she had seemed to dismiss the relationship. Her square face resettled into its previous lines of discontent. 'I'd better go through to the platform now.'

Rosemary left her at the barrier, watching to make sure she got on the train. Miss Gardner never looked back. The WDC no longer existed for her, if ever she had done.

THE TEAM WENT about its tasks, severally on loan and passing back information as netted to Mike Yeadings who shook out chaff from grain and sent on what he thought fit to Divisions A, C, and E. In the absence of a major investigation such team break-up was inevitable, but he prepared an emergency list in case it suddenly became necessary to reassemble an operational unit.

He had thought they might have such a case with the Winter death, but the police file was closed now. It struck him as unusual, however, that no outbreak of similar cases had occurred locally. Salmonella was the cause of 65 per cent to 70 per cent of all food poisoning, yet it seemed this was an isolated case. Possibly the defective fridge had played a major part, with alternating warm and cool temperatures acting on an otherwise negligible presence of bacteria in the pâté at the time of purchase. If only the woman had eaten it earlier, or shared it with someone so that the onset of symptoms could have been observed and dealt with in time. If, if... Pointless applying hindsight. She was dead; nothing could be done. Yeadings grunted and slipped the last relevant paper into the file—a note on the enhanced postmark found on the scrap of wrapping paper in the dead woman's purse. The date was confirmed as two days before she died, and the office of origin had been Harwich.

HARWICH WAS TO FEATURE again within a matter of days. By then the Datchet 'arms cache' had been revealed as a schoolboys' hoard of homemade fireworks, dangerous enough if mishandled but without any terrorist implications. Mott was peripherally involved in a rape investigation at Holtspur, while Rosemary Zyczynski, together with an Asian policewoman borrowed from Slough, was deep into the community problems of parentally arranged marriages which warred with personal attachments in Wycombe.

DS Beaumont was meanwhile sloping round Amersham helping with a case of criminal damage for which no less than three organizations claimed responsibility, and was happily recommending 'Charge the perishing lot!' It was to him that the first message came through and was then diverted to Mike Yeadings, just twenty minutes before he was officially contacted by the Senior Superintendent, Crime, for Essex.

It appeared that a blue Bedford van had been observed parked for four or five days on a patch of waste land at the end of a terrace of small shops, and because it blended with its background—modest, fairly clean and generally unremarkable—it had not come to police notice until a complaint was lodged by the householder whose upper windows overlooked the site. This man, an artists' supplier and picture framer, had been on holiday at Cromer and returned to find the intruder partly blocking access to his rear yard. For two days he had endured the inconvenience of something like a seven-point turn required to get his own estate car out on to the road, before he finally exploded with exasperation and rang the local station.

Such a minor matter warranted only inspection by a bicycle-mounted PC who reported back that the vehicle was locked and apparently, as far as could be ascertained from peering through the rather greasily misted rear windows, densely packed with items of furniture.

Having completed an external examination PC Morris affixed a formal notice requiring the vehicle to be removed. On the following day, since the van was still there and a computer check had proved the local licence plate to be a false one, the relative merits of a controlled explosion as against an internal search were mooted. Since it was agreed that possession of stolen goods was a more popular Essex crime than the booby-trapping of vehicles, a patrol car was sent with a set of keys to check on the Bedford's contents. These confirmed the PC's report, the van approximating to the description of one regularly seen in the area visiting antique shops and buying 'junk items' from farm cottages, but with Dutch licence plates affixed.

Since no claim of ownership was made within the next three days the van was removed to a police pound and an antiques expert asked to evaluate the contents. These he declared to be of above average quality; collectors' items of small furniture, china, oil paintings and glassware. All were at least eighty-five years old, with one remarkable exception.

This last, packed inside an inlaid mahogany chest, dated from little more than two decades back. It too had once been beautiful, but was so no more. The girl had met her death at least a week earlier.

'No means of identification,' the Essex superintendent declared, 'though we'll be circulating an artist's impression throughout East Anglia.

'About the van we know more. It customarily made a wide circuit, buying at auctions and from country antique shops, the two dealers invariably paying cash. Both men were foreign, one early twenties, the other middle-aged. They claimed to be Dutch, and certainly the van always left on the North Sea ferry from Parkeston Quay, Harwich.

'The reason I'm contacting you, Superintendent, is that we found a car park sticker issued in High Wycombe and dated June twenty-fourth; which involves the Thames Valley Police force. It had been used and the sticky surface will almost certainly match with smears of adhesive lifted from the van's windscreen. The ticket had been removed, screwed up small and stuffed in a pocket of the girl's jeans. We thought you might like to send someone to look at her, and at the van. A nice day out with sea air for one of your more deserving men, Mr Yeadings.'

It fell to DI Angus Mott. He drove east, committed himself to the treadmill of the M25 and came off it to a vista of broad, bleached cornfields under a cloudless sky. He felt in holiday mood, wishing Paula had been free to come along for the ride.

A CID sergeant had been allocated to show him around. Since the car pound was nearer they went there first, but the blue Bedford told him nothing. The furniture and bric-à-brac had been removed and put under seal, but there was a complete list, together with photographs, to compare with the schedule of recently stolen goods which Mott had brought with him from Thames Valley. On first sight there appeared to be no correlation between the two.

The DS nodded. 'We guessed most of the stuff was from round here anyway, some of it already identified as legitimate purchases. But if everything's above-board why was this load ditched, with false licence plates on the van? And where are the usual two dealers?'

'They'd hardly welcome a connection with the body in the chest,' Mott reminded him drily.

'So why didn't they simply off-load the body and carry on as planned, exporting the lot by ferry to the Continent?'

'Was that the plan? Had they booked their passage?'

'For the night of twenty-fourth June.'

'Pushed for time, perhaps. But what are the chances you've two more bodies to come?'

'We don't think so. The death looks like a massive heroin OD. It's anybody's guess how she came to be in the chest with the lid fast closed, but I'd say somebody panicked, hid her and ran.'

'Nasty.'

But Angus wasn't to know how much it would affect him until he was there in the mortuary looking down at the body which had been straightened out, cleaned up and decently sheeted.

DS Philby turned back a corner of the cover and moved to one side. 'Nice-looking bird once.'

And Mott was confronted by a strangely familiar face. Grotesquely so, because when he had seen it before it had been vitally young, unheeding, eager for experience. And he had so nearly provided a part of that.

Sight of the dead girl was like an accusation. He knew he must declare involvement in the case, but surely not such great involvement that he'd need to be taken off it?

'Yes,' he agreed sombrely. 'As it happens, I can put a name to her.' No, to *it*, he thought, because this wasn't any longer the girl he'd touched, kissed, laughed with, coming home crushed together in the back seats of the red Porsche Cabriolet.

'Anneke something, a Dutch national.'

She'd mentioned once where she'd come from: a town near Hilversum. Maybe the address would be in the register at Chardleigh Place.

The local man was looking at him curiously. 'What was she?'

'How do you mean—*what*?' Instantly—too swiftly—Mott had reacted with anger and betrayed himself. 'She wasn't a whore,' he followed it up. 'Nor a student. Her English was good, accent-free most of the time. She wasn't a career girl either, just picked up jobs as she went along. Liked living over here, I guess. EC citizen, after all. Why not? A lot more of our kids would be working in the Netherlands if they'd troubled to master the language.'

Even to himself it sounded defensive, as if he had something to hide. Then he remembered. 'Vroom. She called herself Anneke Vroom.'

'Cyanosed,' said the Harwich DS, watching him keenly. 'Case of death asphyxiation. Pulmonary paralysis because she was stoned on almost uncut H. And, incidentally, pregnant. So was she settling for out?'

Pregnant. It rocked him back on his heels again. Had Anneke already been pregnant that day she'd made such a set at him when they'd gone as a foursome to Portland? When he'd given her her head, to needle Paula who was acting hurt and distant.

He closed his eyes and he could feel her again, eager against him, warm and voluptuous. Remembered her deep-throated laughter, the eye language, thigh language. Remembered his own instinctive reaction and her strong hands on his body.

FIVE

MOTT ADJUSTED the car's visor to cut out as much as possible of the low, westering sun and settled to the long drive back to South Bucks. Less than twenty minutes out of Harwich the motorway by-passed Colchester. He was dimly aware of the city spread anonymously over to the left, beyond the slower-moving build-up of container trucks, commercial traffic and occasional holiday caravans.

At the moment of his passing the city's access road a London train was drawing into Colchester station. In the second, non-smoker carriage Miss Freda Gardner crushed her empty chocolate wrappings with stubby fingers and stuffed them deep inside her simulated leather handbag.

Her pale eyes scanned her immediate surroundings, encountered nothing else derogatory to herself and passed on to the three other passengers in her compartment, noting the teenager's bitten nails, the old man's porcine ear-hairs, the meretricious woman's garish make-up. Not until the final squeal of brakes and shuddering jolt did she move her closed knees aside from the door's edge and permit the old man to fumble arthritically with the stiff latch.

It failed to respond and forced him to run the window down, hang out and grope for the exterior handle. Miss Gardner gave a barely audible sigh at his incompetence and her own need to return from the stolen delights of a day in London.

She had experienced no difficulty in getting away, having simply stated her intention of looking up Ronald in the capital. Instantly Mother had submerged the score of odd jobs she required done beneath the urgent need to resume contact with her doted-on younger offspring.

From the chaos of Liverpool Street station she had gone by Underground to Oxford Circus, treated herself to coffee and éclairs in Dickins and Jones's restaurant, confirmed that the fashion goods on show there were fit only for the scarecrow models seen in glossy magazines, and moved on to John Lewis's where she bought a metre of checked seersucker to make a cloth for her bedroom table.

From there she walked to the National Portrait Gallery and sat gazing glassily at seventeenth-century notables until such time as she should have enjoyed herself sufficiently. Lunch she took in the bowels of the National Gallery, regretting she hadn't ventured farther and done so at the British Museum.

There had been a time in her young days when she would regularly meet an aunt up from Brighton by arrangement in the Ladies Room of the Strand Corner House. Such a terrible pity the old Lyons had disappeared. To her it had been the peak of sophistication to be served an adult portion of plaice, chips and peas in the Trafalgar Room by a 'Nippy' in her crisp black and white uniform. Alas, such days were gone, and the adult world wasn't at all what it had appeared from the perspective of a seven-year-old.

At two o'clock she paid the bill and made her way up Charing Cross Road and through Cambridge Circus, anxious now to rest her tired feet. It was still impossible to get returned tickets for *The Mousetrap* matinee, but she found a children's theatre workshop in a side street, where they were putting on *The Firebird*, most of which she slept through.

None of the eating places in the neighbourhood looking suitable for the cup of tea she later fancied, she bought two blocks of chocolate for the journey home. She didn't approve of eating on trains, but it wasn't like a meal of packed sandwiches, which would be downright common.

As her final act before boarding the return train she took out her diary and rang the number she'd copied down from the screw of paper left in Ronald's wastepaper-bin on his last visit. It was a billhead from a car showroom in Hounslow and she'd gathered from an overheard telephone conversation that Ronald had lately been working there.

A girl answered the phone. Freda could almost see her: sheer tights and indecently long legs; not much on the top, and even less between her ears. But all the edge you could imagine. 'Mr Gardner? Oh, *Ronnie* you mean. No, he's not been here for some months now.'

Asked if she had any idea of his present whereabouts the girl hesitated.

'I'm his sister,' Freda insisted. 'I need to get in touch because our mother's critically ill.' Mention of a recently dead ex-wife and two motherless children in need of claiming was hardly proper, she felt.

The girl said she'd see what she could find out. After a short wait and some paper shuffling, during which Freda had to feed the phone twice more with her carefully hoarded coins, the girl came back with an address. It was for a road in Beaconsfield, Bucks, and it sounded like a superior flat: 12 Carrington Court.

A phone number? No; Ronnie had asked them particularly to write if anything promising came up.

And had it? Freda asked. Come up? No.

She'd thought not. Ronald would seldom be employed a second time anywhere, probably. Just as he'd not been asked back again to parties when he was a little boy.

Freda folded her lips firmly over the information and spent much of the journey home planning how best to prolong divulging it to her mother.

ON THE M12 MOTT drove on, dazzled as the sun came too low for the visor to afford protection. His head buzzed gently and he recalled he'd had only a liquid lunch.

Reporting back to Yeadings on his discovery of the Dutch girl's body would put him in a spot, because Mike was well aware of his engagement to Paula and, with Nan, stood almost *in loco parentis* to the pair of them. The Anneke business would be embarrassing to come clean about, not that it had been at all serious—except as a lowdown means of getting back at Paula.

Admittedly the fact that he hadn't ended up in the Dutch girl's bed wasn't entirely due to his recovered judgement, the final scenes of the Chardleigh Place weekend having hit the lowest level of a West End farce.

It had been a scorcher of a day on the Saturday and they'd all been set for fun, except Paula who'd privately expressed misgivings about the Porsche's advertised 149 mph and what trouble it might cause on the motorway south. He'd had reservations himself on that score, but Paula's voicing hers had raised the mule in him.

And in the event she'd been wrong. Coleman handled the car competently, with a little too much panache—as he had done the snooker cue—but with a care for the machine and other road users that Angus hadn't expected. Perhaps as an insurance adjuster he had experience of some really bad pile-ups and acted on that knowledge. Only once or twice in overtaking had he taken risks, but his time and steering had been controlled. There'd been nothing Angus wouldn't have commended a police driver for on an emergency call. In the restricted space of the rear, Anneke had raised an occasional wild, rodeo cheer. Paula, beside her, had stayed silent.

Arriving at Weymouth they had swum, lunched, swum again, then gone to view the damaged sailing-boat at Chesil

Beach. And at that point Angus had felt his antennae quiver, because after Coleman had done his survey he made a casual suggestion: that if the boat was written off it could be bought for a mere song and made good again. Not by himself, of course: professionally that would be improper. But anyone with a little capital to spare... He knew a few young lions keen to be sea-wolves who might jump at it. Maybe a syndicate—equal shares, equal rights—like part-owning a racehorse.

He had looked long at Angus then, smiling through the toy moustache with those perfect white teeth, 'What do you think? Doesn't that grab you?'

There were obvious risks and, keen as he was to get back into sailing, Angus wasn't fool enough to go blind into a partnership with strangers. He'd have given it to Coleman straight, except that Paula was biting her lip, looking anywhere but in his direction. So, demon-driven, he'd grinned along with it, said he'd give it some thought and sleep on the suggestion; as it happened, he'd some capital for which the immediate need had just fallen through, so who knows?

Which hadn't mended any pre-marital fences, and when Anneke had pulled on his arm as they sorted themselves for the return journey, Paula had accepted the seat Coleman offered beside himself. Which left Angus no choice but to share the cramped space at the rear with Anneke's voluptuous overflow.

They broke the journey towards its end for dinner, Coleman again the life and soul of the party. Since he had stood everyone's ploughman's lunch it was now Angus's turn to pay—all four courses with wine—plus champagne for the girls at the end, this time at Paula's request. She had sat opposite him, bright-eyed, never more desirable, perhaps a mite too sparky to be genuinely delighted with the occasion.

Ruefully, he had to admit he'd gone into sulk mode for the rest of the journey. By the time they reached the hotel he was seething, unfit for anyone's company, so he'd gone for a long walk, got lost in unfamiliar leafy lanes, and not returned until almost two on Sunday morning. To find that Paula's bed hadn't been slept in, although her day clothes were still around.

So, remembering Coleman's attentions and the way she'd enjoyed his stories, he'd assumed the worst, packed his bag in thunderous mood and, not knowing the number of the others' rooms, gone down to the car, intending to settle the bill as soon as Reception opened. Flung the case in on the seat beside him, slammed the door. Paula, curled up on the rear seat was startled awake, sat up, wounded and as hornet-mad as himself.

When both had taken stock of the corner they'd driven themselves into, he'd stiffly offered—observing equality of the sexes—to toss for who should return to the creature comforts of the hotel room. But even as he flicked the coin the tension broke. He felt his face twitch and crack apart in a grin. Paula's shoulders were shaking as she bent forward, her dark wings of hair swinging to hide her features. As he reached to lift her chin the little moans of laughter started to bubble out, but he couldn't be sure because of the tears on her cheeks. 'Hell's bells!' he said. 'What are we doing to each other?'

And kissing her had been the end of it all; no inquest, no recriminations. They'd clung desperately and turned their backs on their own hurtfulness. Until now, and the need to tell the Boss everything he knew about Anneke Vroom.

All that Yeadings had gathered of that horrendous weekend was that by common consent the wedding was postponed till Paula had served her extended time with Wheatman. So how little of his own stupidity could he give away, while presenting a clear picture of the Dutch girl and her way of living?

In fairness to himself, he didn't really know her. He'd been far too preoccupied with his own hard lot to appreciate her as a person. She was free and easy, a grabber, no better than she had to be; but what her aim in life was, what made her unhappy or how she saw other people—that was a mystery.

You think that when you've laughed at the same things with someone you've quite a bit in common, but it isn't that at all. Sometimes the laughter comes between, as a convenient insulation. Really, the one person Yeadings needed to talk to was Paula. She, if anyone, had her eyes wide open that weekend. She would have missed nothing.

By common consent Paula and he had classified the whole incident as a limbo file, but it wasn't expunged. There was nothing for it now but to recall it in its entirety. Which he must clear with her before discussion with an outsider. Angus devoutly hoped that her day in court had gone well for Paula, yet not so well that she would now be out celebrating with her colleagues.

He turned off the M25 and headed towards the city. Rush hour was long over and traffic thinned as he made for the Embankment. Threading the maze of the Temple's Inns of Court, he doubted she would still be in Chambers, but twenty or thirty cars remained parked under the long line of dignified Georgian windows. 'My fiancée, Miss Paula Musto,' he demanded with macho terseness of the only woman left in the outer office. And then didn't Paula, at that very moment, come prancing down the stairs behind him, briefcase in hand, calling back to some half-visible man lounging above. And the lounger, following her down, revealed nothing more threatening than the grizzled and simian features of Bellows, the senior clerk.

'Angus,' she exclaimed joyfully, 'this is great! Are you taking me out to dinner?'

'Why not? But with a time limit on it, I'm afraid.'

'Ah.' She gave him a shrewd glance. 'You're on the job, then?'

'And I badly need your help. Personal, not professional.'

'In that case—' she turned and gestured upwards— 'we could just make it coffee. We'll have the place to ourselves and an undisputed claim to the percolator. Let's go talk.'

She listened gravely while he outlined his call to Harwich and the disconcerting discovery there. 'Poor girl,' she said. 'Nothing so grim has happened before to anyone I know.'

'It's shaken me too. Especially because...' His voice trailed away. He gestured helplessly.

'Because you were just using her.' Paula nodded. 'To get back at me.'

'And because, dammit, I can't remember much about her. I ought to, but I never really considered her. Just saw a big, easy blonde—'

'No, that's a type. Anneke was a real person, Angus. I've thought about her since, partly because at first I was afraid you would find her dangerously attractive.'

'Well, I didn't. Look, I'd hoped we wouldn't have to go into this, but it's because you did see her properly that I need your help now. Remembering details.'

'You want me to tell you what Anneke was all about? How can I? I was with her less than you were.'

Paula stopped short, tilted her head. 'There was one incident, though. It might be a key because for a split second she was different. I guess we both had the impression of a brassy, thrusting female, who didn't want to miss out on whatever came along; someone easy to please and over-ready to please others, provided they didn't tread on her toes or threaten her.'

'I'd go along with you on that. But what about this other, untypical thing? Could it be because she was on drugs?'

'Oh no. It was as if momentarily the image shifted and I saw another person underneath. It was all an act, Angus. You thought of her as a type because she was doing that type, dressing the part, working her way on that ticket. Underneath, I think she was different, even if the mask was beginning to mould her to itself.'

'Go on.'

'It was in the powder room before dinner that first evening. I hadn't noticed she was there because there was a crowd round the mirrors. A loo came free and I went across to take it. Anneke beat me to it and said, "Hey, that's mine." '

'Well, we agreed she was pushy.'

'But then she stood a moment looking back when she realized I was someone she'd met. She said, "I've become much more assertive since I've come here." She said it with quiet pride, almost marvelling at her own progress. I thought at first she was jeering, trying to needle me, but later I recalled her tone of voice.'

Paula looked at him searchingly. 'You see what it means, don't you? Or am I reading too much into a few words?

'Angus, there's something that I'm appreciating more and more in court. Prosecuting counsel and defending counsel sometimes each read out a single statement quoted from the accused. One reading damns him and the other doesn't. It's all in the timing and inflection, and the expression in the eyes—which can't be presented as evidence because it's a matter of opinion and interpretation.'

'Where does this get us with Anneke?'

'Just for an instant she stopped in her tracks and looked at me for approval. She was friendly then, not hostile. What she meant was, "Look at me, how far I've come!" Assertiveness being something she'd tried hard to achieve, and now it was coming naturally.'

Angus nodded slowly. He must try to square this with what he remembered of the girl. Paula could be right. When Anneke had got too familiar in the Porsche's rear seat he had chopped at her exploring hand. She had turned her face away and he'd seen a crimson flush start up the side of her throat. He'd taken it for anger, but it could have been something else. After that she'd left him alone, just shouted excited comments to the two in front as they passed anything of interest: a gawky schoolgirl covering up a gaffe.

'Do you suppose,' Paula asked, starting on another tack, 'that she knew she was pregnant at the time we met her? And could it have been Coleman's child?'

Angus shrugged. 'We'll know eventually, when the full post mortem report comes through,' he said heavily. 'I don't know how far the pregnancy had gone. They'll do a DNA test on the foetus too. We'll have to trace Coleman and find out how long he'd known her. He might have picked her up that very weekend, as he did us. I'll be going on to Chardleigh Place next, to see if they can provide addresses.'

'Poor old Angus,' Paula said affectionately, squeezing his arm. 'You're going to have a bad time telling Mike Yeadings, aren't you? I wonder what he'll make of it?'

'UM-UM,' YEADINGS appreciated. 'Sounds as though you're sailing a trifle close to the wind there, Angus. But if you say there was nothing more to your relations with the dead girl than a passing flirtation to needle Paula, well, I'll accept that. So let's summarize it this way, in terms suitable for an ACC's ears: a fortnight ago you and your fiancée chance to make up a brief foursome with another weekend couple, one of whom now turns up as a corpse at Harwich.

'A Dutch girl. In a van full of antiques and bric-à-brac apparently abandoned near the quay where it had been booked for the Hook of Holland. And in the dead girl's pocket was a screwed-up sticker for a car park in High Wycombe, dated earlier on the very day the van was booked to travel to her home country.

'Yes, put like that I don't see why the ACC should expect any more of you than an identification and full description of the girl. We'll circulate the photographs provided by the Essex police and see if any antiques dealers recognize her locally. Did she mention to you that she was connected with that sort of trade?'

'No. I gathered she was picking up whatever jobs she came across and fancied. The assistant manager at Chardleigh Place admitted to me today that she'd been taken on as casual labour there; possibly one of those tax-free dodges such places offer foreigners when they're hard pushed for staff. Certainly the first time we met her she was behind the bar, yet she was free to take the whole of the next day off. Ate with the staff and had a room in their part of the hotel, but was allowed to join the guests in the evening if accept-ably dressed. A bit of amateur hostessing, you might call it. To help out the bar sales. She'd been there seven days.'

'So what was she officially entered as—kitchen help, front desk or chambermaid?'

'General duties, sub-management, I gathered.'

'How about her relationship with the man you men-tioned?'

'Coleman. He'd stayed on for the weekend after a train-ing session for Cosmos Assurance. An organizer, appar-ently. I saw it as casual companionship, which he pushed for what he could get.'

'One of those, than whom there's none with more endur-ance, eh?'

'Something of the sort. Doesn't sell it, though. He's an insurance adjuster, goes around investi—'

'Thank you, lad. I know what an insurance adjuster is, to my cost.'

'Yes, well, he's a sharp one. Tried to do a part-share deal with me over a sailing-boat he was writing off.'

'We can't all be as honest as policemen. Or as unenter-prising!'

Mott ploughed on. 'I got their addresses from Chard-leigh Place on my way back. Coleman's is in London's new dockland development zone. Upmarket. The girl just wrote down "Amersham", though she didn't seem too sure of the spelling; scrubbed out the end and wrote it again.'

'So get "A" Division to circulate her photograph there as well as in Wycombe. That should bring something out of the woodwork. Is there anything else Harwich wants?'

Angus rubbed his chin. 'They're dead keen to mark the case up themselves, leaving us the donkey work.'

Yeadings rose stiffly, flicked off the desk lamp. 'It's their corpse, their job. Of course, there's no telling how it will strike the ACC. Doubtless he'll hobnob with the Essex Chief and we'll pick up whatever they pass our way. Well, I'm off now, lad. Time I showed my face to the family, or they'll start dialling 999 when they see my unfamiliar bulk around the house.'

He turned at the door. 'I'm glad you told me how things were with you and Paula. We'd hoped there was nothing sinister in the wedding postponement.'

IN THEIR COLCHESTER semi-detached, Freda Gardner stood squatly at bay, facing her mother whose dropsical legs were painfully stretched out before her on the kitchen sofa. The older woman's face had an unaccustomed flush. 'But didn't you find out *anything*?' she insisted. 'Anything at all? Where did you look? Who did you ask?'

'I went everywhere,' Freda ground back, provoked by her mother's tenacity. 'Do you think I liked making a nuisance of myself to people I've never met and wouldn't have anything to do with if it was my choice? You don't care a damn, do you? It's your precious Ronnie who matters, and it always has been!'

'Don't you start using swear words to me, Freda. This is a God-fearing house...'

'It's a pity it wasn't so God-fearing earlier, with your fledgling son under your wing! And I wouldn't be so sure your wonderful new husband's such a paragon either, going off to all his meetings and blowing himself up with words. Making an exhibition of himself in front of all those women with his amateur Bible-thumping!'

'Freda, don't. Don't, dear. I can't stand it!'

'Oh, it's *dear* now, is it? Took you time enough to get round to it.'

'I'm sorry, Freda. I didn't realize just how tired you were. And it *was* kind of you to go looking for Ronnie. I really do appreciate it. But I'm so anxious. You can't know how much I worry, cooped up here. It isn't as if I can get around myself with my legs like this, and then having to keep going for dialysis as I do. It seems to take all my time and energy. And I can't ask Bertie to do more than he does. It's awful feeling you're a burden to everyone.'

Freda looked coldly at her mother. She had intended stonewalling longer, but suddenly she was as tired as she'd claimed to be. It was too much trouble to prevaricate. Let her have the address. Part of it, anyway. Much good would it do her. Ronnie would lie low for fear of being made responsible for the children.

'Well, as it happens, I might have something.'

'Someone's seen him? Where?' Her eagerness was pathetic.

'I contacted a firm he worked for once in London.'

'And what did they say? Oh, Freda, you must tell me! Think of those poor little girls without mother or father.'

'You didn't think much of their mother when they had one.'

'I don't know how you can talk like that. I'm sure I gave her every chance. And so did poor Ronnie. She broke his heart with her sluttish ways. He should never have married her, but with Ginny on the way what could he do?'

Freda snorted with impatience and lifted the kettle on to the Aga hotplate. Summer and winter alike the room was overheated, with the monster devouring expensive solid fuel. Almost at once the kettle started singing.

'In my opinion they were ideally matched. They deserved each other.'

'You're only saying that. You don't mean it, not in your heart of hearts.'

My stone of stones, my granite core, thought Freda. 'Beaconsfield,' she said abruptly, as she lifted the kettle and poured water on instant coffee in a mug. 'They think he may be living there with some girl he picked up.'

'Beaconsfield, that's not terribly far away, is it, Freda? Couldn't you go there and make inquiries? You know I can't, and Daddy's so busy.'

'Don't call him that! No, I can't go traipsing off to Buckinghamshire again. It would mean taking another day off work and having to find someone else to step in for me. My job's important. And how would you manage without my pay? No, you'll just have to wait until the spirit moves Ronnie—as your sainted husband would say. Maybe he'll get in touch. Anyway, he must know by now what's happened to his precious ex-wife. For all we know he's over there now, helping the police with their inquiries.'

'The police? Why should they want to talk to him?'

Freda shrugged. 'Well, they came here looking for him, didn't they? And it was a policewoman who went with me at High Wycombe to identify the body. They've an interest.'

Mrs Boulter looked stricken. 'They couldn't think Ronnie had anything to do with what happened.'

'Why not? No, I suppose you're right.' She looked speculatively at her mother under her short, sandy lashes as she sipped at the hot coffee. 'Of course, Beaconsfield *is* right next to High Wycombe, about thirty miles west of London on the A40. If Ronnie's living there, they'd have been almost neighbours.'

Mrs Boulter seemed to be struggling with some other consideration. 'I don't suppose they mentioned—these people who thought they knew where Ronnie was—what the girl's name was, the one he was, er—'

'Living with? No, why?' She looked sharply at her mother. 'You know something, don't you? Ronnie let something slip last time he was here. What did he say?'

'Oh, nothing. Just—well, only that he'd met this lovely girl and he thought this time she was really right for him and—'

'And she just happened to have money, and a house or a flat, and he thought he might be falling on his feet—again! What was her name? Come on, tell me. I'm your only chance of finding her, after all.'

'Janice. That's a beautiful name. She must be a nice, refined girl with a name like that.'

'And her surname?'

'Oh, he didn't say.'

Well, knowing Ronnie, of course he wouldn't. It might make it too easy to check up on him; whether it was true or a complete load of rubbish.

'There's not a lot to go on,' admitted Mrs Boulter sadly. 'Just their names, Ronald Walter Gardner and a friend called Janice living at Beaconsfield.'

'No,' Freda agreed, smiling as she remembered the paper with the address buried deep inside her handbag. When her mother had gone up to bed it would go into the Aga's flames along with the chocolate wrappings.

ALTHOUGH IT WASN'T strictly their case, the body having turned up at Harwich, Thames Valley found that the Anneke Vroom death was now overshadowing the rest of the workload occupying Superintendent Yeadings's team. Especially since the address given by the girl's companion at Chardleigh Place had proved to be a false one. The luxury apartment in London's converted dockland certainly existed and was occupied, but no one there had ever heard of an Arnold Coleman.

'Trace the car,' Mott told Beaumont. 'There can't be all that number sold of an expensive item like that. It was red, brand new and unsullied. Three figures and three letters. A personalized licence plate.'

But again, when the year's sales list for the UK was completed, the name Coleman didn't feature on it. 'He was using an alias,' Yeadings suggested, 'or else he'd borrowed or hired the car. There's nothing of the sort on the stolen list. What did Personnel at Cosmos Assurance give us about him?'

Another dead end. Cosmos had never employed anyone by that name. Yet an Arnold Coleman had certainly been at Chardleigh Place for the entire week of the Cosmos Assurance training course. His single room was one covered by the firm's umbrella contract, and a billing for the extra two days he had stayed on was even now with Cosmos, being queried.

A senior director was convinced that it smelled of blatant commercial espionage. He threatened immediate dismissal of the conference clerk responsible for binning all minor paperwork in the course, as well as wiping clean such files on her computer except for the programme, final report and candidates' gradings.

But the police scented an alternative artist. 'We've got ourselves a new local conman,' Beaumont gloated. 'Essex can't follow the girl back without him. And so far he's only been observed operating on our patch. What's the betting we take over the Vroom case completely now?'

The Thames Valley grapevine rumoured considerable telephone activity between Kidlington and Chelmsford as top brass put their minds to the same question. The final outcome followed on the post mortem report that Anneke's pregnancy was of over three months' duration. The timing of her death lay between fairly wide limits, but it was unlikely that she had been alive when the van arrived at Harwich.

Nothing was known to connect her with the antiques dealers apart from her body's arrival in their vehicle at the end of a journey from South Bucks. It was possible that she had begged a lift to Harwich with them from somewhere in Thames Valley and that, intending to return to Holland, she had been overtaken by circumstances. Somewhere on that journey, by known means but by agency unknown, she had met her death.

Inquiries were being made with the ferry company and in Holland to establish whether the two Dutchmen had actually sailed back on the day for which the van was booked. Nowhere, to date, had any luggage or papers relating to them or to the dead girl been found. If they had been involved in her death, they could have taken her effects along with their own and lost them overboard in the North Sea.

On balance, because of the need to investigate her movements over the past few weeks, Anneke was now more Thames Valley's concern than East Anglia's, whose main inquiries would follow up the antiques end of the affair. A detective sergeant from the Essex force was being sent to liaise with Superintendent Yeadings's team, while a member of that team would look into the girl's earlier background in Holland, find the date she left for England and hunt for a putative father to the baby she'd been expecting. The Dutch police had not yet responded with the information requested, but it was expected hourly.

'I'll be sending you, Angus,' Yeadings warned.

'I'm not sure I'm the right one to go. Why not you, sir? You're not involved, and your rank would carry real weight.'

Yeadings closed the file with finality and stood to clear his desktop. 'Mine the strategy, yours the tactics, lad. Don't hedge. You'll be suggesting next we send old Acky.'

Mott gave a wry smile. 'His the paperwork. No, I guess I've drawn the short straw. I just wish I hadn't met her before.'

Yeadings froze. 'That's not guilt you're feeling, by any chance? Take the positive view. Having seen her alive, heard her talk, watched her actions, you're way ahead of the rest of us. If I didn't believe you could achieve the necessary detachment I wouldn't be sending you. But I am, and all I want from you now is to keep in touch by phone and give a full report on your return.'

'Yessir,' Mott was suddenly official, respectful, little short of clicking his heels.

Yeadings watched him go, grinning inside. What was the expression DS Beaumont used in like circumstances?— 'Sent him off with a flea in his ear.' Well, here's hoping the flea has a mighty big bite so that the lad gets stung into action. This is no time to go broody. Only one sure way to get out of the doldrums, and that's work. Work, with a pinpoint of success gleaming in the distance

ON ARRIVAL BACK from HQ, Yeadings sent again for Mott. 'The Dutch trip is sanctioned, and only a DI will meet the ACC Operations' requirements, lad. The chief constable has every confidence that you will combine tact and initiative. You can fly out of Heathrow tonight. We'll telex for someone to meet you with an info update at Schiphol airport.'

'I'd rather travel the way Anneke meant to. It's longer by sea, but I want to get the feel of it. It'll give me a chance to watch other Dutch youngsters, see where they congregate on arrival. I might make some useful contacts that way.'

'Days after she was meant to travel? Well, it's worth trying, and demands less from Finance. Let's hope we get a family address from the Dutch before you leave.'

'As to that, you remember she told me that she came from near Hilversum?' Mott said. 'I've been looking at a map, and there's a town called Amersfoort. Well, in the Chardleigh Place staff register she gave her local address as Amersham, but she messed it up, had to rewrite the last half. I think she was starting to write Amersfoort and then thought better of it, in case anyone used it to trace and contact her family. When you're communicating with the Dutch police, they might like to check on that.'

Yeadings buzzed switchboard and asked for the connection. 'Our DS from the Essex force reports at nine in the morning,' he said over one shoulder as he waited. 'Name of Bunter. I'll say goodbye, Angus. You've probably things to do.'

There were no hitches in making the call to Holland. A fluent English-speaker took the message and read it back correctly. Yeadings was thanked for the Amersfoort suggestion. The investigating Commisaris would be grateful, if he hadn't arrived at the address already.

That puts me in my box, Yeadings told himself. Still, the Dutch lad was covering for his guv'nor, and that was always a healthy sign. He hoped his own team did as much for him behind his back. He reached for the phone again and asked for Rosemary Zyczynski to step into his office.

'Sir?' she said hopefully, arriving within seconds.

'Z, how's your domestic science?'

'Passable. I can clean and cook.'

'You may need to mince and flounce a bit too. I want to put someone into Chardleigh Place to pick up whatever gossip's going. They're advertising in their local paper for various staff, including a temporary assistant housekeeper. Think you could manage that?'

'I'd need references, a hotel recommendation, sir.'

Yeadings was dialling again. 'I've a friend who is General Manager of a chain of South Coast hotels. He'll give you the background you need. Hallo, Charles . . . ?'

The waggish conversation ended on the superintendent's chuckle. 'Well, he insists on seeing you in person, so pop down to Brighton and his staff will give you an intensive four-hour course. If you pass his test at the end you'll get the best five-course dinner that you've ever had in your life. No, forget the driving. Get yourself a travel warrant and stay on overnight. Beaumont can drop you off at the station. I can't afford to lose you to a breathalyser on the way back.'

With Harwich, Holland and Chardleigh Place covered, that left Beaumont, Silver and the supernumerary Bunter for this end. Thin on the ground as they were, no one could object if he deserted his desk for a share of the action.

SEVEN

DS GEORGE BUNTER arrived next morning in a green Lada with a blue replacement nearside front door. He was lanky and ginger-haired, with a lopsided carroty moustache. His navy trousers and Fair Isle pullover were covered in long grey dog hairs. 'That'll be my springer,' he explained in his slow, country voice, brushing at the offending wisps with the heel of his hand. 'She's moulting in lumps. Must have got in sometime when I left the car door open.'

'A right wurzle,' Beaumont described him in the canteen, but unknowingly George was the bearer of information that was eventually to set the investigation on new lines. It came in the form of a request about another case. Arising from the telephone message from Mrs Bertie (Doris) Boulter of Colchester, Thames Valley were asked for help in tracing her son Ronald Gardner, widower of the late Penny Winter. He was thought to be staying with a young woman forenamed Janice in Beaconsfield.

Beaumont, instructed to deal with it, gave Bunter the phone number of Social Services so that they might do their own researches. He went himself in search of DCI Atkinson to insist that transport for any joint sallies with the Essex DS should be authorized in his own less remarkable Ford Escort. 'In case,' he said woodenly, 'the yokel's spilt cowpats or pigswill on the seat.'

They were summoned together to Superintendent Yeadings's office and further briefed on tracing the red Porsche Cabriolet of the inaccessible Arnold Coleman.

'I need that car by midday,' he told them. 'You two plus DC Silver will be tackling it through Cosmos staff present at the Chardleigh Place course, and also from the lists of Porsches available for hire within the Home Counties. Settle between yourselves how you share it. You can't have Z because she's undercover elsewhere.'

IN BRIGHTON Rosemary Z enjoyed the challenge of a busy holiday hotel. She spent the first two hours of instructions with the senior housekeeper and two chambermaids. While the girls serviced the bedrooms and private bathrooms of one section, the housekeeper kept up a commentary on their actions, stressing where they would most likely fall short of good performance. There followed an hour when they talked theory and covered stock holdings, laundry requirements, insurance liability, staff management and rights, liaison with kitchen, maintenance and front desk.

'At least you've seen the tip of the iceberg,' the formidable lady summarized. 'Now I want you to help set up three new suites in the next hour. When that's done to my satisfaction you can take a bath—and I assure you you'll need it—and join Mr Gadsby in the penthouse for drinks and dinner. By then we'll have a written appreciation of your ability ready and signed.'

A crash course, quite literally, Rosemary admitted to herself as she fell exhausted into scented, steaming water. 'Do I have to clear up afterwards?' she called through to the chambermaid completing the final touches to the bedroom.

The girl put her head round the door, grinning. 'No, this one's reserved for you. From now on you can be as mucky as any other guest. We'll ''do'' you tomorrow.'

'Fabulous!' Z said, luxuriating. 'I'll certainly leave something under the plate.'

She left Brighton next morning by an early commuters' train to Victoria, crossed to Marylebone for the Chiltern Line and arrived back at her digs in time to catch her landlady still at breakfast. There was a message waiting: the assistant manager at Chardleigh Place had telephoned inviting Miss Zyczynski to an interview before midday if possible. It seemed they were hard pressed.

Rosemary put on her burnt-orange suit and an ivory blouse, added a pair of plain-lensed froggy spectacles to add gravitas and went forth to the encounter.

The housekeeper herself was not in evidence and it was the assistant manager who interviewed her, escorted her round and appreciated the show she put on. Noncommittal, she surveyed the first empty conference hall from its doorway, drew on white cotton gloves from her handbag, and applied the fingertip test. Dust on the cross bars of the nearest chair, above the film screen, all over the shade of an elaborate adjustable lamp she ordered to be lowered from the ceiling.

They moved on to the first of the bedroom suites. Here the upkeep was better, but a light powdering of talcum fell from the stiff upper folds as she agitated the shower curtain. Emerging from the bathroom she displayed her nail file draped with an ugly residue from the plughole.

'OK,' the man said, 'see if you can make the girls do better. Come and look at the books. I've got an agreement made out. Four weeks, which just overlaps with the new permanent person who's coming. You can start today or tomorrow, if you're free.'

'This evening at six,' Z stipulated. 'I have to collect my things first. Perhaps I could see my room now. Then I'll need a lift into Maidenhead.'

'Ah, that last may not be so easy. We've a courtesy coach for Heathrow, but nothing in the opposite direction, unless the gardener or a visiting tradesman's going that way. One snag about being out here; you do need your own car.'

They jockeyed round each other over her demand for a taxi back and another to bring her with her luggage that afternoon. Clearly the job did demand her own transport.

'A CAR?' BEAUMONT complained when she appealed to him. 'I don't know. Everything's in over-use already. Except—' He eyed the ginger newcomer who was regarding the trim little WDC with slightly astonished admiration.

'Bunter, how about yours? We'll be in harness together for the most part.'

'I understood,' Yeadings interrupted, 'that there was some drawback to that vehicle?'

'It's piebald,' Beaumont retorted. 'An odd door, and it needs vacuum-cleaning inside. But it goes, doesn't it?'

'It's reached a hundred and twenty on a chase,' said Bunter modestly, with his slow, countryman's smile. 'Kind of sneaky. It has a replacement 3.5 litre engine under the bonnet. People don't expect it.'

Yeadings watched the man and something clicked. Kind of sneaky yokel as well, in all likelihood. He hadn't become a DS that young just because Essex had nothing else but turnips on offer. There could be something quite high-powered under that ginger thatch too.

'If it's just a matter of one door, Bunter,' he considered, 'and you'd let Z borrow your car, we could get the door resprayed today and you could drive it to her tomorrow. Get a look at the layout of the place while you're there, just in case we ever need to follow up.'

'How'll he get back?' Beaumont demanded. 'It's at the back of beyond.'

'You'll follow in your car. I'll authorize the respray, so set it up with the garage. Now, while on the subject of transport, how far are we with the red Porsche?'

'A no-no from the Cosmos Assurance transport officer. Two grades of company car for the staff on the Chardleigh course; Peugeot 305s and 505s, all silver. Our con artist wasn't with Cosmos, sir. We're still going through the lists of current registration models available for hire.'

'Best get back to it soon, then, if there's nothing more to discuss. You trot along too, Z. Ring me every evening after eight at home. Nan will take a message if I'm not there. We should have word from DI Mott soon. If he caught the 21.30 crossing last night he'd have been due in at the Hook of Holland at seven this morning.'

ANGUS MOTT, tall, athletic, blue-eyed, blond, had the ability to shed years when he needed to look the carefree student. He was travelling the hard way, as if every coin had to be counted to spin out his vacation, and he'd had no difficulty joining the polyglot herd of young people under the same restraints. Not for them the overnight berths or the first-class lounge and bar. He spent some time fiddling with a strap as he lodged his backpack in the luggage compartment on boarding the ship, and chose his company with care. Not the obvious Dutch sex kitten, but the overweight little one with the cheerful grin and the snub nose. He managed to walk back on her toe as he stacked his gear and, apologizing, offered gauchely to put it right with a cup of coffee. Fruit juice; she was into a caffeine-free routine, she told him. Trouble was it had turned out high in carbohydrates.

Energy food, he agreed happily, ignoring the inference that she had surplus flesh to be ashamed of. She glowed, tried a bit of eyelash-fluttering and they were away, instant friends. They talked walkers' backpacks; whether metal frames were all they'd been cracked up to be. Squishy, she said was her criterion: something that sat easy on the back of the hips, and then two sausages of equal weight hung on long straps from the shoulders. Worked fine, if you'd plenty of pockets in your shirt and pants for tickets and passport.

She eyed his lean-line jeans and denim jacket. 'You haven't done this much?' she asked. Then hastened to assure him he looked fine, but just a bit, well—last year's news, like.

Lord, she was going to patronize him! Still, she did seem well clued up on singles travel. He asked where she'd visited in England, learned she'd moved around, 'done' all the main cathedrals, was crazy about church architecture. No, it wasn't her profession: she worked in a bank, intended one day to be a manager.

Like Anneke, Yolande spoke almost perfect English but wasn't condescending about his lack of languages. She admired much that was English, British even, but she thought that the native young were on the uptight side. Except the yobbos; they were the pits. There were hooligans in the Netherlands too, of course, but the kids mixed more freely. It sort of diluted the nuisance.

Which led on naturally to where young people got together, and what Mott must be sure not to miss seeing.

'Amsterdam,' she said definitely. 'Everything's there. All the other big towns are stuffy, run by the crumbly stiff-shirts. Go and see Rotterdam, Delft, the Hague, but *stay* in Amsterdam. You'll love it.'

Having handed out this advice she admitted that she lived in Utrecht, but would make for the capital the minute a vacancy came up in a branch of her bank there. It might be a long wait, because everyone young, but everyone, wanted the same.

He had to reciprocate with some personal history, passing himself off as a clerk to a legal partnership in Berkshire. Over fruit juice and a cafeteria salad they shared a little moan about the depressing respectability of their chosen professions, the restrictions exercised by their seniors and the lack of opportunity for promotion.

Eventually, as the upholstered seats were mostly occupied, they set up camp in a quiet corner on a li-lo Yolande produced, complete with pump, from the lumpy sausage bag she had been humping around. This bag, still padded with anonymous belongings, they shared in moderate comfort as a bolster. As Mott drifted into sleep he congratulated himself on having fallen in with a peach among women.

After breakfast when the cafeteria opened at six they sat about waiting for the official docking, saying goodbye on land, when Mott's luggage was being examined while Yolande's was passed through on the nod.

I must look a wrong 'un, he told himself. Anyway what would a UK tourist be bringing into Holland? Wasn't all the drug- and gem-smuggling in the opposite direction?

When Mott had decided the Customs officer was just relieving his boredom with a random search, a fresh-faced civilian appeared, smiled broadly and introduced himself as Constable First-class Pieter Sebens who would see him to the train for Amsterdam. Mott let himself be nannied along to his reserved seat. On arrival, he was told, a municipal police officer would meet the train. Either the Dutch were over-polite or they'd little confidence in a British CID-man getting from A to B on his own.

It was four or five years since Mott's last visit to the Netherlands but the memory was instantly revived as from the moving windows he recognized the same pearly morning light striking comfortable farmhouses, glinting on canals. At Amsterdam he let the crowd clear before starting for the exit, certain that his description would have been phoned ahead. His eyes met those of a melancholy-featured lounger who dropped a half-smoked cheroot and stamped on it once with killing finality. 'Detective-Inspector Mott? I am Adjutant Jan de Vries. Welcome to Amsterdam.'

Police HQ was not far from the central station but they went by car, de Vries shouldering his way to it through a group of South American musicians playing weird, thin pipe-and-drum music on the cobbled forecourt. Their faces were impassive under the long hair and black felt hats. The women had richly coloured ponchos and the undersized children used their huge, sad eyes in silent begging.

'Where do these people come from?' Mott asked, looking back at them from the moving car.

'Who knows? They say Surinam, but their papers could be false. They are our new Europeans. You have some similar influx in Britain. Perhaps these are from Colombia, Brazil, Peru, any place which they think should make us suffer for having once had an empire. And they bring their problems with them.'

'Last time I was here every sixth person was Indonesian.'

'No shortage of those either. From the East they bring the heroin, these others from the Americas the cocaine. We police should be happy to have so much employment.'

A cynic, and possibly a racist. Wouldn't have a great opinion of the Brits, come to that, Mott decided. Why had he been allocated this long-featured, fiddle-faced misery? And where did the rank of adjutant fit into the Dutch police hierarchy? It sounded important, but he suspected it was just above sergeant and one down from his own. Not that it mattered, because everything would be done on the basis of host and guest, with no question of seniority; yet if it came to the crunch...

'We have traced the girl's family,' de Vries said, suddenly. 'Such as it is. A grandfather, retired Reformed Church pastor, aged eighty-four. Very strict. Not surprising, perhaps, that the eighteen-year-old Anneke Vroom chose to run away and seek her fortune in the capital. In his eyes, of course, she made a pact with the devil.'

'And did she?'

'Can't say. We think she joined the young flotsam of the streets and squats. You will see them, mimers or pavement artists or musicians or pickpockets or muggers. They sell what gifts they have and they share what they get with other young people who are on the way out.'

'What happened to Anneke's parents? Are they both dead?'

'Her father was killed in an automobile crash in Germany six years ago. His wife had died some ten months earlier. Not a fortunate family at all. The father was a heavy goods driver, working across Europe, so when the mother fell seriously ill the child was sent to the maternal grandfather. This is the old man you will be meeting: Maarten Coornhert. After you have reported to the Commisaris I shall be driving you to Amersfoort.'

Such misfortune detailed in de Vries's lugubrious tones was gloomy enough. But as it was the vital Anneke he spoke of, whom Paula had described as proud of newly acquired assertiveness—so newly that she wasn't quite sure how to handle it, overdid the familiarity, stepped on a few toes— this had a special pathos. Angus felt immeasurably depressed as he was led through an office of young detectives curious to observe him, and after a short wait ushered into the Commisaris's presence.

And he, in rank equivalent to Mike Yeadings, was small and rotund and merry-eyed, a younger, unwhiskered Santa Claus in whose world surely nothing could go very much

amiss. A born public relations man who had only to an-
nounce a disaster for the public to be reassured. Perhaps it
was as well that such as de Vries were out on the streets
keeping in touch with awful reality.

Yet as Angus related what he knew of Anneke Vroom's
last weeks in the UK the little man sat, head cocked like an
intelligent robin waiting on the windowsill for scraps. At the
final description of how she was found crammed in the
dowry chest intended for export to Holland, Commisaris
Stuyvesant sat back appalled. 'Poor child,' he said simply.
'A terrible thing. We must do everything possible to bring
to justice the people responsible.'

'We can't prove murder yet,' Angus warned him. 'But
someone certainly packed the body away and secured the
hasp on the chest. And that person may be the one who ad-
ministered the heroin first. Apparently she wasn't a habitual user. A full pathology report is due shortly.

'Meanwhile we have particulars of the two antiques dealers and artist's sketches drawn from customers' descrip-
tions. They made at least three journeys to the UK in the
past six months, collecting small items from the Home
Counties and East Anglia. This seems to be the first time
they drove as far west as South Bucks. As the girl had been
in that locality for several weeks the change of route may
have been connected with her. On the other hand they may
have met up by chance and she accepted a lift with the intention of returning to Holland. But Sealink can't trace an
advance booking for her, and unfortunately no handbag,
papers or passport were found with the body.'

'So identification,' said Commisaris Stuyvesant, fixing
him with his bright, shrewd eyes, 'might not have been possible even now, had you not already been acquainted with
the young lady?'

'That's so. I was sent by chance to look at the van because a car park sticker from our locality was found on her body.' It sounded apologetic, almost over-protest.

There was a significant silence. Mott looked from the Commisaris to de Vries and back again. In both men's eyes he read the same doubt. For the first time he realized that Yeadings had sent him here to confront their personal suspicion. They were distanced from the crime, and he was their only connection. The only suspect on offer.

'That would have been quite a considerable—*shock* to you?' The Commisaris made the question silkily sympathetic. Synthetically.

'It was.'

De Vries cleared his throat, no more. Mott's gaze swung back. The slitted, world-weary eyes looked through him. There was nothing new left to shock the Adjutant.

Commisaris Stuyvesant sighed. He appeared to be thinking, barely aloud. 'We shall need to know what attracted Anneke Vroom to your part of the world. And why she apparently decided to leave it.'

EIGHT

SUPERINTENDENT YEADINGS replaced the receiver with a wry smile. Angus had walked right into it, as was inevitable. The Commisaris was quite properly concerned about a fellow-national found dead abroad. Sides must be seen to be taken. What had happened to young Anneke Vroom was pitiable, and the UK was to be held answerable that she hadn't returned in the same good order that she had arrived. Angus represented that other party, and furthermore, he had met the girl, spent at least a day in her company, in suspicious alien eyes could even have been personally involved with her.

Well, the lad was fit to cope, and it would do no harm in the long run for him to experience the other side of the interrogation table. Their Dutch opposites had to be satisfied that every possibility was being checked, even to sifting the motives and opportunity of any investigating officers peripherally involved. To have removed Angus from the scene totally might at first sight have seemed proper, but that would have been negative. In this way he'd get positive clearance. After a certain, hopefully brief, discomfort.

The Amsterdam Commisaris had asked for an independent report on the weekend Angus and Paula had spent with the other two at Chardleigh Place, and Yeadings had assured him that the staff had been questioned and an officer was also working undercover on the inquiry.

In Yeadings's opinion it would take a few days for her to penetrate the establishment and shake out the tittle-tattle. Her first call-in would be tonight. He was determined to get home in time to take it direct. There were questions he'd need to ask. Rosemary Z was a bright girl and learning fast, but she hadn't a lot of CID experience. On the positive side, he was eighty per cent sure she wouldn't be in any danger working there alone.

Meanwhile, George Bunter: already gleams of solid worth were showing through the chinks in his gangling yokel disguise. And Yeadings had confidence that DS Beaumont was astute enough to catch on, so making him more vigilant in competition with the outsider.

They were still following up the lists of new red Porsche Cabriolets. Despite talk of a recession, there were more of that pricey and eye-catching model than expected. All hiring agencies in the Thames Valley area had been exhausted and Bunter was now checking on the whereabouts and recent history of privately owned local models, while Beaumont worked through a list of other Home Counties and London agencies.

It all took time, locating addresses, then setting up meetings for personal interviews. The name Arnold Coleman had not appeared anywhere yet, and it seemed unlikely that Z, in her housekeeper role, would unearth any clue relating the car to the man, although if he reappeared at Chardleigh Place she would be on the spot to tackle him.

Quite what he hoped she would discover, Yeadings couldn't say. The Dutch girl's few effects at the hotel had offered no clues and the management had volunteered little about her. It looked at first as though they would have denied all knowledge, until DI Mott had insisted he'd met her as a casual worker there. Even if nothing further was officially admitted, there might be some tenuous personal link so far unexplored. Someone must have told the Dutch girl about Chardleigh Place and that temporary help would be taken on without close inquiry into references. And how had she reached there, having no transport of her own? Coming from where? And how recently arrived in the UK? Rosemary had met the resident staff the previous evening and the daily chambermaids when they came on duty at eight. Forewarned at Brighton, she sanctioned the traditional coffee session on arrival, because their scramble to rally their children for school and husbands for work left little time for snatching breakfast. She greeted them cheerfully, announced they had a clear run until ten-thirty when she would start on her bedroom rounds. She implied they would wish her to find everything in good order. And as they moved off to collect their gear she overlooked the barely audible comments this drew. There always had to be one of these under-the-breath mutterers. Among the police it was much the same.

When she checked their work she found no major instances of corner-cutting, and sympathetically agreed the universal difficulty of cleaning behind taps. She insisted that the guests' radios be kept at lower volume while the girls worked, and later returned to the channel originally set.

The official housekeeper made her first appearance at senior staff elevenses, which was served from a running buffet next to the main kitchen. She was a thin, elderly woman with blue-rinsed hair folded back into a French pleat, and she walked painfully with the aid of an elbow-crutch. She explained to Rosemary that she was recovering from a thigh fracture which had not improved her general arthritic condition. The woman's surname was Denison, the same as the middle-aged general manager's, and front desk later confirmed Rosemary's guess that he was her son.

At the woman's departure, Z became aware of the others huddling over a printout sheet with varying exclamations of delight. She decided against appearing curious, made some excuse about checking laundry and left them to it. In snippets gathered from the far side of the partly closed door she heard sums of money quoted, and assumed that a book was being run in which a number of them were winners. But if so many won, who were the losers? The answer came to her during the early afternoon when a junior from front desk circulated urgently whispering, 'Dollar's falling. Buying yen,' followed by a marked general movement towards the hall to initial a paper.

Legitimate or not? Z had no idea, except that actual currencies had to exist to back up the paper exercise. And where else, so close to the world's biggest international airport, than the money which foreign guests exchanged officially or used for cash transactions? They would be given the going rate for the day less a handling charge, but apparently the hotel's senior employees had a syndicated fund which acquired these and used a front desk broker to play *bureau de change* Monopoly. But didn't the hotel inquire into the loss of its own expected profits?

During the late afternoon the fine weather broke dramatically. Thunder rumbled in, followed by a downpour with no sign of letting up. A phone call from the bodywork men respraying Bunter's piebald car's door regretted that due to slow dry-out it couldn't be delivered until next morning. Now if Z followed her intention to use the nearest public telephone kiosk rather than risk an internal call routed through the switchboard, she would be a sodden wreck before walking the necessary half-mile there. But the Boss expected her to ring after eight.

At ten past, with coins piled ready, she waited at the crossroads, shivering and dripping, for the connection to be made. 'Hullo,' Yeadings answered, offering no name. 'That you, Z?'

She assured him the line was clear and summarized the day's pickings: a check on the register which showed Cole-

man's name only once, and that for the Cosmos Assurance
conference week; his overlapping of five days with Anneke
Vroom who, according to the staff day book, received full
board and a pittance against 'general duties' from the latter
half of the Cosmos booking.

Rosemary explained she hadn't yet managed any gossip
with staff about the Dutch girl or pricey cars: they were
amiable on the whole but still unsure of her as an outsider.
She mentioned the currency scam, but the superintendent
agreed it was probably irrelevant: a mere smirk on the face
of private enterprise.

'How d'you find Bunter's car?' he asked finally, and
clucked on hearing it hadn't arrived. 'Are you speaking
from Chardleigh Place, then?'

Rosemary explained and he caught on at once. It was
deluging with him too. A lovely drop of rain for the garden, but he could see the drawbacks.

'We'd better fix it so that you can ring me discreetly from
work,' he said. 'Ask for your auntie if you're likely to be
overheard. Better use Nan's name. Auntie Nan if there's not
a lot to report; and cover what you have to say in waffle.
You'll find she's quick to catch on, and I have a recording
switch. With anything more important, or in an emergency, ask for Aunt Laura. Then we'll send someone out to
you. How's that?'

'Fine, sir. Thanks.' She replaced the receiver, smiling.
Laura Norder, much-quoted by DS Beaumont. She was
hardly likely to forget the name.

ADJUTANT DE VRIES drove a small Volkswagen at a reasonable speed but steering with one hand—the other occupied
with the inevitable cheroot and dismissive gesturings to explain the landscape they were passing through. For the first
time he showed some animation, as though this trip to in-

terview Anneke's grandfather represented a kind of social outing for them both.

They left the built-up area quickly behind, travelling through farming country with occasional glimpses of water, then by forests interspersed with stretches of heath. Passable riding country, de Vries declared, though Mott saw only bicycles on the rough tracks beside the motorway.

Anneke's sometime home lay on the far side of Amersfoort, a pleasant, scrubbed-clean sort of town perhaps a fifth of the size of Amsterdam. Maarten Coornhert sat waiting in the shade of a small verandah on the front of a modest, old-fashioned house.

He seemed an extension of its slightly dingy pepper-and-salt shabbiness, tall and dried-out, with an unhealthy pallor. The long moustache, white at its tips but stained from tea round the mouth, drooped and gave his whole face an appearance of sagging melancholy. When he rose at their approach his lean frame stooped too, his weight resting on a hand-carved Indonesian walking-stick. He observed them with tired grey eyes which seemed to despair of all passion but condemnation. Inside the tannin stain his mouth took on a bitter twist. Mott, pitying him for the talk they must have together, felt a greater rush of sympathy for Anneke. She dead, while this forbidding old image lived on: it was a mockery. Perhaps the man recognized that too and suffered for the irony of it.

De Vries, having met Coornhert before, performed the introductions. Formally the old man invited them into the parlour, a small room with drawn blinds which seemed crammed with empty china bowls balanced on jardinières. Mott traced its musty smell to a bunch of dried grasses and wild flowers stuffed in a black iron pot in the unused fireplace, all bleached now to a uniform parchment shade. He felt that if he should brush against them as he moved past to the table they would crumble to papery dust.

De Vries helped out Coornhert's halting English as the old man produced a photograph album and indicated who the stiffly portrayed characters were. First came old monochrome prints of himself and his wife with the baby who grew up to marry—disappointingly, one gathered—the long-distance heavy-goods driver Johan Vroom. There was a studio shot of the couple with the child Anneke aged about five, stocky and solemn, standing awkwardly with one arm behind her back, the hand clasping her other elbow. Her uncut hair was strained back into two equal plaits and she frowned as if its pulling gave her a headache.

Coornhert closed the album abruptly, but not before Mott saw that photographs had been torn from later pages, leaving parts of their pale backs stuck to the darker sheets. These must have covered periods of which he preferred not to be reminded. From inside the back cover of the album he produced a bundle of loose snapshots showing Anneke, older, with schoolfriends. Some of the later ones had this house in the background.

'Dead,' said the old man flatly. 'The others—my wife, my daughter, the man—by then they are all dead.'

He looked at Mott with fierce accusation. 'And now Anneke. Everyone dead. But I go on.' He turned to de Vries and made demands loudly in Dutch.

'Mr Coornhert wishes,' the police Adjutant translated emotionlessly, 'that you should tell him everything you know about his granddaughter's stay in England.'

THE DISAGREEABLE BUSINESS with the old grandfather over, de Vries displayed some discretion, or possibly fatigue, in driving up-country into open heathland, parking, and falling asleep in his seat with a cheroot dying on his lips. Angus removed the soggy thing for him, quietly abandoned the car with the door still ajar and trudged to a private point some two hundred yards off. There he sat, cross-legged on the heather and buzzed about by bees in the hot afternoon sunlight, and wrote up his notes for Superintendent Yeadings.

Keener to demand an account from the Englishman, Coornhert had given him little fresh information, but every moment in his company had underlined the depressing circumstances which had driven the young Anneke to look for life elsewhere. The *pre-assertive* Anneke, Mott granted, because Paula's assessment of her as proud of newly acquired self-confidence was proving true. The image of the younger Dutch girl which Angus now carried with him was of a lumpish, slightly overweight eighteen-year-old, disciplined to be undemanding, inarticulate but avid for a freedom guessed-at yet still unidentifiable.

In Amsterdam, had she found it? She had anyway started out on the trail which led ultimately to Harwich and her cruel death.

But perhaps Harwich was irrelevant. She had most likely been dead before the van reached there, the killing enacted along the way, possibly in the Thames Valley area where she had lived for an unknown period, unremarked by anyone in the job except himself over that short, abortive weekend at Chardleigh Place.

When had she first arrived in England? Coornhert had known nothing of her movements for the past two years, and even her passport, which was still missing, would have held no clue, stamping no longer being necessary for EC citizens. The only way to find an answer while details of travel bookings were still unavailable was to follow in her tracks to Amsterdam, identify what friends she'd made in the capital, work on whatever recollections they might willingly offer—or, if reluctant, let slip.

To say that de Vries awoke refreshed would be to underrate his faculty for personifying world-weariness, yet even he seemed to respond to the natural surroundings. He yawned, paused in the act of removing a cheroot from the crumpled packet, squinted sourly at the honey-scented heathland rolling toward distant blue-green conifers and said, 'Suppose I shouldn't.' Regretfully he replaced the cigar, only to go for it absently five minutes later as they mulled over their meeting with the grandfather.

Mott told him what he hoped to follow up next and the man nodded. 'Meet some kids, yes. But first we make you look less British, I think.'

By now Angus had got the message. People, as they passed them in the street, had let their eyes slide over de Vries, but they lingered on him. A noticeable foreigner unable to fool the natives.

It was the tailored jeans mainly. Here the Asian-droop pants were universal but they'd taken on the national ballooning character of two centuries back. In a street market Angus found something suitably bulgy in washed-out blue-grey cotton. With his denim jacket left in the car, and wearing a black T-shirt dingily printed with a circuit diagram, he passed muster with de Vries.

Back in Amsterdam, they got rid of the car and took to their feet, ploughing through the evening crowds on Damrak where eating-places jostled in polyglot abandon, and exuberant Italian chefs performed competitively in the front windows of pizzerias, slapping pastry on marble slabs and whirling the doughy discs on the end of a finger before loading on the tomato paste, cheese, mushrooms, artichoke hearts, peppers . . .

'Time for a drink before dinner,' the Adjutant announced, leading him into a maze of little streets. It was genevar he ordered, with a throat-searing fire in it which gin in England never had. De Vries was more practised, Mott calculated as the empty glasses on the table proliferated, but he was also smaller and less fit. England expected, and all that: one must see what benefit there was in a greater volume of blood to be polluted.

He was getting owlish, he admitted, as de Vries lifted a finger towards the girl at the bar yet again. Next time, when it was his turn, Angus would fetch the drinks, prove to himself he wasn't legless. They went on 'having a drink before dinner', but the food never came. Eventually they made it to the men's room and silently declared a truce. Mott and the Adjutant slunk out into the night.

The dive where de Vries had put him through the crash course of geneva had seemed at first sleazy, then taken on a womb-cosiness which he was now loath to quit. Out here he felt defenceless without the low-volume compulsive music, steady as a pumping heart, in which the downbeat timpani was complemented by some unknown instrument producing the audible effect of a large cow-hoof squeegily removed from an unyielding bog.

Now there was no consecutive experience. Stills of individual scenes, figures, faces, patterns of coloured lights presented themselves and were withdrawn. Between them he chugged on mentally in a hazy maze. The two men let themselves be borne along by the crowds. In the open cobbled space before the royal palace—unguarded by bearskins, railings or protocol; just grimy stone sullied by pigeon-droppings—there was a thin English boy, stoned half out of his mind—top hat, grease-painted face. Union-Jack singlet—pathetically failing to juggle with three skittles.

Nobody minded, no policeman moved him on. Of course, their royal family rode out on bikes, didn't they? Anything else would be hardly fitting. None of this would do for EIIR.

Among the greasy, strutting pigeons sat the unwashed young and stood the bemused not-so-young feeding the birds. Mott leant a moment against a shop front. More detached frames of film. The fiddle-shaped face of the Dutch Adjutant loomed close in fish-eye lens treatment. Then they were weaving through traffic, joining a standing queue, Angus grasping a horizontal bar in a sort of sheep pen while de Vries groped in his pockets for money. The single frame of a notice-board came up and Mott read the words on it: *'It's nice to be important, But it's more important to be nice.'*

He shook his head. It was still there, in English only. Other nations didn't need to be reminded.

Well, he was doing as suggested, being nice, putting up with the Commisaris's snide suspicions, letting de Vries lead him around like a bull on a nose-ring, yielding up his virgin British stomach to their neanderthal Nederland firewater.

A pair of lovers joined the queue, abandoning their bicycles on the ground, secured together with a single chain. Mott removed his eyes from the strangely copulative sight. 'Nice,' he insisted to de Vries as they steadied each other in boarding the glass-topped canal boat and sank on to a double seat in the stern.

Then, as the rows of façades floated by above, it was de Vries's face repeated over and over again in the Dutch gables of the old houses crowding the Singel and all along the Herengracht: stepped gables, baroque gables, necked gables, fiddle-shaped gables; all de Vries with different expression and electrically lighted, sometimes curtained, eyes.

And all having hoist beams—a long shaft stuck out of the centre of their forehead like a crossbow bolt.

They bobbed, throbbed, slobbed through wide docks lined with old sailing ships, sleek passenger liners. The tilting and tossing became critical as they reached open sea. A period of acute enforced body control, and then mercifully they were back in the Singel, tying up, stumbling on to dry land, vomiting behind the little hut with the notice about 'more important to be nice'.

Mott was shamed. De Vries grinned groggily, slapped the Britisher on the shoulder. 'Now you are ready,' he said, 'to meet the young on their own terms.'

MORE SIGNBOARDS in English: 'Young Budget HOTEL KABUL' advertising 10-bedded rooms, with an address in a street he'd surely seen. An Afghan youth hostel?

'Not there, I think,' de Vries told him. 'I know somewhere country girls are more likely to have heard of.' They followed more dark and twisting streets.

Wherever it was, this squat had never taken in an Anneke Vroom. The group leader suggested another address which equally drew a blank. At their third stop, slightly less downmarket, a scribbled list of past guests included her name, but she had stayed only three weeks.

'She had a friend Cornelia,' the woman in charge said. 'I know where she works. I'll write it down for you, but you must promise not to inform her family. These young people trust us, you see.' De Vries had not mentioned that Anneke was dead.

'We go there tomorrow, then?' Mott supposed.

But Cornelia's work was at a night club where she helped in the kitchen. They moved on there, to be told that weeks back she had been obliged to leave. After a little pressure from de Vries the girl's last address was unearthed.

They were back among the canals, or it could have been the Amstel; by now Mott's bump of location had flattened out. De Vries was shining his torch on the bows of barges, looking for a name on the greasy hulls.

'Ah, *Hippopotame*! Here we are.' He rapped on a dimly lighted window and after a moment the curtain was twitched back. A silhouette with bunchy hair appeared against the glass to peer into the dark outside. A girl's voice called out in Dutch, de Vries answered and there followed scrabbling sounds as the door on deck was unfastened.

'"Have you brought it?"' de Vries translated sourly for his colleague.

'And you said "yes".'

'My "it" is you, fellow-pig.'

'But it's a fix she's after?'

'A fix she's before, most likely.' The Adjutant's long face twisted in a savage grin at his own wit. He stepped up and hauled Mott after him. They shouldered their way past the old timbers of a narrow doorway, stumbled down rough wooden steps, overriding shrill protests from the girl when she saw they were strangers.

'We speak English together, understand?' de Vries demanded, thrusting his face close as she fell back against the curving wall. 'My friend here needs to find someone he's fond of. Anneke, remember her?'

'You can't come here so—'

'We *are* here. Sooner you tell us how to find her, sooner we leave, eh?'

'She went. Long ago. I don't see her no more. Now you go. I am sick. Soon my friends come back. They don't like you.'

'They won't if we bust 'em, put 'em in the wagon.'

She gave a long wail followed by a flow of invective in incomprehensible Dutch.

'Cut the compliments. Anneke—she was here with you. When did she leave?'

'A year back. No, more. Eighteen months, twenty perhaps.'

'Where did she go? She surely told you her plans.'

'Just that she gets a man. Perhaps marries, yes? His first name was the same as her father's, but I forget it.'

'Johan?'

'Yes, it was Johan.'

'There are a hundred thousand Johans in this country, perhaps in Amsterdam alone.'

'Hard luck, then.' She had found anger enough to overcome her fear.

De Vries approached her closer. 'Rubbish person, empty out that raddled brain of yours. What more did she say of him? That he was big and strong, small and old, dishonest? Stank? Took size forty-eight shoes?'

'She did not speak much. We were not much friends then. Just that he was clever, had a medical job but would not give us any—' She stopped, shivering, covered her face and began to moan, turning her head from side to side as if in mortal pain.

'Had access to drugs and wouldn't deliver?' De Vries couldn't disguise his interest. 'This medical position?'

'I don't know. Go now. I am ill. Anneke's gone.'

'Here.' The Adjutant planted himself squarely between the girl and Mott, so he couldn't see what was put in her hand. 'Go wash your snots off. Then come back and remember some more.'

She scrambled away from him and scuttled through the cramped space towards a door at the far end.

'You were blind and deaf then,' de Vries told Angus.

The Englishman sat back on a chair. Something she'd said was circling inside his mind, unable to surface.

'They are friends when they share. Enemies if they break away.' De Vries was all cynicism.

'That's it! She said, "We were not friends *then*." Meaning they were friends at another time.'

'Before your Anneke decided to go her own way.'

'I don't read it like that.' Muzzily Angus paused, asking himself quite what he did read it as. 'I think she'd seen Anneke since, shared confidences...'

The girl Cornelia came back, sullenly vicious. 'You are mean, that's what. You could give me—'

'You could give me something first. Information. After Anneke left, you saw her again, of course. We get to know these things. When was the last time?'

Sulkily she answered in Dutch, slid on to a dilapidated couch and crossed her legs high up, looking at Mott hopefully under her eyelashes.

Although still foggy from the drink, his intuition was alerted. He couldn't find the questions to ask, but he knew at once, sensed, when the right answers came.

The girl with the bloated white face—a swollen, drowned fish belly—started wittering on, returned to stumbling English, was vacuous, irrelevant, then said suddenly: 'I tell you something. Anneke, she has dish- dis-illusion. Last thing she says to me, "Men are not nice persons."' Cornelia shook her head, seemed to float off into her own thoughts. 'Anneke is good, wants loving. To respect someone. But he sends her away.'

De Vries let the silence build up, then, 'This was just over three weeks back? How can you be sure?'

'My birthday,' said the girl. 'I am seventeen. I see her by the river opposite the Muziektheater. We walk and she takes me to L'Opéra for a drink. To celebrate.'

'This man she went away to,' Mott said, rousing himself at last to question her, 'where had she first met him?'

Her answer was incomprehensible, but de Vries nodded. 'I know the place. We'll look for him there. Are you sure Anneke didn't say what her future plans were?'

'She says nothing, except—'

'Yes?'

'Perhaps she goes abroad. For time to think.'

MIKE YEADINGS took the call from Holland at a little after 7.30 next morning. He came back to the breakfast-table looking thoughtful. 'How is Angus?' Nan demanded over the cereal packets.

Her husband adjusted to her line of questioning. 'Oh, all right, I guess. A touch jaded, now I come to consider. Spent most of the night chasing rainbows.'

'Pot of gold,' said Sally solemnly.

'Well done, chick. You remembered. But Angus hasn't found it yet. Today he'll be following up the odd clue in Amsterdam. He's been taken around by an adjutant who sounds quite a case.'

'An army officer?' Nan sounded puzzled.

'It's a police rank. Sort of junior inspector.'

'Mummy, Mummy—'

'I know, Sally. I'm trying not to notice.'

'Has he done that before?' Yeadings inquired, looking through, rather than at, his son who had upturned a pot of yogurt over his head and now looked delightedly astonished as it trickled down over his face.

'If we take it calmly it may be a unique performance. He wouldn't have wasted a fruit one. I only had that plain one left. We'll just leave him to feel uncomfortable for a moment.'

'So end all protests,' said Mike, rising to leave.

'Fascist!' Nan put up her face to be kissed and Sally followed suit.

Yeadings considered Luke's slimy condition, lifted a corner of the tablecloth to clean a space on the child's cheek and planted a smacker. 'Point taken, lad. Tomorrow you get a strawberry one.'

BY ARRANGEMENT Yeadings drew up between DS Beaumont and DC Silver in the library car park. The other two climbed out, joined him in the Rover and wound the windows down. George Bunter, Beaumont told him, was sweating it out in London car marts.

Since the replacement of Serious Crime Squads by Intelligence Support Teams their CID unit had survived but with an increasingly low profile, meeting at odd places, avoiding divisional offices, 'operating out of vehicles' as the CC chose to call it. It gave them greater cover, left them more on their toes, travelling light. 'Like living out of suitcases' was Beaumont's way of putting it.

The superintendent brought them up to date on the other two's activities. 'DI Mott's expecting to find Anneke's ex-lover today. They both used an eating place near the Netherlands Cancer Institute. A number of its staff pop in for meals. The dead girl's photo should jog someone's memory. The significant thing is that she was seen by this Cornelia boatperson as recently as three weeks ago. So, unless she was in the UK on an earlier occasion, we don't have to look for the baby's father here. It's a fifty-fifty chance whether Anneke suspected she was pregnant when she saw Cornelia. She didn't mention it.'

'Wouldn't that have been a welcome chance to let her hair down?' Silver suggested.

'Possibly, but it seems they weren't all that close, and Anneke was a pretty private person, modestly brought up. She may have hugged her secret for fear of coarse reactions. Her "Men are not nice persons", seems as far as she was prepared to admit things had gone very wrong with her expectations. At least we can gather she'd left, or been abandoned by, her lover.

'The Netherlands police should be able to turn up her travel application in the narrower time frame we have now,

and see whether there's any correlation with the two antiques dealers' movements. It's confirmed that they travelled home as planned, abandoning the van; so to my mind
they knew of its grisly contents and possibly had more to
hide which wouldn't take looking into. We can't overlook
the heroin connection. So far they've failed to surface on the
Continent.'

'I thought they were regulars on that route. Wouldn't
Customs make a point of tooth-combing their loads, sir?'

'Ideally, but if there were distractions there's little choice
sometimes but to let a lot through on the nod. All Customs
ever expect to score on is the tip of the iceberg. So—' he
shrugged— 'as they were regulars, unless there was information lodged against them... So many lions, so few
Christians to knot their tails together.'

'Leaving us to more of the same?' Beaumont assumed,
taking this as the wind-up of Yeadings's little homily.

'Turn up that damn red Porsche of Arnold Coleman's. As
soon as you've located it I can withdraw Z from the conference centre. We need her back here on the drugs end. So
make it this afternoon at latest.'

ROSEMARY ZYCZYNSKI (Miss Seal to the staff at Chardleigh Place) was stepping out of her office with a sheaf of
laundry lists when she almost collided with a waitress carrying a tray of used crocks from the first-floor bedrooms.
They grunted apologies simultaneously and passed on, then
the WDC heard the clicking of heels cease, and turned to
catch the other woman's slow double-take. Recognition
wasn't instant; more a sucked-in-cheeks, narrowed-eyes look
of 'Where have I seen her before?'

'Something wrong?' Rosemary demanded.

There could be trouble there, Z decided. She too knew
she'd encountered the other before, but where? Small, nar-

row-hipped, with an unremarkable face except for the high forehead under strained-back dark hair, the waitress could have served coffee and doughnuts anywhere in the Reading area when Rosemary called in wearing uniform.

The context would probably come to her in time, but would it reach her before the other woman? And could this chance encounter blow her cover? She looked at her watch, decided that retrieval of lost memories was best left to the subconscious. Senior staff elevenses were due: time to start prattling about her fictional boyfriend's super sports car, and see what envied models were put up in competition. Maybe a red Porsche Cabriolet belonging to a recent visitor? Then on to a little subtle teasing out of anecdotes about said customer.

THAT MORNING Angus had arrived at Amsterdam police headquarters to find that de Vries was out on a job and had requested he should wait there for him. He repaired to the canteen where young uniformed men asked him respectful questions about UK procedures and barely hid their disappointment that he wasn't from the Met. To hail from Scotland Yard still held the overall blue riband.

At a little after 9.20 de Vries swept in with a diabolical smile and an upturned thumb.

'You've scored?'

'Here we are. Johan—as Cornelia informed us—Groeneveld, not very high in the medical world, it seems; a laboratory technician.'

'Does that preclude him from obtaining drugs?'

'Not totally. He might well be able to get his hands on the right keys for long enough to take an impression and steal small amounts for personal use. The difficulty would be in covering up any losses—perhaps by mixing in chalk or some other substance to make up the weight—because these places are meticulous in their accounting for prescribed drugs. Anyway, I assume Cornelia's friends get their nasty habits from crack, which wouldn't be available there. But work with cancer patients could involve the use of diamorphine for pain suppression.'

'Heroin, in fact. Big H.'

'I knew you would wish to come with me when I visit the young man. The administrator's secretary told me he works shifts and we should find him at home before midday.'

JOHAN GROENEVELD sat gloomily waiting. He had sent his lover out with a list of shopping which should ensure no interruption until the threatened visitor had left. He had no idea why a detective should ask for him at work but it could do his reputation no good, however discreet the man had been. He must avoid drawing attention to himself, and even to witness a street accident was regarded as a scandal by the dried-out stiffies in admin. He wished that Arrielle on switchboard hadn't rung through to warn him, or that the shared phone downstairs had been out of use as it so often was. Even in that you could not rely on it. Waiting was so much worse than the real thing.

He heard steps on the stairs and men's voices. Expecting first to hear their car draw up outside, giving him time to pull himself together, he felt outraged, stood up facing the door, fists bunched, waiting for their knock.

It came as a knuckled *rat-tat*, with a flourish. 'Come,' he said, then remembered the bolt and went across to open up. There were two of them, the dark one sardonic, long-faced, the other younger, tall and athletic, with crisp yellow hair. It was the older one who began the questioning.

The detectives saw a tall, loose-limbed young man with a handsome profile and flaxen hair that flopped over eyes of innocent blue. He would have been attractive, certainly, to a young country girl on her own in Amsterdam, but right now he was uneasy.

'You are Johan Rinus Groeneveld?'

Groeneveld nodded. The man waited, so he added, 'I am.'

'Adjutant de Vries, Netherlands National Police. My colleague, Detective-Inspector Mott, is from England. Because of him we will talk in English.'

'I speak some, yes.'

'Can we sit down?'

'I suppose, yes.' This was terrible. They would think he was afraid of them if he said yes all the time. He struggled to assert himself. 'I have no idea why anyone comes from England and sees me.'

'Don't you know anyone over there?' This was the other policeman now.

'Perhaps I have friends on holidays. I can't say. Nobody I can think of.'

'Name of Vroom mean anything?' The older man sounded casual, but he looked up suddenly in the act of lighting a cheroot.

'Anneke? She is there?' It was clear he hadn't known.

'Anneke Vroom. You know her quite well, I think.'

The young man looked embarrassed. 'Once she lives here with me.'

'For quite a long time.'

'For over a year, perhaps nearly two. There was nothing wrong in our relationship.'

'When did she leave?'

'It would be a few weeks ago. Three, four maybe.'

'Did she leave anything behind? Here in your room?'

Groeneveld frowned, looking round. 'Some pots, dishes. A few magazines.'

'Did she have any post delivered, either while she was here or later?'

'Perhaps. I am not here always. There were some papers came at the end. But after she went, nothing.'

'And why did she leave?'

'That is not your affair.'

'Yours broke up, you mean?' The dark man was cynical. It annoyed him.

'It did not work out. These things happen. She was jealous.'

'You had someone else and she found out.'

'I have a friend she does not like.'

'And that friend—?'

'Out shopping. I ask you go before my friend returns.'

De Vries looked across at Mott, eyebrows satanically arched. Angus took up the questioning.

'Did you know where Miss Vroom was going when she left you? Make any arrangements to ensure she would be safe? I think she had few friends in Amsterdam.'

Groeneveld faced the Englishman. 'She is free to go, make her own arrangements. She learns typing and knows other students. Also she waits in restaurant, evenings, to make money.'

'I need the name of the restaurant, and the place she learned typing. Here, write them on this.' Over the boy's bowed head Angus passed a query to de Vries who took over.

'You did not know, then, that Anneke was dead?'

It shook him, the mention of death. He was shocked, even saddened. So she had meant something to him. 'No. Who would tell me? But she was well, strong. An accident, then?'

'No accident. Deliberate. An overdose of drugs.'

It seemed to puzzle him and distressed him even more than the fact that she was dead. Yet it was a way young people commonly chose to die. Crisis suicide from whatever drug they could lay their hands on at the time.

'Murdered,' said de Vries coldly, 'with diamorphine.'

For a moment they thought the boy would collapse. His face lost all colour and he swayed on his feet, put out a hand and lowered himself to a nearby chair. 'Terrible,' he said, after a moment with his face averted.

'In England?' he said suddenly, as if there was hope in that fact. 'What was she doing there? Where would she get heroin from?'

'We thought you might tell us. Some acquaintance you had in common who might have travelled with her?'

'I know nothing. Nothing at all. And now you must go. I have answered everything, but I cannot help you. I am sorry Anneke is dead. She was a good girl, an innocent. She takes no drugs when she is here, I am sure.'

'We shall need to see you again,' de Vries told him implacably. 'The same questions over and over, perhaps, but also some new ones when we know a little more. Shall we come here then or will you go to headquarters?'

Groeneveld looked sick. 'If you must, I come to you.' He stayed seated as the two detectives left.

On the way downstairs, 'At least we have two addresses to follow up,' said the Dutchman. 'But little else on Anneke. We might pass Groeneveld's name to the Drugs Squad for them to shake something out. There was a definite reaction when we mentioned diamorphine. And he preferred to call it heroin. Not the name they'd use where he works. A Freudian avoidance, would you say? That is certainly something that he does not care to have mentioned.'

'THREE, POSSIBLY FOUR, weeks since Anneke left Johan Groeneveld,' Angus said. 'And Cornelia ran into her just three weeks back, with sufficient funds to stand them both drinks at L'Opéra. So where was she living then? She could have stayed with a friend from the restaurant where she worked evenings or with someone from the typing school.'

'We'll tackle the restaurant first,' de Vries decided. 'If we arrive at the beginning of their lunch rush we shall worry the management. They'll spill all we need just to be rid of us.'

But there was little joy from that quarter. It was a small place of twelve tables. There were two other waitresses, both nieces of the Indonesian proprietor. De Vries, accustomed to the elasticity of the term, accepted the relationship in this case as strictly familial.

The 'Ari' of the restaurant's name could have been taken for the girls' considerably older sister, so slight and delicate was his physique. About forty years old, he had the same glossy, dark hair worn long to the shoulders, golden skin and long-lashed, slanting eyes. Dishy, if you had that homo kink, de Vries admitted.

The nieces were recently from Jakarta, servile and a little silly, but the trio made an ethnic unit. Working, they would have kept the Dutch girl at a distance.

'We know no friends of hers, and Anneke doesn't speak with customers. Just to take orders and be polite. More, our uncle does not like,' one of the girls told them and, judging by the blackly scowling Ari who chaperoned the interview, Mott could well believe this.

The girls had worked six evenings a week, Anneke having Wednesday free, the other two Monday and Tuesday, but from Thursday onwards, when the work was more intensive, all three worked flat out. Without a permanent replacement for Anneke they were at their wits' end.

'So check out her Wednesday evenings, and pin our hopes on the secretarial school bringing results,' de Vries summarized the options as they walked away. 'But after we have eaten. At present I have a quite abominable thirst.'

At a restaurant in the Rembrandts-Plein they enjoyed cheese omelettes with green salad, washed down by chilled beer and followed by enormous slices of spiced apple-cake.

'Classes will restart at two p.m.,' de Vries guessed, 'which gives us time enough to shake this meal down. We eat light lunches now because tonight my wife gives us dinner and among her many virtues she is a prodigious cook.'

Thank God, Mott thought, there'd be no second night of geneva. Happily he ambled in the Adjutant's wake for a second touristic round, this time on land.

'Here,' said de Vries suddenly, and they went in by a heavy oak door, mounted uncarpeted stairs, and entered a first-floor office.

Mevrouw Henstra, the school's principal, was making shorthand transcripts. She sat tall, was fiftyish, angular with a strong-boned square face, the pale skin papery fine and stretched tightly across wide cheekbones, puckered under shrewd eyes. Capable hands. Someone to be reckoned with.

Chin raised, she removed her glasses to examine the two men, shook her centre-parted grey-blonde hair which fell perfectly back in twin scimitar curves from temples to chin. She tapped her teeth peremptorily with a pencil. 'Gentlemen, I think you have identification to show me?'

Wordlessly they complied. She put her glasses back on to read the cards. Only her eyebrows queried the UK Thames Valley one.

She had had dealings with police before, remained distantly polite, cautiously correct, answered barely what they asked, at first offered little more. At the end of their questions she said, 'Anneke had no real friends. She was too old-fashioned for most of her own generation. Which is why I offered to help her when she was in trouble.'

'You, Mevrouw?'

'Why not? My students work better without stress. I offered her a room in my house when her lover turned her out. You knew, perhaps, that she was pregnant?'

De Vries nodded. 'What did she intend to do about that? Would the father help her?'

The woman pursed her lips. 'He was useless. I tried to counsel her, that she should have the baby and let some responsible person adopt it.'

'Yourself, for example?'

He had scored a bull there. She paused tight-lipped before going on. 'Anneke couldn't make up her mind. One day she would say this, another that. Sometimes she would lock herself away and cry and cry. Terrible. And so unnecessary. As if this was the first time in the world that a girl . . .' She shrugged dismissively.

'It happened to you once.' Not a question. De Vries said it with unexpected gentleness.

Again she tossed her fine hair and it fell back in the smooth grey-blonde curves. 'That is why I understood, why I could help her. My own child was stillborn. Over twenty years ago—a girl.'

And would have been about Anneke's age by now, if she had lived, Mott thought. So what exactly had this determined woman been after when she made that offer to

Anneke—a replacement baby, a grown daughter, or a lesbian lover? Whichever, she had been too strong-willed for Anneke, who had chosen once more to move on.

He leaned forward. 'But Anneke wasn't decisive like you, I think. You said yourself that she would change her mind whenever the wind blew. And perhaps there were others trying to influence her in different directions. What finally happened to make her turn down your offer?'

The woman pushed back her chair, stood and walked stiffly to the window. With her back to them, arms crossed, she drew breath deeply and said, 'Anneke asked me for money. Quite a lot of money. I knew she meant to have an abortion and to go her own way. I couldn't let her. She seemed quite reasonable when I explained why this couldn't be, but when I got home that evening, thirteenth June, she had gone, and taken her few things with her. I never heard from her since.'

'Did she leave a note?'

The woman unlocked a drawer in her desk and took a folded paper from the handbag in it. 'You may read it. It is simply to thank me and say "au revoir".'

'So she meant to see you again.'

'It would seem so.' She glared at de Vries, her mouth a hard line. 'Am I to understand she went to England? Why are you police looking for her? Has she done something foolish?'

'She is dead, Mevrouw. I am sorry. My colleague here is conducting a murder inquiry.'

She gave a soft gasp. Horror, disgust, pain? Whatever she felt, it was instantly gone, stifled under her habitual efficiency. Her shoulders sketched a barely visible shrug, then she held out her hand.

'I must say goodbye, Adjutant. I am due to take a class now. If you wish me to sign a statement I can come to your office this evening. Will that be convenient?'

'Perfectly.' It was exactly what he had been about to ask.

'Chilling!' Mott exclaimed, out again on the staircase. Was this woman the assertive, liberated ideal on which Anneke had tried to model herself?

De Vries was looking at his watch. 'Unfortunately I have an interview now on another matter. Perhaps you would like some time to yourself? I can pick you up from your hotel at eight, which will give us an hour to discuss the case over a glass or two before dinner. By then we shall perhaps have news of our antiques dealers. Such traders cannot disappear off the face of the earth. Maybe they bribe their associates to forget them and it takes a day or so to shake some sense into them.'

He chuckled as Mott darted him a questioning glance. 'No, no! We do not shake them by their collars. Just by reminders of indiscretions past, or of future ones we believe they are about to commit. There's a delicate line between an honest man and a rogue in their dealings, which sometimes makes it easier for us.'

Left to himself, Mott retraced his steps to the flower market, faced a choice of lilies, bright bulbous ranunculus, marguerites, and dahlias. Finally he bought long-stemmed pink roses for the Adjutant's wife.

Stretched out on the bed in his hotel room, he reconsidered Anneke, so cavalierly dismissed by him in the flesh: accepted as reckless, brash, a fun person out for a good time. And why not? Such a beautiful, brazen hussy she'd seemed, with bobbling boobs to strengthen the image.

And pregnant. Had even Paula, more perceptive and sympathetic than himself, noticed that? Pregnant and proud of her new assertiveness. Strangely confident, despite being thrown over by her lover who'd have nothing to do with their child—or perhaps never knew of it.

Why hadn't she *insisted* on his help? Was it that having been supplanted by his new love, her pride was scalded and she despised him for his faithlessness? Men being, as she'd mildly told Cornelia, 'not nice persons'.

Ms Henstra had offered the girl help, but by overmanagement she'd scared her off. Anneke had dithered between having the baby and an abortion. Or had she chosen to give that impression while working to acquire the money needed for the medical operation?

Then, her request to Ms Henstra turned down, she suddenly crossed to England. Why? She could have had the abortion as easily here in Amsterdam. So perhaps it was anonymity she wanted; fear that some account of her exploits might leak back to Amersfoort?

But in England she would still need money. Even more, because of travel on top of medical expenses. So somebody had to provide it. When de Vries confirmed the date of her crossing, the same day's passenger list might show up a significant name. Maybe the two Dutch dealers. Somewhere and at some time she'd linked up with them. Suppose it had been here while she was desperate for help, and they'd offered to employ her, pay her expenses, make it well worth her while.

Doing what?—she had no experience of antiques. But a healthy-looking, personable, backpacking young woman able to merge with the student groups flocking on and off the North Sea ferries—what better courier for clandestine goods? Taking into the UK amphetamines, coke or heroin; smuggling out small art treasures which, if found, Customs would have queried. Plenty of money to be made that way, if you're not detected—and only a very small minority of foot passengers off the ferries ever got searched.

From Amsterdam it had to be diamonds or drugs, and he knew which he thought more likely. The heroin factor in her death was unaccounted for as yet. At Chardleigh Place she hadn't struck him as a user, although the Anneke he'd met was very changed from the one who'd gradually emerged in retrospect over here. Yet he still didn't see heroin as a active factor in her life. She needn't be taking the stuff herself. It would have been folly in her pregnant state, unless she expected it to effect an abortion.

An alternative reason for her new-found confidence might be the Chardleigh job itself. Suddenly she'd found something she could do which paid, without back-breaking drudgery and unsocial hours. She could swan about, for the first time in her narrow life afford to enjoy herself a little in a role she played well. And it had been only a role: he remembered her embarrassed reaction when he'd rebuffed her in the rear of Coleman's Porsche. Not a case of the strictly brought up girl who threw her cap over the windmill, but an uncertain venture into new freedoms.

He wished he had Paula here now to talk it over. He was trained to observe, but she had the greater perception. She would understand Anneke so much better, being a woman herself. He needed to contact her, but it wasn't a subject he could foist on her at Chambers. He must leave phoning until she returned to her flat tonight, and there was no knowing at what time he'd get free from the de Vrieses.

THE ADJUTANT arrived a few minutes early, straight from work, and surprised him by heading for home instead of some favoured drinking place. And there were more surprises: Eva de Vries was small, dark-eyed, caramel-skinned with the glossy oriental hair of her maternal grandmother from Bali. She was also plumply vivacious, intelligent and full of laughter.

'So now, I imagine,' Eva said, 'you work backwards through this poor girl's life?'

'No. Forwards from the earliest point we could find,' said her husband. 'And still there is a gap.'

'But we haven't done too badly,' Mott conceded.

'Ah, I knew there was something I had to show you.' Mischievously the Adjutant, having shed ten years and the cares of office, pulled back his cuff, fluttered his fingers and drew a folded paper from the coiled hair behind Eva's left ear. 'Now what have we here?'

'Magic,' she said in her rich contralto.

Mott took the paper. It had a single name written on it. Johan Rinus Groeneveld. He looked at de Vries.

'I don't say he is your murderer, but he travelled to England on the same day as Anneke. Not the first time by ferry, but the second time. Because it appears that Anneke flew back to the Netherlands on Wednesday, twenty-third June only ten days after she had arrived. Then returned to Heathrow the following day. And Groeneveld was booked on the same flight. More than a coincidence, wouldn't you say?'

ELEVEN

ROSEMARY ZYCZYNSKI had made some progress in the quest for Arnold Coleman. The conversation, leading to upmarket cars, reminded a waitress of an incident three weeks back. As they sat out on the kitchen's walled lawn after clearing lunch the girl asked, 'Remember that flashy car the feller saw you home in once, Yvonne?'

'A Porsche,' said the other. 'He said it was German for "posh". And wasn't it? If you want to give me a prezzie...'

'What model?' Rosemary inquired, but the girl wasn't into technicalities. 'Couldn't say. An open one. A lovely red, it was.'

'Cabriolet 944S2,' said the sous-chef superciliously. 'That's about 3000cc.'

Police inquiries hadn't elicited that detail. Rosemary looked at him thoughtfully. Either he had suppressed the information or he'd missed out when Beaumont and Silver interviewed the hotel staff earlier.

Envy prompted him further now. 'It wasn't that Coleman bloke's, though. He was driving for one of the Cosmos bosses. Swanned about in the Porsche himself when it wasn't needed and after the others left. Fancied putting on the ritz to dazzle the women.'

'Did he come in daily, then?' Rosemary asked naïvely.

'Nuh. Was booked in with the rest of them. Full board. Bit of a perks fiddle, I'd say. Letting Cosmos pick up the tab. Same as for the car hire. Directors! You can get away with murder if you're high enough up the tree.'

The scorn in his tone didn't necessarily detract from the statement's validity, Rosemary thought.

'And you were the lucky girl who caught the chauffeur's eye, Yvonne,' she said admiringly.

'Not really. He just happened to be by the stables when I found my bike with a flat tyre. So he offered. Anyway, next day that Dutch girl turned up. Remember, Rene? She got a sleeping-in job. I reckon he helped her with that and all.'

There was a low snigger from the men. The quiet waitress with swollen feet said, 'It's not nice to talk like that about the dead. Anyway, she wasn't promiscuous, just friendly.'

Since nobody took her up on that Rosemary thought she'd better. 'What do you mean—"dead"?' she demanded, sounding shocked.

'Mr Denison said we're not to talk about it,' said Yvonne primly. 'Especially since the police came asking questions. Still, it was in all the papers. She was found murdered in some van on the east coast.'

'Harwich,' said the sous-chef, who liked precision. 'And there wasn't any mention in the papers of her having been here. Which is how the management want it kept.'

'Oh, I think I did read something of the sort,' Rosemary said vaguely. 'And that was the Dutch girl you said was working here?'

'If you can call it working.' This was Rene, following it with an audible sniff. 'Only here about ten days, and precious little she ever did. Junior assistant manager, they called her. I reckon Mr Denison was sweet on her. Doesn't get a chance for much you-know-what, always under his mother's thumb.'

One of the waiters made a spluttering sound. 'Don't be a wally. Denison's never heard of women.'

'Mebee. He didn't object to her hanging around with the Porsche bloke, anyway,' agreed another.

Rosemary put the Denison item on a back boiler for the present. 'So how did the Dutch girl come to be found so far away?' she pursued.

'Killed in a van. Vans have wheels, don't they? In any case she'd overstayed her two days off. Maybe she didn't intend coming back. I reckon she picked up with some delivery bloke who was a bit crazy. They'll trace him through the van. And whatever you say about Mr Denison, he nearly went spare when he heard she'd been killed. Bet he wouldn't have if it was one of us!'

And that was the sum total, a hotch-potch of reportage and vague innuendo, but it suggested lines to follow: at near hand, the hotel manager's possible interest in Anneke; and at Cosmos Assurance, a director who liked to make a personal splash and could include private expenses among legitimate claims. Because Coleman wasn't an insurance man, just his driver. All of which Superintendent Yeadings would need to know promptly.

There was a further matter, probably minor. She was still worried by the dark-haired waitress who had half recognized her as they passed in a corridor. Inquiry had by now produced her name—Hannah Minton—but it rang no bell. Rosemary had the feeling that when they met earlier she herself was in uniform and the other woman looked different as well. It remained to be seen which of them first arrived at full recollection of that other encounter. Meanwhile she watched out for her, noting that she hadn't been one of the recent group discussing Anneke's death, so might be taking a free afternoon.

Z went back to her little office, a cramped space off the kitchen corridor. From outside came the perpetual hum and clatter of the ice-making machine, constantly being raided for the restaurant and bars.

Detecting a discrepancy in the laundry accounts she decided to take it up with her theoretical senior, Mrs Denison. There might be some useful spin-off from that if she could bring the subject round to the woman's son.

At the foot of the staff staircase she again ran into Hannah Minton, but this time heavily made-up and dressed for some social outing. The woman's hair was crimped, pulled low over her forehead and fluffed out to fall like a spaniel's ears to her shoulders. She wore a broad, black patent-leather belt between ruffled satin blouse and bright emerald mini-skirt.

Their mutual recognition was simultaneous. Rosemary's air of competent officialdom, with the sheaf of papers in one hand, must have recreated an instant image of the courtroom WPC who gave evidence of arrest against the woman's brother, Dan Gray. It had been a charge of wilful damage to a motor vehicle. A plea for leniency had been made by his sister Mattie, with an unconvincing testimony to his previous good character. Mattie, well known to the uniformed branch for repeated soliciting. And here in a decent job, calling herself Hannah Minton.

For a brief moment they confronted each other, then the woman swept past, hissing under her breath.

Blown, thought Rosemary. How long before everyone knew there was a police spy on the staff? There was nothing she could do now to recover the situation. Best to carry on looking into the Denisons, and be prepared for getting slung out, bag and baggage, before nightfall.

After the laundry query, over which Mrs Denison was unhelpful and disinclined to prolong discussion, Rosemary had exchange bedrooms to check, those which hadn't come free for cleaning before noon hand-over. She went up now to see what progress there had been.

A bottle of red wine spilt over a beige mottled carpet and allowed to dry in overnight had delayed some of the team. Three girls were taking turns at scrubbing at the stain. Rosemary took a hand herself with a cup of lemon juice, but to little effect. Nothing for it but to get a maintenance man in to replace the carpet from stock.

There seemed no prospect yet of getting away to contact the superintendent. Her true identity could soon be common knowledge in the hotel—unless Mattie's own need for secrecy made her think twice about exposing Z.

By 4.45 p.m. the carpet job was nearing completion. Harris, the senior handyman, had located some matching Wilton which he was setting in competently enough. One of the chambermaids would stay on and clear up after him. Rosemary had exchanged the booking for this room with that for a similar room allocated to guests not due until an 8.00 p.m. arrival at Heathrow. Now she risked running down to the stable yard for a wild dash in George Bunter's car to the crossroads phone-box.

Only to find the car's engine dead.

The starter whirred desperately but no sparking followed. After three or four attempts she lifted the bonnet and did a quick survey. Wiring was all in place; plugs OK. Hell!—no rotor arm.

That was no accident. Had 'Hannah' removed it from spite, because her young brother had been run in for malicious damage to cars? Surely she wasn't into irony.

Whatever and whoever was responsible, enough time had been wasted. Z would have to phone from here and risk the switchboard operator listening in.

She returned to her office, buzzed through for an outside line. Then she pressed out Mike Yeadings's home number.

The dialling tone was repeated four times, ceased, and instead of the answering machine's recorded message came an uncertain voice. 'Yes? Who's that?'

'Sally?' At least she'd remembered the girl's name, but she dared not give her own. 'Listen, dear, is Mummy there?'

Clearly the youngster had been schooled to give nothing away. There was a short silence, then, 'Is that Z?'

'Yes. Can I speak to Mummy, please?'

'She's not here. Mrs Osborne's not well next door.'

'I see. Well, do you know the button for recording messages?'

'Is it the black one?'

'I expect so. Just push it, would you. I want to leave a message for Auntie Laura, and it's rather important.'

'All right. Do I say goodbye now?'

'Yes, please. Goodbye, Sally.'

After the girl's voice there was a slight pause, then some clicks like dialling sounds. With luck she'd have hit the right button. 'Aunt Laura?' Rosemary said. 'It's me. I've a bit of trouble with the car. Could you send George over to see to it? Something's blown, I think.'

Surely that last bit would be hint enough? The trouble was that Nan Yeadings might stay on with her sick neighbour and the message would remain unnoticed until the Boss got back tonight. Which could be any time.

She sat back in her chair, and suddenly was conscious of fresh air behind her. The door to the corridor was open and Gerald from front desk was leaning against the jamb.

Rosemary turned, wondering how long he had been listening there. He had a smooth, unreadable face but just now he was avoiding eye contact. 'We wondered,' he said, 'if you'd care to come in on our currency fiddle. You must have gathered how it works.'

His eyes met hers briefly with a hard stare, then swept on towards her desk. She could feel his hostility.

'Well, thanks, but I'm not sure I'll be here long enough to benefit. What do you think?'

'Easy enough to include you in. It's just a case of programming another code name into the computer.'

'Actually, I'm not much of a gambler,' she confessed.

It was the answer he'd expected. He looked long at her this time, and the intensity of dislike in his eyes belied his casual voice. 'As you wish. You had your chance.'

He was gone as silently as he had arrived.

I should have agreed, Rosemary thought: then I'd have been equally implicated with them. It's no big deal, 'Hannah' must have warned him who I am, and now he's afraid I'll make trouble over the money game. Still, if she leaves it at that there's not too much to worry about.

AFTER LISTENING to the depressing ten o'clock news, Mrs Denison switched off the television, grumbled under her breath that her son had again left her to her own devices and, feeling her arthritis peaking through the pain-killers, decided to order the new assistant housekeeper up for a game of backgammon or Scrabble. The girl had come up earlier on some pretext, probably fed up and ready for any company.

But Miss Seal was not in her room, the bar or the restaurant. Mrs Denison, knowing it was her duty night, expressed extreme displeasure. Minions were dispatched throughout the hotel and staff building to find the defaulter, without result. It was reported back that her car was in its usual place but nobody had seen her since the affair of the carpet.

It was not until after one a.m., when the night porter helped himself to the wine cellar keys for private reasons of his own, that anything sinister was suspected. Young women, especially those taking temporary hotel posts, were known to be unreliable. Probably some male guest she had taken a sudden fancy to...

But Wharton, the not-so-secret-drinking night porter, considered himself owed a modest bottle of claret, and he went about setting the account straight. He used his flashlamp on the tricky cellar steps because, apart from a rope handrail, one side was open to the stone floor ten feet below. At the bottom he rested the torch on a ledge and switched on the main lights. Breathing in the wondrous aroma of bulk alcohol, he turned towards the Bordeaux racks, and saw, crumpled, on the flags, the pale limbs and dark dress of a woman, lying face downward.

Wharton was as soft-hearted as any other ex-sergeant-at-arms who has bitterly come down in the world, and it seemed to him then that if she was dead there was no real need for him to declare he'd ever been present. He could simply slip away. Best not take the bottle after all.

Just the same, he was both alarmed and curious. Reluctantly he went forward, squatted down beside her and moved back the darkish hair that covered her cheek. It was that Miss Seal from housekeeping.

He put a hand on her cold arm, felt about for a pulse in her throat, and his fingers met a caking of dried, congealed blood.

DURING THE COURSE of an entertaining evening Eva de Vries had elicited that Angus was engaged to be married. He explained how Paula and he had met at a degree presentation, both of them graduating Bachelor of Laws, he as an external student working in his precious free hours.

'Paula,' she said, then 'Pow-la' the Dutch way. 'I like that name. Is she very beautiful? When will you marry?'

Jan-Willi, rolling his eyes, disappeared to load the dishwasher and left them to it. There was no escaping telling Eva the whole story of the postponed wedding and the weekend at Chardleigh Place when they had come across the girl who was later murdered.

'So Paula is concerned with this case too? Surely you would like to ring her. Please use our phone.'

He tried three times but there was no answer. After midnight he gave up. He shared a last round of drinks with the Dutch couple, thanked them warmly, and then Jan-Willi was walking him back to his hotel.

He was wakened by a bell shrilling close to his head. Telephone. His travelling alarm clock showed 5.30. Must have stopped. But no; morning was already here. A dim line of light marked the wall to each side of the heavy curtains. He reached for the phone. 'Mott here.'

'Angus! Darling, I do know the time, but I thought you might have been trying to reach me.'

'I did, all right. God, are you just getting home? Some junketing, wasn't it?'

'Idiot, it was an Inner Temple dinner. I was back by one a.m. Now we're about to dash off again, down to Devon. I'm driving old Wheatears to a special client. Elderly lady he's known all his life. I think I'm along as chaperone. Sorry about the early hour, but we aim to be well on our way before the roads clog. How are you, Angus? Any progress your end?'

'We're filling in a few blanks. It looks as though Anneke was some kind of courier. She doubled it with coming to England for an abortion after her boyfriend ditched her.' Briefly he told her of Groeneveld and Ms Henstra.

'Are you sure?' She sounded doubtful.

'About the courier?'

'No; that she'd meant to have an abortion. It doesn't fit, does it? She was so pleased with herself when we saw her; on top of things. Besides, time was running out for a legal operation. There's a limit set, you know. Leave it too long and the medics won't touch you.'

'Maybe she had to wait in a queue.'

'No.' Now Paula sounded quite sure of herself. 'If Anneke had meant that originally, then she'd finally changed her mind by the time we met her. Don't you see?—that would explain her new confidence. She was hugging a special secret, finally *looking forward* to having a baby. Another life to be responsible for. The female thing. Think about it. And she was only flirting with you; wouldn't have gone all the way. On reflection I know I'm right there. Must dash now, darling. Ring me tomorrow night at ten. I promise to be in. Love you.'

He thought about it, as she'd advised. Perhaps her view made sense. There had been nothing apprehensive or strained about the Dutch girl; none of the mind-changing uncertainty Ms Henstra had spoken of. So what had made her decide (if she *had* decided) to take on the unknown problems and expenses of being a single parent?

The likelihood that someone would share it with her? An offer of some more or less permanent relationship? It was going rather far to imagine that this hitherto quiet girl had suddenly found the courage to brave it out on her own.

Yet she had made just such a positive decision once before in quitting Amersfoort. Once away, she hadn't hankered after going back but made the best of what she had. And when Groeneveld gave her the push it seemed that, however upset, she hadn't insisted on established rights but shook off the old life, finding herself alone again.

Only, with a baby coming she wouldn't be on her own any more. She'd belong in a totally new way. Could a woman really think like that? He remembered his mother once saying that pregnancy brought more than a physical change: it included all the mental and spiritual ingredients for motherhood. At the time he'd considered that overstated and possibly a purely personal experience of a dear old innocent.

Well, Anneke was being increasingly revealed as rather a dear young innocent under the adopted worldly-wiseness, wasn't she? He could well have read her wrongly at first. Could he accept now that she was no wanton, but fancy-free, just newly into self-discovery and, having accepted her pregnancy, hugging the exciting secret which had freed her from all her earlier unsatisfactory experiences?

He wished he could talk with Paula again, or with Nan Yeadings, who'd been through the mill of child-bearing twice and was no stranger to personal crises. True, she'd had a husband backing her all the way, but she'd be able to put herself in the single girl's place to think it through.

A lone parent. Or, supposing there actually was a potential partner in the background for Anneke, who would it be? Groeneveld had his new woman. Coleman, although teamed with Anneke when they met her, was obviously a good-time bachelor with no serious intentions. Certainly Anneke herself had shown no real attachment to him, willingly swapping escorts and making mild come-on signs to Angus. She'd been in England little over a week then.

It seemed possible that she'd been counselled by someone experienced who had put the case clearly to her, the pros and cons of ending the pregnancy. A professional? It was essential to find out what clinic or hospital she had contacted. By now maybe Z would have picked up some clue to that from the staff at Chardleigh Place.

WHARTON REACHED the top of the stone steps and paused by the door to the kitchen corridor. He'd pulled it shut after he slid in, carefully pocketing the keys in case any night wanderer, however unlikely, should happen to see the ring hanging from the lock.

But what key had the girl used? He knew which ones were on the housekeeper's bunch, and there was no reason for her to have had anything giving access to supplies in the food and bev department.

Her hands had been empty, so if she'd had a key ring with her it would be in her pockets or under where she'd fallen. Fallen ... or been pushed—because why should she have locked herself in? After all, he'd had to unlock the cellar door to get in here himself.

He'd have to go down there, move the body and grope about to see if she had had keys or not. Because if not there was only one conclusion to be drawn: she hadn't come here alone and, whoever had accompanied her had gone away, locking her body in.

And that was invading his territory, since he was responsible for everything that happened during his hours on duty. Better to make a row now than let one break over his head when the body came to light. He'd be immediately suspect. But if someone else was involved, that someone must take the rap. He could say he'd heard noises and come to investigate, went for the right keys and by then the killer had gone.

So he turned round and went back down. No stranger to death, though he'd never had to handle a woman's corpse before, he knelt and lifted the shoulders, trying not to disturb the clothing. He propped her against his chest while one hand explored the ground and the front of her tailored dress. Luckily the bleeding had ceased. A little marking of his clothes might seem normal, but not more.

'Right, gal,' he muttered, 'nothing saucy intended.'

And suddenly her eyes were open, wide with terror.

It went through him like a stab of pain. Gawd, he'd walked out on her alive. He'd have sworn on oath she'd fluffed it, cold and stiff as she'd felt to him before.

'Don't scream,' he begged. 'For gawdsake stay shut. It's me, Wharton. I'll haveta think of some way to get us out of this.'

TWELVE

YEADINGS HAD TAKEN the call from Amsterdam in person before breakfast and was poring over the dates Angus had given for Anneke's movements. He laid his notes out on the kitchen table and Nan came to stand behind him, reading them over his shoulder.

June 7 Anneke left Johan Groeneveld.
Accepted Ms Henstra's offer to share her flat.
June 11 Met Cornelia: said, 'Men are not nice persons.'
June 13 Left Ms Henstra, took night ferry for England.
June 14 Arrived Harwich. With antiques dealers?
June 15 to June 22, at Chardleigh Place.
June 23 2 free days. Flew to Schiphol, Holland.
June 24 Flew back to Heathrow.
Not seen at Chardleigh Place.
Killed?
June 28 Body found in van at Harwich.

'There's a night missing,' Nan said. 'The night of the fourteenth/fifteenth. Have they traced the antiques dealers yet?'

'No. They're hopeful it will be soon. The ominous thing is her return to Holland by air on her first free day from the hotel and an almost immediate second journey back here. Plus the fact that the girl's ex-lover came to England on the same flight. According to the pathologist's report she's thought to have died that very day or in the early hours of next morning. The Dutch police will be pulling the young man in today for questioning.'

'So that could be it? End of your case.'

'Apart from the small matter of proof. Even if he confesses, there are a lot of loose ends to follow up before it's over. By the by, someone's fiddled with the hall phone. The recording button had been cancelled and it was left on "open speech".'

'That must be Luke, then. I'm sorry, love. I didn't realize he could get up there.'

'Probably no damage done, but Z was supposed to be phoning in last night and we seem to have lost her message.'

Sally, halfway through her bacon sandwich, started coughing and almost choked. Nan poured out a glass of orange juice and tried to calm her.

'Miss Z!' said the girl, and spluttered again.

'Take your time, love,' Yeadings encouraged. 'Big breath and a little cough, that's right. Now, what about Miss Z?'

'She phoned,' Sally managed after a moment or two. 'Mummy was next door.'

'So you answered it?'

'M'm.' Her parents exchanged cautionary glances.

'What did she say?'

Sally screwed up her face and concentrated. ' "Push the button." And I did.'

'You didn't use the handpiece at all? And Z's voice was still coming out of the box instead of the phone?'

'Yes, all the time.' Sally looked pleased.

He hadn't the heart to explain that using 'open speech' had prevented the whole conversation being recorded. The second button Sally had pressed, at Z's request, must have been LR, which would merely reconnect her with the caller.

'Anyway you heard everything she said, Sally,' Nan said cheerfully. 'Now you can tell us what it was.'

'About somebody's car. It wouldn't go.'

'George's car? George Bunter?' Yeadings prompted.

'George, yes. She wants him to go and mend it.'

'That was all?'

'Yes. I think so.'

'Well done, love.' Yeadings rose to leave and kissed her forehead. 'I'll send George over this morning, then. Tonight we'll have a talk about the phone's gadgets and I'll show you everything it can do. How's that?'

'That's nice.' She beamed, proud of being helpful. As she took up her sandwich again she hesitated. 'Daddy?'

'Yes, pet.'

She looked uncertain. 'Who's Auntie Laura?'

He stood frozen and turned on his heel. 'Did Z ask for Auntie Laura? Are you sure, Sally?'

'Yes. Who is she?'

Nan faced him, recognizing trouble. 'That's your code word. I was to let you know at once if—'

'Shi— Sugar!' swore Yeadings. 'Nan, you know Beaumont's number. Tell him to get to Chardleigh Place at once. Say I'm on my way and it looks like trouble.'

He got as far as the door and changed his mind, rooting in a jacket pocket for a card. 'No. Ring this number first and ask for Miss Seal. Make up some excuse.'

Impatiently they waited while the ringing tone sounded. Then a cool male voice answered, 'Chardleigh Place Reception. Can I help you?'

Nan explained she was Miss Seal's aunt and she needed to speak with her urgently.

There was a pause, then 'I'm sorry, madam, but it's not possible at the moment. Could you call back later when the manager's available?'

'But I don't want the manager. I want my niece. It's very urgent. My husband's been taken to hospital and he's asking for her. He's been seriously injured.'

It was a good try. Yeadings noted her crossed fingers at the lie about her husband. No need to tempt fate.

'It seems Miss Seal's not here at the moment, madam.' The voice was less cool now. 'She went out quite early. I couldn't say when she'll be back.'

Nan questioned Mike with her eyebrows and he shook his head. 'I see. Well, be sure she's told when she does get back or phones in.'

'Yes, madam. Who shall I say rang?'

'Her Auntie Laura. Thank you. Goodbye.' She replaced the receiver and called after Mike. 'She could be on her way to report to you.'

He waved in a negative way. With his talent for picking up vibrations he knew the man answering the call had been flannelling. Whatever had gone wrong was under wraps. Going out he shouted back, 'Get on to Beaumont just the same. I've a nasty feeling about this.'

GERALD ON FRONT DESK was biting his lip as he put down the phone. He hadn't asked the woman which hospital her husband was at. The fact was he'd panicked, and that wasn't like him. Nor was what he'd done to the girl last night after Hannah told him she was The Bill. He shuddered. There'd be hell to pay when the police got on to it. But play it cool and maybe they'd not think of him.

He'd instruct his relief to put the aunt's next call through to Mr Denison. Let him deal with it since he'd left no instructions on covering up. And the Old Gorgon was loose, whingeing around on her elbow crutch because the girl wasn't here to check on the chambermaids. She'd make more chaos, sticking her haggish old nose in. It was already a pretty frightful morning. He thought he might report sick and lie low once Peter took over front desk.

He suppressed a sigh and went silkily forward to greet new guests arriving from the airport courtesy coach. They were all Terminal Three intercontinentals out of Kennedy, jet-lagged and inclined to be tetchy. He rang for porters, proffered the register, answered queries, made a play with the computer, smiled and soothed and charmed till his face ached with the effort.

Eventually, with rooms allocated and luggage removed from the foyer, one man remained. Gerald didn't care for the look of him. No bags beside him; a local trying it on. Not at all the sort they wanted at Chardleigh Place.

'Sir?' he said coldly.

The man gave him a hard stare, reached inside his jacket for a square of leather with a plastic window. 'Thames Valley Police, "C" Division. Detective-Constable Boyes. I'd like a word with Mr Denison.'

DC BOYES WAS STILL there, seated beside a stone gryphon on the front terrace wall when Superintendent Yeadings swung his Rover up to the front entrance, ignoring the notice directing cars to a park at the rear.

'Sir,' said Boyes in astonishment, recognizing both the car and a senior CID officer for South Bucks.

'What are you doing here?' Yeadings demanded.

'Got a call from the hospital about an incident. The guv'nor sent me to question the manager.'

'What incident? How serious?'

'One of the staff took a tumble down some stairs. Concussion, a couple of broken ribs and crushed cheekbone. Could have been pushed, from the sound of it.'

'Name?'

'A Miss Seal. It seems she was—'

'Acting housekeeper, yes. In the job. Surveillance.'

'They didn't say, sir.'

'Nobody here knew. Shouldn't have, anyway. Maybe they found out and didn't like it. How is she? And where?'

Boyes reddened. 'Out cold when I saw her at Windsor General, sir. Not too good, they said. Had to wait for the neurosurgeon to get there. He was driving down from Oxford. The fractures could wait till later, if she...'

'If she pulls through the other. I see. Who found her? Let's get the story direct.'

Wharton the night porter was in his pyjamas, huddled in a blanket before a single-bar electric fire in his room in the staff block. A motherly-looking woman let them in and insisted, 'I hope you're not going to bother him, like. He's in shock, that's what he is. Can't stop shivering.'

The room was like an oven. Wharton looked up apologetically. 'Silly, innit? All the gory things I seen in my days and I get the willies over this. Because it's a girl, I guess. Nasty vicious thing to do to anyone, mind.'

'You're not as young as you were, Mr Wharton,' said the woman and he glanced back at her.

'I'll thank you, Mrs Gilliat, not to harp on the fact. Best leave us now. We got men's work.'

'No offence meant, I'm sure,' she said, less motherly. 'Well, you know where I am if you need anything.'

'Fussy old cow,' said the man when she had gone. 'Better make sure she's not listening outside. I s'pose you're the Old Bill. Find a seat, can you? I'll be all yours when I've finished me cocoa.'

Through the window Yeadings caught sight of Beaumont coming at the double round the shrubbery dividing the block from the main house. He heaved up the window, leaned out and shouted. Behind him Wharton muttered about the risk of pneumonia.

With Beaumont to cover questioning the staff here, Yeadings ordered Boyes to the hospital to watch over Z until Division could arrange a rota to sit with her. He wanted to see her himself, but there were more pressing things to attend to until she recovered.

He let Beaumont question the man, only cutting in when Wharton wandered off the point, and eventually they got the full story of his discovery of the girl, badly injured and unconscious, on the stone floor of the locked cellar.

'And she didn't have no keys with her,' the man insisted. 'So it stands to reason, dunnit, that somebody else musta been with her. Left her for dead, they did. That's what I thought she was meself, first time I touched her. Out stone cold and stiff.'

'You didn't attempt to move her?'

'Gawd, I know better than that. Ran up to me office to dial 999. Got shouted at by Mr D because I didn't let him know first, but that woulda wasted time. I told him—'

'Yes, so you said. And Mr Denison insisted on going to the hospital himself with Miss Seal?'

'Thass right. In a real tizzy, he was. You know what I think? I think he was shit-scared because of that other girl before. The murdered one. Didn't want more trouble coming here so the hotel'd get a bad name.'

'Did he say anything to connect the two incidents?' Yeadings put in, leaning forward alertly.

'Said, "Oh God, not another!" Well, I sussed what he meant all right. And he said to stay shut and scarper.'

'So how did Reception know this morning that Miss Seal wasn't on the premises?' Yeadings demanded.

'Gerald took over early from me when I was sent back here. He saw the ambulance take her. Mr Denison told him to say she'd gone out early to run some errand for him.'

'There was a cock-up over Z's call-in last night,' Yead-ings told Beaumont briefly. 'Her coded mayday didn't reach me until this morning. She must have been on to something here, and an attempt was made to silence her.'

'So we make it hot for all of them till we know where and when she was seen last. Do we get a team over?'

'I'll contact "C" Division.'

'Here, I'll tell you something,' Wharton said, wagging a finger. 'She'd disappeared before half past ten last night. That was when old Mrs Denison tried to get her paged and couldn't. And wasn't she on her high horse about it. I'll say so!—because Miss S was supposed to be on call. Lot of tit-tering among the kids on staff. They thought she'd shacked up with one of the men guests.'

'And you found her when?'

'After one, it musta been. Ambulance got here one-thirty. I'd got her a blanket and hot bottle by then.'

'You did all the right things, Mr Wharton.' Yeadings looked down at him. 'But I don't think part of your story rings quite true. You didn't hear anything suspicious on your rounds, did you? Because if Miss Seal was missing be-fore ten-thirty her attacker wasn't still coming out of the cellar at a little after one a.m.'

The night porter sank lower in his chair. 'I thought I heard a noise,' he insisted.

Yeadings stared at the man's lowered profile. 'Try again. At the worst this could end up a murder case. Even with simple GBH you'll be needed to give evidence in court. On oath. If it's obvious you're lying, we could think you were involved in the incident. After all, you had the keys.'

'That's setting me up!' he protested. 'As God's me wit-ness I never knew a thing till I switched on the light and there she was, dead on the floor, as I thought. It gave me a real turn.'

'It must have done. You were in a spot. No good excuse for being there in the first place.'

So Wharton gave in, with relief admitted he'd popped down for a spot of liquid perk. All the others got it one way or another, only he was a bit left out when hand-outs occurred, being night staff and nothing to do with catering; yet he'd rights like anyone else, hadn't he?

Beaumont warned him that a constable would be back to help him write up a statement, then the two detectives left him to recover.

'And we still don't know what Z had found out,' Yeadings said sombrely. 'Better take a look at the car, I suppose. She used that as an excuse to get help across here.'

'Round the back, probably,' Beaumont suggested, leading him past the old stable block. 'Yes, there it is. Left her keys in the ignition. A bit careless, wouldn't you say?' He sat behind the wheel and tried the engine. 'She really did have car trouble. Let's have a look.'

'Rotor arm's missing,' said Yeadings heavily, peering into the bonnet. 'Someone certainly was out to get her. This would be the point when she decided on the mayday call. Now, who found out what she was up to? We'll trace all her movements yesterday, find out who she was with, and what was discussed. I hope to God she wakes up to tell us herself, but we can't wait for that.'

'It looks as if the Dutch girl discovered something fishy here too and had to be silenced,' Beaumont added blackly. 'Chardleigh Place could be the centre of some right criminal goings-on.'

And the DS didn't even know about Anneke's sudden flight to Holland, returning on the day she was probably killed, Yeadings told himself. What had the girl gone back to do, and had she known that Groeneveld had followed her when she returned? Somebody here must have seen him;

possibly someone he had business with. There was heroin in the case and he'd had access to it at work. But surely not in the sort of quantities needed for regular trading?

They could do with Angus Mott back on the team. The Dutch police had enough to work on now without him. Yeadings stomped back to the main building, confronted Reception and demanded a phone call to Amsterdam.

In a few minutes he was connected to Commisaris Stuyvesant. They exchanged civilities and Yeadings was told that Angus was even then accompanying Adjutant de Vries to interview Johan Groeneveld at work. Certainly it would be possible to pass on a message and have facilities laid on for Mott to fly back on an afternoon plane.

Stuyvesant's manner was different now, quite purring, Yeadings observed with wry detachment. Angus had clearly made a good impression and the Commisaris, scenting the case's end in sight, was happy to have the foreigner withdrawn and the glory of arrest left to his own men.

Well, he could be wrong. As for himself, Yeadings sensed no urge to stand by for the final curtain, no CID equivalent of the orchestra's homing in on *doh*.

'I don't think we're out of the wood yet,' he cautioned the Dutchman, 'and I need Inspector Mott here. We've quite a widespread new aspect to cover.'

His next call was to lay on the operation for Chardleigh Place. News of Z's injury had already leaked through and Acky was on his toes, anxious to hear what news there was from the hospital.

'None to date,' Yeadings replied curtly. 'Have the family been informed? There aren't any parents. I think the closest relative is an aunt. If she cares to go and hold Z's hand, keep talking till she comes round, I'd be happy. I'll be taking a turn myself when I get free.'

He put down the receiver. 'One more,' and he dialled his home number. 'Nan?... Yes, I thought you'd be worrying. She's in Windsor General, possible concussion and a few breaks. Still out, but Houghton-O'Neill's coming over from Oxford to have a look. Well, yes, if it fits in with... Fine. How? Pushed down cellar steps and left for two or three hours, we think. Dodgy, yes. Bless you, love. See you, but God knows when.'

I thought so, he told himself. Nan's trotting out the universal mother touch. Z'll have every chance if we all rally round and keep on at her. Amazing how much the old subconscious goes on taking in when you're out to the wide.

THIRTEEN

IF IT HAD BEEN a murder investigation the Superintendent would have had no reservations about freezing the entire organization, setting up an Incident Room on the spot, and isolating both staff and clients irrespective of who or what they claimed to be. With GBH he hadn't the same excuse, even though by nightfall the issue might become a much graver one. The hotel was, after all, very much a going concern with staffing levels already low to ensure that everyone was fully occupied for their periods of duty. Some of yesterday's staff were off and unreachable; others were busy about necessary tasks.

He and Beaumont set up offices independently in a commandeered conference suite, each with an assistant and recording facilities. Gradually they began building up a general picture of Z's movements on the day leading up to the attack.

'I want reconstructions of every conversation Z had, a description of every sighting of her, so that we can plot her progress from room to room, person to person,' Yeadings told the duty manager. 'Somewhere my WDC picked up vital information. We need to know what it was, and who was threatened by it. We need to know above all just who knew what she was here for. When did the word first get put around that she was plain-clothes police?

'As far as possible I want today run exactly like yesterday, same staff duties, same routine. I'll walk the part of Miss Seal myself. The rest of you can prompt.'

Mr Denison was fetched back from the hospital. 'I want him in here with me before anyone speaks with him,' Yeadings ordered the DI from 'C' Division. 'And after him I'll have another go at Gerald from front desk and the worthy Wharton. Both could do with a gentle squeeze.'

The first jewel of information arose from a repeated conversation including mention of up-market cars and a mite of gossip about recent guests. The knowledgeable sous-chef was asked to repeat the description of the red Porsche he had admired over a fortnight back.

'It was brand spanking new. I had a good look under it when no one was around; only you couldn't tell its age by the registration because the licence plate was personalized.'

Unfortunately he hadn't committed that to memory, it not having any mechanical virtue. The sous-chef's interest was purely in bodywork and performance.

'Personalized,' Beaumont pressed him. 'You noticed that much. So it was someone's initials. What did it remind you of? Did it apply to anything or anyone you knew?'

The sous-chef thought there had been something familiar about it, but he couldn't remember what. JR, would it be? Maybe JC. Or even CJ. No, three letters. He'd have a think about it; see if anything surfaced.

'So Z was aware of the model number,' Yeadings summarized, 'and also that the Arnold Coleman we need to question about Anneke was actually nothing to do with Cosmos Assurance itself, but a car-hire chauffeur brought in by a director as a bit of flashy front. We'll have to pull in the Cosmos top brass who were here and question them again in the light of this.'

'That information wouldn't have been enough to make Z put out a *mayday*,' Beaumont said bluntly. 'From that point she must have probed somewhere sensitive. So who was she likely to have tackled next?'

Yeadings turned the tape back on the after-lunch conversation. 'Discussion passed from the car to Coleman and his picking up the Dutch girl working here. Then Z got them to tell her Anneke was dead. They mentioned her body being found in a van in Harwich, but they'd been warned not to discuss the murder because it might rebound on the hotel's reputation, Mr Denison having put the ban on. Finally a surmise that he was "sweet on" Anneke.'

'You can't be sure we got the whole story,' Beaumont doubted. 'It stands to reason if they were dishing the dirt among themselves they're not going to give us the juiciest scandals. They didn't know then that Z was in the job. You can reckon they sanitize what they pass on to us, out of self-protection.'

'I reckon we got most of it,' said Yeadings. 'The waitresses, Rene and Yvonne, were competing to remember every word. Hotel scandal's probably the spice of life for them, their very own soap opera lived out daily.'

'In Z's place,' Beaumont announced, 'I'd have wanted to know a bit more about Mr Denison after that.'

'Mm. After the gossip party Z returned to her office to work. Maybe she made some notes on what she'd heard, but nothing of the sort has turned up. She was next sighted about thirty minutes later on the back stairs bound for the upper floor where the Denisons have a flat.'

'Whose testimony is that?'

'Let's see. A Mona Butterworth, rushing out to catch a courtesy coach leaving for Heathrow. Apparently the staff make use of it when there are spare seats, then get a bus from the airport to wherever they're ultimately bound for. Mona had fixed a foursome date with another girl who was going to hold the coach for her.'

'Do we have a statement from that one?'

Yeadings looked through his list of names. 'Doesn't look like it. Better find out from Mona who she was. If this other girl met Z earlier on the stairs she may be able to fix a more accurate time for it.'

Beaumont grunted assent and ran the tape on to the point of Mrs Denison's interview. She had been rather high-pitched and protesting, couldn't pin-point exactly when Miss Seal had come to her with the laundry query. It was a point she didn't need to advise on: the girl was merely being fussy. And anyway it was the time of day she usually took a little rest. Yes, she'd mentioned to Miss Seal that her son wasn't available just then, being involved in checking the Food and Bev reports.

'Would that involve him going down to the cellars at any point?' Beaumont wondered.

'Not necessarily,' said Yeadings, 'unless he came across discrepancies in the paperwork and decided to hold a mini stock-check. I have a statement from the Food and Bev Manager that squares on this.'

'So the next appearance of Z is with the chambermaids, and all that kerfuffle over the wine stains on the bedroom carpet. Nothing significant in that, is there?'

Yeadings was frowning over the papers in his hands. 'Doesn't sound like it, but... Only fifteen minutes after she finally left the maintenance man to get on with things she was putting in the phone call to my house, using the code calling for assistance.'

'Which means she rang from here, where she might have been overheard by someone on the switchboard. And by then she knew her car had been fiddled with, and she couldn't get to the call-box at the cross-roads to talk openly.'

'That operator doesn't come on again until tomorrow morning,' Beaumont said. 'I've put one of "C" Division's sergeants on her job for the present.'

He was reading off the duty roster. 'Crazy sort of shift system, alternating a.m. and p.m. Got the girl's home number here, though.'

'Don't ring. Brief a uniform man and send him to question her. Pick a bright one who might spot if she's lying. He's not to let her get away with saying she never listens in. We need to know who else knew about that call, anyone in the switchboard room at the time, anyone she may have mentioned it to.'

The phone on the desk beside him suddenly rang and Yeadings lifted the receiver, listened, nodded, and said, 'Right. Send him on down.'

Over his shoulder he muttered to Beaumont, 'Denison's back. I'd like you in on this one.'

The voice on the other end spoke again sharply and Yeadings grunted. 'Put him through, then. Hold Denison back until I'm finished... Hallo, Bunter. You have? At last. Right. Is he co-operating? Is that so? Well, jolly him along, make him hang about a bit, then deliver him here for six-thirty. I'll arrange a confrontation with Inspector Mott.'

He turned to Beaumont, smiling grimly. 'Bunter's run Arnold Coleman to earth. He's manager of a car dealer's in Croydon. Has a couple of Porsches in the window right now. One's a red Cabriolet which has been "out on trial runs". He denies knowing where Chardleigh Place is, let alone having ever stayed here.'

HUBERT DENISON was a large, fleshy man with pink jowls and soft white hands. He blinked earnestly at the two detectives through gold-rimmed spectacles, and a little nervous tic under his right eye fascinated Beaumont. The DS kept his own gaze fixed meanly on it.

'Very upsetting, all this,' the manager said, seating himself opposite Yeadings.

'The second attack on one of your staff,' the Superintendent led off.

'Oh, you mean the—er, Miss Vroom. But that wasn't here. Dreadful, of course, but with no connection to our hotel. She accepted a lift, as I understood it...'

His voice trailed away. He gulped, straightened himself and decided on a different angle. 'Miss Seal is not really one of us. We took her on temporarily to bridge a gap. Miss Seal had an excellent letter of recommendation and I had no cause to think...'

'To think someone would need to kill her?' Beaumont suggested flatly.

Yeadings tapped his papers with a pencil. 'Surely Miss Vroom's was also a temporary appointment?'

'Er, not exactly. If she had seemed satisfactory on trial we intended to keep her on until...that is, for the rest of the season.'

'But yours isn't a seasonal operation, is it? So near a major airport, within easy reach of London, and equipped as a conference centre, you could expect full bookings, even overbooking, all the year round.'

'Er, one hopes so, of course. But it's early days yet.'

'I understand,' Yeadings probed, 'that Miss Vroom was pregnant. Perhaps what you meant was that she could work here until the baby came? You did know about it?'

'I—yes, she told me quite frankly when I interviewed her. She was a pleasant girl, friendly, and spoke almost perfect English. We considered she would fit in well.'

'Whereas you say Miss Seal was "not one of us". Am I to understand you didn't know she was actually one of *us*?'

For a moment Denison appeared puzzled, then a dull flush stole up his neck and flooded his face. 'Do you mean she was *working* for you, Superintendent?'

'Miss Seal is a detective constable assigned to look for background in the Anneke Vroom case,' Yeadings said. 'I see you were ignorant of that.'

'But her testimonial... Do you mean it was forged?'

It was odd, Yeadings considered, what popped out when people were knocked off balance. Forged documentation, in this man's eyes, must rate as a major crime, perhaps on a par with GBH.

'Perfectly genuine,' he assured Denison. 'Miss Seal worked hard to earn the reference.'

He seemed deflated. 'I don't know what to say.'

'You can tell us what you think happened here during the night, and how she came to be attacked and left for dead in a locked cellar.'

'I am quite appalled. There is no way I can account for it, Superintendent. It would seem that there was a criminal element within the hotel. I can't speak for the guests, of course, but as far as my staff are concerned it is quite—unimaginable.'

Yeadings let a silence build up, then nodded to Beaumont, who resumed the questioning briskly. Denison turned in his seat to meet the new onslaught.

'Yesterday the policewoman you know as Miss Seal discovered new details about a guest staying here shortly before Anneke Vroom's death. We hadn't had those details before because the sous-chef wasn't listed when police officers questioned your staff earlier about that period.

'The young man tells me he has been working here for four weeks. His name isn't in the staff wages ledger, but I'm certain he doesn't put in kitchen time purely out of love of feeding the starving masses. So what about him, Mr Denison? Would you care to explain?'

'An oversight, it must be.' The man looked wretched.

'Could it be so that the Inland Revenue never heard of him? He works three days a week. The rest of the time he's a student, on a full grant. What you pay him, Mr Denison, isn't a large sum. Easy enough to lose among sundries in the accounts as "potatoes" or "fresh pineapple" or chicken wire to mend the fences. Don't think we were born yesterday, Mr Denison, just because we're not in the trade. We need to know what other little dodges are on, because Miss Seal uncovered some racket here just before she was almost killed. And we'll find it if it means taking the hotel to pieces, brick by brick.'

DENISON LEFT THEM a shaken man, but they were satisfied that he had kept back nothing. His only crime was weakness, a willingness to turn a blind eye in the cause of acquiring good staff and keeping them happy. He hadn't been party to the currency swindle, didn't even quite understand how it worked, but he knew who ran it and that most of the junior management team were probably involved.

So long as a certain proportion of visitors changing currency received official receipts and the counterfoils corresponded to the amounts entered in the books, he had been satisfied. Other unofficial transactions, undertaken for guests less likely to examine their receipts closely, had financed the staff's own currency-swapping game.

'As I see it,' Beaumont said, 'being a simple man, if these people are making money somebody must be losing it.'

'The guests would receive the official going rate accepted by the hotels in this area,' Mr Denison insisted. 'They are reminded in our brochure that we offer the exchange service at a slightly less advantageous rate than at the banks. It's common practice all over the world.'

'And the hotel takes the legitimate difference? But in this case, it doesn't. What you're permitting is misuse of the

hotel's profits, Mr Denison. How would your directors see
that? I think you must bring it out in the open now. So you
can start by naming the wheeler-dealer who's in charge of
the fiddle.'

Which brought them back to Gerald, Front Desk Assistant Manager. 'The lily-lad himself,' Yeadings marvelled.
'We shan't need heavy tactics to get the truth out of him.'

'Consommé on a fork, that one,' Beaumont agreed.

They put their notes together and prepared to go across
to the staff house and confront him. 'All the same,' Yeadings pointed out, 'Z mentioned this scam the previous day
and I played it down. I still think it's irrelevant, except to use
as leverage.'

Gerald Manning had been hourly expecting their visit. He
knew someone would crack under questioning and give him
away. But such an enormous sledgehammer to crack a mi-
nuscule nut! Still, everyone knew the police went berserk if
you touched one of their number. It was bad luck he'd
thought of getting back at her when he'd overheard Hannah
say Miss Seal was fuzz.

He thought of the rotor arm lying in some clump of this-
tles behind the stable block. If only she'd searched around
a bit she would have found it without all this bother. In
putting it back she'd have covered his dabs with her own.
Now, since she was out of the running, these unspeakable
oafs would be searching the area and sending the damn
thing to Forensic lab to find who had spiked her car. Which
was bad enough, without their assuming he was also the one
who had attacked her last night and left her for dead!

He had opted to plead fatigue (having done overtime re-
placing old Wharton) and reported sick. Now the reality had
overtaken pretence. His whole inside was seething and
surging. Twice he'd rushed to the bathroom and voided it
all. Now there was only a thin, bitter dribble and an omi-

nous pain that went on long after the retching. He was in for an ulcer at least. And still the CID men hadn't come to wring the truth out of him.

'WHAT DO YOU THINK?' Beaumont asked as they left the staff building after their short sharp interview. 'Is there more to our Gerald than meets the eye?'

Yeadings grunted. 'Nobody could act that scared. Too green about the gills. To my mind waspish spite is his line, as in the rotor arm incident, but if he had given Z a pettish shove on the stairs, he'd never have stood up to our questions.'

He sucked in his cheeks. 'We'll chase up this Hannah Minton and find out how she discovered Z's identity and who else she spilled the beans to. From the times quoted it looks as if she must be the one who was to hold the courtesy coach back for the girl we spoke to earlier. We seem to be narrowing the field. I believe the lily-lad when he says he kept it to himself about Z. He's a loner, and his only use for other people is to make money or put one over on them, as in the currency exchange.'

'So we leave that to the hotel to straighten out?'

'It'll give Denison an opportunity to drag himself out of the mire with his board of directors. Little Jack Horner pulling out the plum. Look at this naughty fandangle; and now that I've cleverly unearthed it, sirs, your profits will be greater.'

IN THE FOYER they found Angus Mott, newly arrived from Holland, bright-eyed and rarin' to get at Arnold Coleman. 'Thought you'd like to be there when we meet, Guv,' he said with a broad grin. 'So I hung on.'

He dug a fist in Beaumont's ribs. 'Hi there, Skip. I've a mini pair of china clogs for you somewhere in my luggage. Or, as alternative, geneva.'

'Haven't got mini feet,' the DS asserted, following the other two.

Coleman was standing at the window and turned to face them as they entered. A uniformed constable pulled out chairs positioned so that light would fall on the man's face. Yeadings saw a tallish, olive-skinned Mediterranean type with drooping eyelids and a thin thirties' moustache. Perhaps his similarity of name had made the man model himself on Ronald Colman without the 'e'.

'Mr Coleman?' Yeadings inquired, and when the man agreed, introduced himself. 'And this is Detective-Inspector Angus Mott.' He stood aside so that the two should come face to face.

'Indeed I am,' said Angus, the spark in him instantly dimmed, 'but this is an Arnold Coleman I've never seen in my life before.'

FOURTEEN

ARNOLD COLEMAN stuck to his story: he had never been to this part of the country before, knew nobody here, had never heard of the Chardleigh Place hotel and conference centre. To back this up, nobody at Chardleigh Place recognized him, and George Bunter had to admit that beyond trial runs the garage bookings included no mention of a Porsche having been hired.

When the alibi Coleman offered for the week in question was checked and confirmed by Croydon police, Yeadings had no option but to let the man go. He drove off, tight-lipped, in his own BMW. Next morning the real Arnold Coleman would be hunted from a different angle when Angus Mott went to new interviews arranged at the Head Office of Cosmos Assurance in the City of London.

There was no difficulty this time in tracing Mr Alex Brightman as the Personnel Director in charge of the Cosmos course at Chardleigh Place. Elusive during the preliminary inquiries at Cosmos when only a senior manager had been available, he now expressed himself willing to assist in any way, and offered the DI quite lavish refreshments borne in by a leggy brunette with the disdainful hauteur of a *Vogue* fashion model.

Mott watched his man closely. Despite being on his own ground—a large office furnished in chrome, smoked glass and black leather with a wide, high view over the Thames and Tower Bridge—he was less at ease than the presence of a mere Detective-Inspector justified. Even before Mott indicated that the case had expanded from a car-hire inquiry into a full-blown murder investigation there was more cuff-shooting, leg-crossing and recrossing than was to be expected from someone presumably experienced in the body language of interviewees.

'You see, Mr Brightman,' Angus said pleasantly, 'we believe that your chauffeur during your stay at Chardleigh Place was acquainted with the murdered girl and that he stayed on after the course, retaining the Porsche as his private transport to drive the girl about.'

'I assure you he did so without my sanction, Inspector.' Brightman was eager to deny any connection with the dead girl. 'Do you mean that the car would actually still show her fingerprints and so on?'

As he spoke, Brightman had risen and walked towards the window, where he stood looking downriver. Mott quietly went across and stationed himself beside him. The morning light clearly showed a film of moisture on the man's brow and about his mouth. He dabbed at his face with a folded handkerchief and shambled back to his desk.

Mott pursued him. 'The main difficulty we have is one you could easily clear up for us. Perhaps you made a note of the firm from which the car was hired?'

'I—yes, of course.' He snapped finger and thumb in an effort to recall a name. 'It was a garage in Croydon, I remember. I happened to have business down there, saw the car in a showroom, and on the impulse—you know how it is...'

'Croydon,' Mott reminded him helpfully.

Instead of ringing for his secretary to look it up in official files, Brightman had recourse to a personal diary which he produced from an inside pocket. 'Let me see. I must have booked it just over a month ago. Yes, here we are. The firm was "Simpson and Carmichael". I have their telephone number if you'd like to copy it down. The person I dealt with was the manager, a Mr Coleman.'

'Who delivered the Porsche and himself chauffeured for you throughout the course?'

'That is correct. But not in uniform, you understand, due to his position.'

Mott digested this. He received the impression that it had been a sore point with Brightman. 'Could you give me a description of this Mr Coleman, sir?'

'Oh, medium everything, really. Not dark, not fair. About my height. Neither fat nor thin. Had a small moustache. Self-assured, with just a touch of the cockney or something. More in his manner than his speech.'

Certainly not the Mediterranean type Bunter had produced the previous day. But the description fitted the pushy type who had driven Mott and Paula down to Portland with Anneke Vroom.

It would seem that Bunter had turned up the right firm in the right area, but there was a discrepancy over the chauffeur. Mott felt pretty certain that Brightman wasn't deliberately clouding the issue, and there had been no recognition of the Mediterranean type yesterday by any of the Chardleigh staff. So his own and Paula's 'Coleman' could have been a stand-in.

'Tell me, sir, did you first meet Mr Coleman on your visit to the Croydon showroom?'

'No, I was a bit rushed. It wasn't until I got back here that I really decided to go for the Porsche. I rang through to the garage and asked for the manager. We made the deal over the phone. I have a good company car, of course, but I thought that on this occasion it would be as well to have something really eye-catching and challenging—to put across the visible rewards of getting to the top. One always needs to be presenting a target to work towards, which sorts out the truly ambitious from run-of-the-mill candidates.'

Wanted to make a personal splash centre-stage, Mott translated. 'Yes, I see, sir. And the car you fancied was for hire with chauffeur?'

'Well, actually no. I had to haggle somewhat. Cost me a pretty penny in the end. It was a showroom model allowed out only for trial runs to potential buyers. At first Coleman was reluctant to meet my requirements, but then we negotiated an extended trial period with the car's return at the end of it, but one of his stipulations, in view of the distances likely to be covered, was that it should be chauffeur-driven at all times. Since the arrangement we came to was a little irregular, I imagine that is why he chose to offer that service in person.'

And why the car's hire hadn't featured in the books of 'Simpson and Carmichael'. To compensate Coleman for the risks taken without his employers' sanction, Brightman had paid through the nose for his showy pretentiousness and thrown in hotel board and lodging charged to the Cosmos account. Which would explain his present embarrassment and his refusal to come forward when inquiries were first made at Cosmos. Deception and petty fraud on both sides of the deal.

However, one mystery was solved: the genuine Arnold Coleman had made the deal by phone, but for some reason had sub-contracted the driving and sent a substitute. Coleman's would be the name Brightman included among the Cosmos bookings at Chardleigh Place, so the stand-in had taken over his identity, with or without the real Coleman's knowledge of the name-switch.

Yesterday Coleman had denied all involvement, for fear of ditching himself with his bosses. Without Brightman's statement the police might have accepted his story and continued to look elsewhere for the red Porsche.

Mott wondered how far the man was cheating his employers in other ways. Knock one worm out of the woodwork and there was no knowing how many other unpleasant forms of life would drop out too. Well, Mr Coleman, next time we meet it will be on 'Simpson and Carmichael' ground, and you will tell us everything about your stand-in.

'He was a very careful driver. I must say that for him,' said Brightman, still bluffing away.

Yes, he had been. But then he'd needed to take care. Imagine the backlash if he'd crashed that car on the Portland run, with false personalized plates and a Thames Valley CID Inspector incognito in the passenger seat beside him!

Mott rang through to Yeadings at Chardleigh, told him of the development and announced he was off to Croydon to pin the car dealer to the floor. 'Any news yet of Ros Zyczynski, Boss?' he asked at the end.

'I'm just off to see her. She's still in intensive care but it seems the readings are improving. She surfaced briefly during the night and then went off again. I'm hoping I'll catch her eyes open and her memory returning.'

'Tell her we miss her,' Mott said shortly. 'And count me in on any flowers.'

There was no need to take a second officer to Croydon. Whatever information Coleman—the genuine one—let out would be acted on immediately. Mott would take pleasure in having him hauled back to Thames Valley again at a later date to make his signed statement.

He found the garage showroom and parked his classic MG out front. A grey-haired salesman seated at a paper-strewn desk treated him to a charade of being busy, but a younger one polishing a model in the window came forward enthusiastically. Mott asked for Arnold Coleman.

He had just left with a customer on a trial drive. The older man had overheard and came across to offer his help. 'Arthur Carmichael,' he introduced himself.

Angus replied with his name but not his official card. 'It can wait,' he said, 'until Mr Coleman is free.'

He was told to try again at 3.30. The younger man came out and gazed enviously at the MG. He suggested a couple of places where Mott could get a late lunch.

There was a blue BMW with a personalized ARC licence plate on the forecourt when the DI returned. Coleman hadn't reacted to Mott's name but came forward to inspect the MG, which his assistant had described. He walked round it with professional approval before looking into Mott's eyes. Then his jaw dropped.

'What do you want here?' he demanded tightly. 'I told you all yesterday, I know nothing about any business at that place I was taken to.'

'Just a further question or two if you don't mind, Mr Coleman,' Mott said calmly, getting out.

'I certainly do mind. This is most inconvenient. Anything you need to say to me can be said after my hours of work. I will not be harassed.'

'Mr Carmichael still about?'

'This has nothing to do with him.'

'Just as you like. I can question you or I can question him. Which shall it be?'

The man hesitated for only an instant then he went into smooth cruising gear. 'I can show you a 944S2, sir,' he said loudly. 'Capacity 2,990cc, its maximum speed . . .'

' . . . is 149 mph,' Mott finished for him. 'That's what the other fellow said. The one who wasn't actually Arnold

Coleman, but thought he should take on the same name as on the car's temporary papers.'

The car salesman looked sick. 'Perhaps you would like me to demonstrate the car, sir?'

'Why not? Nice to take the weight off my feet, sit for a while on something more comfortable than police-issue chairs. You'll get to dislike them yourself in time.'

They walked together round the side of the garage to where the assistant was gently leathering the wheel arches of the red Porsche. 'Ah yes,' Mott said, surveying it, 'we've met before. And frankly, for anyone of my build, the rear seats are on the tight side. Let me show you my driving licence, then I'll take it for a turn round the block. Jump in, Mr Coleman.'

MIKE YEADINGS left Beaumont and Silver to get results at Chardleigh Place and drove over to Windsor with the spray bottle of eau de cologne Nan had bought for Z. 'Give her a whiff behind the ears and on the pillow,' she'd instructed. 'It'll do more for her morale than you'd believe.'

He found the girl awake, but only just. She looked deadly, bruises discolouring the whole of one swollen cheek and her dark curls brutally cut away to accommodate the strips of plaster dressing. She appeared to be naked under the covers and unaware that the fact was obvious. Yeadings patted a bare shoulder in a fatherly manner and unobtrusively drew the sheet higher above the strapping.

'How goes it, then?'

'Fighting fit,' she lied limply.

'You've done well, Z. Keep it up.'

'I'm sorry...' Her face screwed like a child trying not to cry. 'It's no use. Can't remember.'

'Don't try too hard. It'll come when it's ready. You know about memory shadow. You were out cold for quite a period. The blank patch can extend backwards over the same time as after the trauma.'

'So—frustrating.'

'Just lie back and let it all happen.' He realized as it came out that that was almost the cynic's advice over rape. He shut his mouth with a snap and reddened. At the same time he saw that she had made the same connection and her face twisted with laughter.

'Ooh, mustn't—laugh.'

He reached in his pocket. 'Nan sent this. I hope it's a pong you really go for.'

'Lovely. Could you puff some—'

'Behind the ears and on the pillow,' he said. 'I've had my instructions.'

'Kind. Thank Mrs Yeadings, please.'

'I'll not stay and tire you. Everyone sends good wishes. Angus is back from Holland. He thinks he's caught up with the Porsche. Mainly Bunter's spadework.'

'George's car—did you . . . ?'

'We found the rotor arm, yes. Just a touch of spleen by Gerald on front desk, when he learned you were in the job and guessed you'd have it in for the currency club.'

'I remember he came and sneered at me afterwards, but there was something else that happened. Something I meant to tell you, only it's gone.'

'It'll find its way back, like Bo-Peep's sheep-tails. I've left Beaumont and Silver over there. They may get to it before you do. I'm going now, so goodbye, Z.'

On impulse, because she looked so small and battered, he bent over and gently kissed her forehead. To cover it he sniffed loudly. 'Just testing. It's a good pong.'

He turned in the doorway to look back. Her eyes were struggling to stay open. She smiled groggily. The uniformed policewoman came in from the corridor and settled again on the chair he'd vacated.

From a public phone in the foyer he rang DCI Atkinson to be brought up to date on current cases. Satisfied that his presence wasn't required elsewhere he set out for home, in his briefcase a transcript of a manslaughter case which was due to go to Appeal. It was the Crown Prosecutor's business, but he wanted to be doubly sure there had been no technical quirks which the defence might use to overthrow an adequate and just verdict.

He found Nan sitting in the garden alone and joined her on the swinging couch. 'I put Luke back in his cot,' she told him. 'The heat has knocked him out.'

In the shaded end of the garden he caught sight of Sally directing spray from a hose on to the clematis fence.

'There was a letter for you this morning,' Nan said. 'I guessed what it might be so I opened it.'

Yeadings waited, wary because of her serious tone. 'And?'

'You remember those tests Sally took about five weeks back?'

'Her assessment? Yes.'

'The results were better than expected. Dr Wilkinson has passed them on to the Education Committee. He thinks there's a chance she'll be offered a place at the Comprehensive school.'

'Oh.'

'I've rather been expecting this. Her reading has come on well, and she does straightforward sums. It's with more complicated reasoning that she panics. But even there she's better. She really does try to work things out.'

'You'd know better than I would, but I've been thinking the same. Remember that tap business—the one gushing water without being connected to a supply? It worried her, but once I told her how the trick was done she caught on at once. And if she hadn't noticed it in the first place I might have been a whole lot slower solving the case I was on.'[1]

'So what if there is a chance of the Comprehensive?'

'I don't know. She might find she is the slowest of the slow. It could upset her, and other children can be cruel.'

'It's a very big school,' Nan said doubtfully. 'There are too many pupils for the teachers to take special notice of one who's disabled.'

'Perhaps there's an alternative. Somewhere smaller. A couple of years back I called at the convent high school to get background on an ex-pupil found dead in the park. There was a Down's Syndrome girl working in their garden-room and the nuns were so nice to her. I mentioned Sally to the Mother Provincial then. Of course, that girl was a novice, maybe seventeen or older. I don't know how they would regard taking a pupil with the same disability.'

'And we're not Catholics. Not religious at all, really.'

'M'm. There doesn't seem much of a chance. But worth a try. Suppose I go and see them, sound out the possibility? They struck me as very human, not so much red tape as with the Education Committee.'

'I'd like to see the place before we decided. There'd be fees and uniforms...'

'Let's take it as it comes, love. We're a long way off September still and things may...' The phone was cooing. Yeadings pushed himself off the swing and went in to answer it.

Mott's voice sounded quietly cheerful. 'The Coleman business is sorted out at last, Boss.' In a few sentences he explained what he'd learned from Brightman and at Croy-

[1] *Cat's Cradle*

don. He was phoning from there now, with the name of the man who'd stood in for Coleman with the red Porsche.

'Ronald Gardner. He's a freelance chauffeur and part-time salesman. Which may mean he draws unemployment benefit and makes a load on the side. Not local. Coleman thought he was London-based. He contacts him through a common acquaintance in Bow, but it seems Gardner's gone missing for the last few weeks. He's moved out from his rooms in Bow and nobody has his new address. If Criminal Records have nothing, we'll have to ask Social Security for a line on him.'

'I've told Angus to drop by for a bite,' Yeadings told Nan as he came back, armed with two tumblers of iced mint tea. 'He'll have missed the rush-hour traffic out of London, should be here by seven-thirty or eight. Is that all right?'

'There's always room at the table for Angus. I thought he'd gone Dutch.'

'Flew back from Holland yesterday. And he may have a second suspect for the Dutch girl's killing.'

'One of the antiques dealers?'

'No, an Englishman, name of Ronald Gardner.' Yeadings stood weighing his tumbler in one hand, printing the other palm with rings of condensation. 'Ronald Gardner,' he said again. 'Why does that ever so faintly ring a bell? Almost a knell of doom?'

'Tell me about it,' Nan invited. 'I don't have to cook. I poached half a salmon and it's ready in the fridge.'

'Right then. You know we were looking for this Coleman fellow?' and he started on the story.

When he reached its end Nan said, 'You'll get Gardner through the DSS, won't you, if he's been on unemployment benefit?'

Mike's face flooded with sudden animation. 'That's it! Social Services. *Ronald Gardner*! The same man. We even have a local connection! He's the missing ex-husband in connection with the death of—what was the girl's name? The one poisoned by dickey pâté who broke her neck falling on the stairs. *Winter*! Penny Winter. She'd gone back to her maiden name after the divorce.'

'You mean he's involved in the death of *two* girls now? An unhealthy person to know.'

'His name coming up isn't the only common factor,' said Yeadings grimly. 'There's Harwich too. Where Anneke was found, and from where a package, probably containing the salmonella pâté, was mailed.

'Nan, we dismissed Penny Winter's death as accidental. But now, identifying the ex-husband as a possible suspect in another case of violent death with a Harwich link means we have to take a second look!'

FIFTEEN

THE TEAM MET UP at 8.30 at the Mermaid Café. Charlie Wigram didn't normally serve breakfast, but he occasionally granted police favours, having once been a PC with the Met, invalided out on losing two fingers to a machete in a minor race riot. The injury didn't prevent him throwing together a satisfactory line in grilled sausages, fried bread, bacon, eggs and beans.

DS Beaumont was in his element, almost silent for once with pleasure at not having to cook for himself. The estranged Cathy was still at her mother's, and his son Stuart, although full of good domestic intentions when he first seeped back, had relaxed into a passive kitchen rôle.

Silver, by habit a toast and marmalade man who made up for it at midday, was tucking in, inspired by DI Mott whose energy and physique required early morning stoking of no mean order. Superintendent Yeadings divided his attention between his notebook, the telephone and a bowl of high fibre cereal with semi-skimmed milk. They were all coffee men, and Charlie had withdrawn, leaving a hotplate with an almost unlimited supply.

'So,' said Yeadings when he'd made his dispositions for the day, 'let's consider Ronald Gardner. What we have to determine is whether Penny Winter and Anneke Vroom had any connection beyond a common acquaintance with him. How significant is the Harwich link and the fact that their deaths occurred within a day or so of each other? Have we a serial woman-killer here?

'Can we go on assuming that Winter's death was accidental, as the resumed inquest is likely to find? While we've nothing that could stand up in Court—even if the Crown Prosecutor could be persuaded to take an interest—the sending of the pâté by post from the very town where Vroom's body was recovered must now be regarded as most probable. But we've no positive evidence of it.

'I'd remind you that the outer wrapping of the package has not been recovered, and any defending counsel worth his salt would claim that the torn-off corner with the stamps came from some unconnected package and was smeared with pâté when in contact with the other garbage. The greasy thumbprint was identified as the dead woman's own. There was no weight and price label on the inner plastic wrappings recovered by SOCO from the kitchen flip-top bin. The postage stamps bore no trace of saliva, but of minute sponge rubbings, grit and gum mixtures such as could be picked up from an ordinary damping pad. So a DNA identification is out.

'Let's recap what probably happened. The package arrived by post and the Winter girl kept it till the children were in bed that evening, then scoffed the lot with dry biscuits. Feeling low, perhaps, she indulged herself—with mint chocolate (which she'd already bought) and the pâté. Made herself sick, but not sick enough to clear the poison.

'Either the sender didn't know about the little girls or didn't care. Or—and this is important—knew they wouldn't be eating any pâté; either because Penny was reputedly a pig over the stuff, or the children wouldn't eat spicy pork. Some won't.

'All this information was available to us within twenty-four hours of the incident. And salmonella poisoning happens often enough, somewhere or other. BUT this was the only case reported at that time. The Public Health Department are adamant on that. They've made extensive inquiries. Now it isn't their job any more; it could well be ours. Any questions?'

'Would she have known the pâté's source?' asked Silver doubtfully.

'Certainly, if there was a note enclosed; and probably, if pâté was a known favourite of hers and she'd been given some before.'

'No note was found,' Mott considered, 'but it could have gone straight into the dustbin with the outer wrappings and been cleared by the council men that day.'

'Unless,' suggested Beaumont, 'someone present took care to remove the evidence after the girl fell—or was pushed.'

Yeadings looked round at their grim faces. 'Beaumont, I want you to find where this Gardner's got to. He's a slippery customer; didn't leave an address even with Coleman; contacts him every couple of weeks, or so, touting for what jobs are going. His family in Colchester are equally in the dark. After the sister-in-law identified Penny Winter's body, Essex police had a phone call from Gardner's mother, a Mrs Doris Boulter, requesting help in tracing him. She thought he was staying with a young lady called Janice at an address in Beaconsfield. The death wasn't then considered suspicious, and the query was passed to Social Services. Check first whether they came up with anything.

'While he's on that, you, Silver, will go through Beaconsfield voters' lists and make a note of all Janices. And thank your stars she isn't a Mary or an Elizabeth.'

He sounded grim, as well he might be, having had the Winter case in his hands days ago and let it slip away like a sliver of soap in the bathtub.

Angus had been away at the Bailey for Paula's first defence case, so it was Beaumont who had been in charge on the spot, plus divisional SOCO team, with himself just looking in. Rosemary Z had dealt with the children and next-door neighbour. No excuse if, between them all, they'd missed something vital.

He remembered the Winter's girl's face, pertly rodent-like in death, perhaps pretty enough before her light went out. Sluttish in her habits, or was that only the outcome of her despair, rejected by her in-laws, without resources and solely responsible for two small children? Surely not at all the same type as the Dutch girl, who was described as warm and generous. Both Gardner's victims? How true was it that a man always went for the same kind of sexual partner? It would be interesting to see what this new unknown Janice was like; which of the two dead girls she approximated to.

The Ronald Gardner who had run out on Penny Winter was escaping from domesticity and debts: looking for freedom and a better life—better in the sense of cushier, not morally elevated. He'd found a touch of *dolce vita* as temporary chauffeur for the Cosmos Personnel Director, then stayed on at Chardleigh Place with the double pretence that he was a senior member of Cosmos staff and that the Porsche was his own. Hotel staffs being notoriously busy on conference occasions, his status hadn't been questioned, but it spoke for some skill in deception that he'd carried it off as he did. Putting over the same kind of pretentious con as the man who had employed him.

So why? Was it merely for the pleasure of the moment, or had he seen some long-term gain in it? If so, from where and from whom? Was the magnet Chardleigh Place and something profitable going on there, or was it Anneke?

If there was drug involvement, the connection could have been with both: Anneke as courier, Chardleigh Place the drop, Gardner distributor. And wouldn't that explain how easily Gardner had passed himself off there as someone of importance?

Yeadings drew Mott aside and sketched his thoughts on this. Angus hummed through tight lips. 'The General Manager Denison, and Brightman from Cosmos: could they be in on some scam together, employing Gardner?'

'You're the one who's met them all,' Yeadings reminded him. 'Try the notion on for size.'

'Gardner's a philandering con,' Angus said thoughtfully. 'Small-time good-time Charlie. Flashy. What I don't know—'

'Yes?'

'—is how far he cons himself. He sounded pretty convincing on the surface with his insurance-adjuster talk, really into it. It might not have fooled a professional, but he'd certainly picked up a lot from the people he was with the previous week, probably mixed with them, attended some of the lectures, eaten with them, absorbed the scene. Adaptable. When they mixed socially the training staff would have taken him for a candidate, the candidates for someone in the firm.

'With hindsight I recognize he was enjoying the rôle. It fitted into his hopes of negotiating the sale of that damaged yacht down at Portland. It wasn't his, but I think he'd offered the owner to pull some suckers in, then happened on Paula and me. I remember we mentioned sailing the evening before when we were chatting in the bar. He picked up that I was an enthusiast who had to hire a boat. Maybe he also picked up the atmosphere between the two of us, which wasn't good just then. Anneke didn't matter enough to prevent him offering her to me on a platter, as compensation for a dead weekend.'

'And Anneke went along with it?'

Mott considered. 'She seemed quite natural; not under orders, I mean. No, she was just playing, I think. A newish game for her. She knocked off when I slapped her down, figuratively of course.'

'Freewheeling, you think?'

'I'd have said so. Rather like her attitude to the hotel. It was there and she was using it, harmlessly enjoying what she could get out of it at the time. But not quite in the same way that Gardner did. I think she was more honest; just idling, though, and by nature she was a worker. She said as much and sounded proud of it.'

Yeadings regarded Mott. He was a good jack, kept pretty well to the book. If he had a fault it was that he didn't enter enough into the minds of the people he dealt with. This time it was different. Since the Amsterdam trip the Dutch girl's death had really got to him. Or the temporary upset with Paula had shaken him into appreciating a new human dimension.

As if he'd picked up what his boss was thinking, Mott acknowledged, 'Look, a lot of this is Paula's observation. We've discussed Anneke by phone and I think she saw her more clearly than I did. At the time I was angry and off-guard. Paula was the reverse, and she was watching everything.'

There was a silence during which Yeadings poured them both more coffee. Then, 'You imply Anneke was coasting,' he considered. 'But she shouldn't have been. If she wanted an abortion—and that's why, presumably, she'd come across from the Netherlands—she should have been moving heaven and earth to get it done before the legal time limit ran out.'

'Ah well, Paula's convinced that Anneke had changed her mind; was riding high, looking forward to having the baby.'

'In that case she couldn't carry on without help of some kind. So who was going to support her when she'd produced the child? Not Gardner for certain. He'd already run out on one family, seems to have had no feelings for the children.'

'Got rid of his wife,' Beaumont intervened chirpily. 'Remember what the Gardner woman said to Z about her sister-in-law?— "Twice removed: once through divorce, now again by death." Suppose Gardner intended it that way. Divorce wasn't enough, because she still cost too much; so second time permanently, by murder. Then along comes another embarrassment likely to interfere with his long-term plans and he tops her as well.'

'It's one possibility we have to consider,' Yeadings allowed. 'But we don't know Gardner had a close enough connection with Anneke to need her put away. She could have been looking elsewhere for support. Someone had suggested she should come to England, must have pointed her towards Chardleigh Place. She seemed relaxed there, so why don't we accept that she was expecting to stay on until the baby arrived, maybe even later? So under whose protection?'

'If not Gardner, it has to be Denison,' Beaumont said. 'He may have met her earlier in Amsterdam, if he ever went across there. Anyway we have it from talk among the staff that he was bowled over by the news of her death.'

'Which almost puts him out of the frame for her murder,' Mott regretted. 'And takes away at least part of a motive for Gardner to have done her in, because if Denison was her protector, Ronnie G didn't have to be. We're going in circles, Boss.'

Glumly they admitted that it had become even more vital to discover just what lay behind the Chardleigh front. The answer could lie in what Z had discovered but could no longer recall.

'I'll get over to Windsor this morning,' Yeadings said, 'and see if anything has surfaced in her mind overnight.'

SOCIAL SERVICES had traced Ronald Gardner's address in Beaconsfield by the same method DC Silver used, sweethearting his way to the terminal of the Community Charge computer. In his case he fed in 'Janice' and keyed in the 'Find' function. Beaumont, meanwhile, had learned that Gardner had been successfully contacted the previous day and had already accompanied a social worker on a visit to his two little girls at St Nick's.

'Not all that willingly,' the young woman told him sourly. Until that grimace she had been a mini-skirted, merry-faced artificial blonde with Elizabeth Taylor eyebrows and a near-skinhead haircut.

'That man is no penguin.' She grinned at his look of incomprehension. 'Number one in my charts for paternal instincts: daddy penguin nurses the egg on his own flat feet, tucked under his beer-paunch, all through the Antarctic blizzards until junior pecks his way out.'

'Then what?' Beaumont demanded, unimpressed. 'That's the stage I find hardest myself, when the young get frisking around under their own steam.'

'The penguin community puts on pressure and junior has to conform to survive. Rather more successful than the human handout system. Usually when I'm sent in it's too late to change things, and anyway I'm hobbled.'

He looked his doubt at this. 'Go on, show me?' he begged.

She checked that nobody was peeking over the office partition, then scuttled round her desk on her heels, feet never more than two inches apart.

Enchanted, the DS grinned back. 'You're as mad as me! Listen, Miss—'

'Alison. We use forenames here. Surnames only for reprimands.'

'Alison, could you take me to Gardner's place, work me in as your assistant, without actually telling any lies?'

'Sorry. Not this morning. The diary's clogged. I'm due a free afternoon, though. I was actually going to choose myself a new carpet...'

'Have lunch with me, take me to Gardner, and I'll help choose the carpet. I'm a dab hand with Axminsters and Wiltons, not to mention underlays.'

She looked at him accusingly.

'I said *not* to mention underlays,' he said demurely. 'We'll likely catch him at home on a Saturday.'

'On those terms how can I refuse? Where and when?'

'I'll pick you up at twelve-thirty—no? One p.m. on the dot. Fancy eating at the Falcon?'

'Lovely. See you then.'

He called DC Silver by radio and walked to where he was parked. 'Let's just take a preview of where Gardner's shacked up,' he suggested. 'The address sounds as if he's fallen on his feet.'

The modern block of flats stood behind landscaped lawns on a corner of the Beaconsfield road to Penn. Three storeys high, built of red brick and dressed stone, it had picture windows, many of them with matching sun blinds throwing welcome shadows over balconies decorated with flower-filled tubs and troughs. 'M'm,' Beaumont appreciated. 'Here be Gentry.'

There was a smoked-glass double front door with an entry phone and only twelve names discreetly listed beside it.

'There you are; J. Furnivall. No title. Does she call herself Ms or Mrs?'

'Miss,' said Silver. 'Rather old-fashioned, isn't it? I never know whether a Ms is ashamed of being single or of being married.'

'It's a snare,' Beaumont said. 'A warm invitation, implying they're open to meaningful relations.'

'Nice to have the time for it.'

Silver was twenty-four, lived with his parents and spent most of his off-the-job hours helping to organize sports at a lively youth club. Beaumont grinned at the plaintive voice. It occurred to him to find out what title skinhead Alison gave to her name in full.

'Is that it? Just a shufti from the outside?'

'For the present. I don't fancy announcing a coming arrest through the entry phone, to get "Not today, thank you." I'm going in incognito this afternoon, with a Social Security escort on overtime.'

'So what now, Skip?'

'Phone in a report, get an OK on the next step.' He ran a hand round his chin and looked smug. 'Then take my buggy to a car wash.'

Silver gave him an odd look and restarted the engine. Beaumont thought he heard him mutter something about two moons in the sky.

'I'VE SET UP A MEETING for two forty-five,' Alison said over their drinks. They had them served at table, to avoid the weekend crush in the bar.

'What excuse did you give?'

'There's plenty to discuss about Ginny and Miranda. He hadn't any suggestions where they should go; just a determination not to be saddled himself.'

'But he is. He can't escape it.'

'He seems very good at dropping things at his backside. Wait till you see how he's living, and his clothes. Nothing

but the best, and there's months of arrears on maintenance. I was a little surprised to catch him in. He seems so
much the sort who'd be running a lucrative job on unemployment benefit.'

'Could do that via his lady-love's telephone account. Did
you meet this Miss Furnivall when you called yesterday?'

'She let me in, but he didn't want her around while we
were talking. I shouldn't think he's been exactly open with
her over his marital arrangements.'

'But he was properly divorced from Penny Winter?'

'Oh yes, and once her solicitor got on to his cohabiting
with a relatively rich partner there would have been demands for a revision of maintenance. Not that she'd necessarily have benefited. Three times nought is nought, after
all. The most she could force him to would be imprisonment for non-payment, and what good would that do, apart
from venting spite?'

'And lining the lawyers' pockets. So they'd just have harassed him until he moved on and got lost again.'

'That's his style. Unless he chose to settle here and pull
Janice Furnivall in on a share of the payments. Of course,
now with his ex-wife dead, there are only the children. A
judge would probably make a settlement which Gardner and
the girl between them could manage quite easily. I expect the
little girls will be fostered. They should be reasonably easy
to place. Some foster parents prefer to take a pair provided
they're of the same sex.'

'You make it sound like choosing gloves or wellies.'

'Sorry. I've been in this business five and a half years.
Feel how thick my skin's grown.'

Beaumont accepted the invitation and took her hand in
his own across the table. It was warm and soft with a cooler
strip on thumb and forefinger where she'd held her wine-
glass.

'So that's my job,' she said wryly. 'Now tell me about you.'

'I decline to be regarded as one of your cases. Just for a change, let's put you under the microscope.'

She gave a bubbling laugh. 'Now which version shall I give you? The By-Dali-out-of-Picasso one, I think.'

'That'll do for now,' he allowed, 'Unless there's a By-Bowie-out-Heavy-Metal one. I've been better brainwashed into modern music than art.'

In Windsor General, Rosemary Zyczynski had been taken down to theatre again because the last set of X-rays had shown a crack in the left cheekbone. Now that the swelling was beginning to subside they intended compressing that and the shoulder. Because it would be painful she had been given a general anaesthetic. When she came round later she would still not be up to answering questions.

Superintendent Yeadings hunted out the policewoman who had been left to sit with her. He ran her to earth in the staff cafeteria lunching with two young doctors. He fetched himself a coffee and joined them.

'She hasn't remembered a thing yet, sir,' the girl said. 'But I had a relief sit in for part of the night, and she said Zyczynski was restless, seemed to be having a nightmare. I thought you ought to know she called out twice something that sounded like "Anna!" I have reported it in, sir.'

'Good girl. And that's the lot?'

'I'm afraid so, sir.'

'At least it sounds as though things are surfacing in her mind,' one of the doctors offered.

'It could be some private worry. We'll find out who she knows by that name. I'll pass it on by phone. If there's anyone at Chardleigh Place...' Yeadings looked grim.

When he arrived there George Bunter spotted him from a window of the temporary office and came out to meet him. 'This "Anna" business, have you turned up anything on that yet?'

Bunter nodded. 'We've two possibles, sir. There's a Mrs Hargreaves, helps in the stillroom. Comes in alternate weekdays, and that evening she went home at ten-fifteen. Her husband picked her up in his van. The time's vouched for by two witnesses. They saw her from the windows.

'She's the only Anna, but for good measure we've a Hannah Minton. Thought she might be worth considering. Boyes is almost sure he's seen her somewhere before. He's gone to look through records. Didn't want to scare her off.'

'She's the one who told Gerald that Z was in the job.'

'She's a live-in-waitress, but she was out at a disco in Slough that night. Didn't get back till the early hours, exact time unknown, according to her room-mate.'

'Has her own transport?'

'Came back by taxi, sir. We're still trying to contact the driver.'

'I want all details when you do. Time and place of pickup, time of arrival here, what state she was in, who she was with, all the rest. Meanwhile I'll have a word with this Anna Hargreaves. In the office. On my own.'

As far as you could go from appearances, and Yeadings took nothing at face value, Mrs H came into the category of decent old body, the type you could work to a standstill and then once she was done she'd fetch out her knitting and keep busy with that.

She had to think when she'd last seen Miss Seal. It must have been about 10.10 p.m., at the end of the corridor when she went to pick up her handbag. She'd left it in the assistant housekeeper's office, but she always did, because she sometimes had quite a bit of money in her purse and she could lock it away there in a drawer.

'Come and show me where you both were,' Yeadings invited. Which she did, smoothing the front of her granny-print apron with large red hands and saying she didn't know what things were coming to when such a thing could happen to a nice young lady like Miss Seal.

Rosemary had been heading for the staff staircase which would ultimately lead up to her own and the Denisons' rooms. Only the male staff lived in the separate block.

'But now I come to think of it,' Mrs Hargreaves said, 'she probably didn't go up just then. She had a folded bit of paper in her hand and she was opening it as she started up the stairs. Then she stopped and put one hand on the banisters. She was reading it, see. I called out goodnight and went out the side door, so I can't say for sure, but I had the feeling...'

'Yes, Mrs Hargreaves?'

'...that she'd changed her mind, like. And she was coming back down.'

As if she'd had a message and was going to check up on what it said, Yeadings thought. Coming down again, but how far? Just to the kitchen corridor—or one floor farther, down to the wine cellars?

'Your husband's car was already waiting outside?'

'His van, sir. He's a joiner. Yes, he always picks me up when I'm lateish.'

'And were there any other cars about? Anyone you noticed near the side door?'

'No, sir. All the guests' cars were parked round by the stable block. Geoff and me were the only ones about outside then.'

SIXTEEN

RONALD GARDNER patted aftershave on his cheeks and chin, peering appreciatively towards his reflection in the bathroom mirror. He wasn't dissatisfied with his morning's efforts.

Saturday, so they hadn't risen early. He had made coffee and heated some croissants, brought breakfast on a tray to Janice in bed, with a pink rose from the balcony climber afloat in a brandy globe for romantic colour. Then he'd climbed back to join her. They'd stayed on, and he'd given her a good time.

With the phone call from the Social Services girl he'd scented trouble. He hadn't had time enough to work on Janice. Yesterday, once she heard about the kids she'd been upset because he hadn't told her before, and then she'd had this stupid idea that they should take them on themselves. He had to be careful there, point out the obvious drawbacks while not letting her get the impression he felt well rid of them.

No way would the kids fit into the scene here as it stood. And as it stood was how it suited him best.

Penny had been a slut, sinking farther with every row between them; and she'd dragged the kids down with her. Spruced up and warned to keep shut, they might pass muster for half an hour, but by then they'd be out of hand. All kids were messy, and just one afternoon of them let loose in this flat would make it look like a bomb had hit it. A treacle and soot bomb.

He'd tried hinting at that, thoughtfully turning Jan's Dresden shepherdess (one of a fragile pair) in his hands as he spoke, to help get the point across. And Janice, silly cow, had said, 'We could sell up here, get a small house with a garden. They'd love that. Between us we could afford it too.'

With her salary and the allowance from her dad; plus his dole? Because what he made on the side was needed for other things. No, it wasn't on; there'd be no financial parleying, especially since Janice had gobbled up that talk about his working freelance for Cosmos.

Besides, a house would be far too permanent. He'd only just got the other one off his back. (Or the Building Society had transferred it to its own broader back, so that he'd had to find somewhere to drop Penny off with the bits of furniture that were left.)

At least he had put some distance between the kids and his mum. She was one of those fussers who wanted everyone permanently round her kitchen table. He wouldn't have objected to her taking on Ginny and Miranda—God, what a name!—except that she was a bit wobbly on her pegs of late. If she fluffed it, there'd be the same old story all over again. Everyone would want to dump the kids on him.

In a way, provided someone elsewhere could be found to foster the little monsters, Janice's idea of a house together wasn't too bad, all the time things kept on as they were. Provided she financed it. He rather fancied a neighbourhood like this. They'd need two garages; he might get a smart little sports job of his own. Only, learning from history, he hadn't much faith that the dice fell his way for long. This might be an up, but the down could be just round the corner. Women were dodgy, and the least incident could turn them from cuddly pets into screaming wildcats. So— better no house, no mortgage, no signings; just like no wedding-bells, no chains. After all, something even more suitable might someday heave in sight, and he had to stay free to grasp it.

He looked at his exposed chest and slapped at the flesh below his ribs; still firm, maybe too pale. He should get out on the balcony in his shorts while the hot weather lasted; and sucks to the old dowager who looked so scathingly down from the apartment one above and one along.

Anyway, this Social Services doll. Luckily a second kerfuffle would be avoided because Janice had arranged to drop in this afternoon on her dad, the almighty Lieutenant-Commander. She'd suggested Ronald should go with her, but he wasn't ready for that much condescension.

Let the old man wait. He knew Janice had someone living with her because twice he'd phoned when J was out and Ronald had answered. It had tickled him to hear the doubt in the old man's voice the second time, as he worked out that the gas man or the electrician wouldn't still be there ten days later. But so bloody well bred! Not the sort to land punches; hadn't even asked Ronald his name.

He pulled on his shirt and buttoned it, went for his cigarleaf brown summer suit in the big cupboard she'd given him for his things. They looked lonely, stuffed in one corner. All good quality, but sparse. He'd have to take Jan on a shopping spree, slip her that emerald ring he'd won off Dougie's friend at snooker, and let her set him up with something really classy.

Meanwhile, check the fridge and totter out for a newspaper. Then a brandy, and he'd be ready to take on Miss Skinhead and go through the poor-little-lambs routine.

HE HADN'T EXPECTED that she'd bring along an assistant this time. Not that the fellow was that impressive, with his round eyes and cartoon face, but it meant modifying one's line a little, cutting out the chatting up.

The girl sat cross-legged in an armchair opposite, with her short skirt riding up her thighs and her free foot rotating so that you had to keep your eyes on her ankles. Which were good. While she prattled on about fostering, adopting, natural parents, all that bilge—and what could that really matter to a girl like her?—the chap with the puppet face stood boggling out the window or wandered aimlessly about, picking up things and putting them down again as if he was at a street market.

They didn't get anywhere, and he hadn't intended that they should.

'We'll have to see,' she said doubtfully at the end.

'So long as you remember,' he said, his voice deep with sincerity, 'that their Gran is in a pretty poor state of health, so she's out of the running. And as for me, well—you must understand it's a new relationship. We've a long way to go to build up to a really stable life together. Fragile things are easily destroyed. The presence of children from an earlier marriage...'

'Oh, you are going to marry Miss Furnivall, then?' Alison stood there wide-eyed, with pen poised as if to write in a date when she could dump the kids on to them.

'It's not quite fixed yet. We're at a delicate stage. Opposition from the family, you see. Hers, I mean, not mine.'

'Well, quite. Apparently yours don't know anything about it.'

'You've been in touch?'

'Of course. It was through your mother's contacting us to find your address that we, er, ran you to earth.'

'She's probably lost the card I sent her. Not quite as bright as she was, you know.'

'Something of the sort...perhaps. Well, I'll make out a report. Some kind of temporary fostering seems to be the best I can recommend.'

'Unless, of course, you have someone suitable who's keen on permanent adoption. In that case I wouldn't want to stand in their way. It would be a wrench, but probably better for the girls in the long run.'

'M'm. I get your point, Mr Gardner. Well, that's it, then. I'll be back.'

Once outside, Beaumont observed the girl's mottled flush. She raised clenched fists and shook them in the air. 'What I couldn't do! The oily, lying bastard!'

'So what can you do?'

'You heard. Make out a report. And leave out the adjectives.'

THREE MILES AWAY, on the outskirts of Penn, the thin red-haired girl and the tall, silver-haired man, whose shared photograph Beaumont had examined in Janice's flat, sat at a table under a lime tree. The sticky flowers, some of which Furnivall dried every summer to make an infusion with slices of lemon, were already over. Occasionally as they talked together, the tiny hard balls that were seed cases fell and bounced gently on the sun-dried grass. When Janice moved her chair to keep out of the glare, they crunched under her feet and split open.

Under the same tree, when she was a child, she had collected them in her pinafore to play shops with, barely hearing Mother at her piano beyond the open French windows. In those days Father had stood tall in his gold-braided uniform, sometimes coming home from a tour of duty with a piratical, scratchy black beard which Mother had quickly made him shave off.

While she ached for that disappeared past, she was fiercely impatient for the future, eager to have what she'd missed all those years when Mother had needed her near, almost dying so many times, but not quite managing it until Janice was in her late thirties.

'I'm glad you brought me out here. The house feels empty,' she said.

He chose not to understand. 'It's much the same as it always was. If there's anything more you'd like for the flat, please take it. I don't need . . . things any more.'

Things not mattering when you've lost a person, someone much loved. She could appreciate that, being in love herself. Yesterday, when Ronald had told her about his wife—his ex-wife—their wretched life together, and the children, it had gone through her physically, a piercing pain.

She'd thought until that revelation that he was like herself, somehow passed over by love. It was something about his springy walk, an almost child-like delight in receiving presents, a rounding of the eyes when she confided something personal which he found of absorbing interest, his constant willingness to please. None of that went with his having been married, having impregnated some unknown woman and given her a child, twice over. And then . . . been divorced.

She had known without having it explained that the fault wasn't his. This Penny had married him before he was old enough to understand how two-faced a woman can be. If he didn't mention her now, Janice respected him the more. She was careful to keep unspoken any bitterness of her own, because now the woman was dead, so one couldn't speak ill.

All the same, she wished it had been different. She would have liked to be the first with Ronald, to feel they were starting out together on a discovery fresh to both; not merely trying to make a better go of it this time. Though he wouldn't see it that way.

But there were still those two little girls; and he hadn't been given so much as a photograph of them to take away.

It was unthinkable that the social workers who had taken them off like orphans could have any doubts that Ronald would manage to bring them up himself. Perhaps now, with her alongside to help, these officials would see sense. When they were married, surely...

She would be glad when it was fixed. His moving in with her hadn't seemed right at first. Wonderful, of course, to be together and needed all the hours of the day, every day. But she read censure in the eyes of older women living in the same block of flats and it made her uncomfortable. It shouldn't matter how outsiders thought of her. But then her father too...

She hadn't been able to talk to him frankly. Over several visits she let a few facts drop, singly like pebbles in a well, and left him to make of it what he could. But she wouldn't have him discuss Ronnie with her. That was out, because once she had broken free, had sloughed off this dutiful daughter business, she had become her own woman. Tough and independent. And—yes, sometimes more than a little lonely. Longing to belong. Then Ronnie had come along, when she was at her lowest ebb.

James Furnivall set his cup down in the centre of its saucer, looking quickly away because he couldn't bear to see the tears squeezed from her closed eyelids. His sight of them would have shamed her.

This earnest little face was the one he had watched over as she took her first tentative steps; the occasional spasm of alarm the same as when she had faltered and almost fallen. But what was new was the heart-aching distance between them now, so that he couldn't gather her up close for comfort—comfort necessary for them both.

She was as vulnerable as ever, but private. He had no place in her present troubles. Pride required that she should cover decently what couldn't be openly admitted.

Somewhere along the line, when she'd been small, he should have taken her on his knee and told her: that success wasn't everything; that seeing your best efforts frustrated or disregarded was part of what life was about. You don't have to show a brave face and command admiration all the time: there's affection too. There's loving and being loved for one's weakness as well as one's strength.

But he'd never explained that, *confessed* that. And she hadn't learned it elsewhere. If he attempted now, with all her spiky defences raised, it would be a voice from outside, something else to defend herself against. He'd failed her for the same reason that she was prolonging her own hurt, from this damnable need for privacy, and the fear they both had of revealing their own wounds.

But perhaps this man she had found was different. Must surely be, because of the physical link, their shared sexual needs. So perhaps he could reach out with comfort.

If only Janice talked about him. In such a covert relationship every facet must be guessed at, so he hadn't yet recognized what kind of man the stranger was.

Perhaps he himself lived in a world that had disappeared, and this modern informal bonding had a spontaneity and a joy that formality had lacked. But if so, where was this joy? He saw only her discontent.

She was gathering her things together, the spilt carrier bag of shopping, her cigarettes, a crumpled tissue fallen by her feet; getting ready to move herself physically farther away. She reassembled her face in front of him, under the flesh seeming to check the muscular control of cheek, lips, brow.

They walked side by side into the house, through the hall. Opposite the ormolu mirror she started sorting strands of her fine, russet hair, shaking her head to make them fall flat against her ears.

Too brightly she turned to him, lips arranged in a tight smile. 'It's a simple choice really. To be lonely or be buggered about.' More than she'd ever previously admitted in plain speech.

There was surely something possible in between the two options, but he couldn't assert that. He did try. 'I just want you to be happy, my dear.'

'So don't fuss me. That's all. I'm doing nicely. I'm fine.'

She didn't ask how he was, insist she wanted him happy. That only occurred to him after she'd gone, leaving behind a pool of soft lingerie gleaming peach under the garden table, silky and pathetic. Something new she'd bought to make herself look desirable. He bent to pick it up and held the softness against his face. It gave off nothing of her, only the smell of some impersonal local store.

THERE WAS A DIFFERENT smell here; less disinfectant than before, more humanity; a lingering of the eau de cologne the Boss's wife had sent her. If she twisted round against her pillows Rosemary Zyczynski now had an oblique view of the outside world. Just before lunch she had been transferred from Intensive Therapy to a women's ward. She marvelled at the difference space made.

She was still immobile but at least aware of life continuing outside her. From beyond the glass pane by her bedhead came sounds of cars and occasional shouting voices, the *hoo-haa* of ambulances. Nurses passing where she lay gave a quick smile, asked if she needed anything; trays clattered with cutlery; women called chirpy greetings from bed to bed. Now and again one of them would come and peer at her. There was no longer a WPC in attendance.

After the duty change and before the public visited, a tall girl with golden curls bouncing on her shoulders came and sat beside Z, quietly said, 'Hullo, Rosemary, feeling better now?'

Z struggled to sit up, hampered by her bandaging. 'Do I know you? Sorry, I must have forgotten more than I thought...'

'Well, I know you better than you do me.'

There was something familiar about the voice, but the face was quite strange to her.

'It's the hair that makes the difference. Look.' The girl swept her curls together, twisted them back and left the sharp planes of her face uncovered.

'Mind, you were pretty woozy most of the time I was with you. At the point when our patients come alive they're always whipped away from us.'

'In Intensive Care. Yes, of course. No hair then. You wore a cap. I have to thank you. For everything.'

The girl rose and smiled. 'All the thanks we need are in seeing our patients get back on their feet. I won't stay, but look in again tomorrow. Might meet some more of your dishy colleagues. Popular girl! We had them queuing in the corridor to peep through the louvres. I thought Dr Mac-Gibbon would have to ring 999 to clear them.'

Z smiled and dozed off again. She was in a corridor herself, walking towards some stairs. The uniformed nurse was ahead coming towards her. Then a strange transformation took place. Her overall turned into the café-au-lait outfit of a Chardleigh Place waitress and now her hair was black, strained back into a brown velvet bow. Z started to laugh, but the girl went on changing, her face coarsening, the hair bursting free into a crimped bush that hung down long like a spaniel's ears. The woman's teeth showed in a savage grimace. It was Hannah Minton coming at her...

She awoke in an instant and cried out. Nobody came, but the woman in the bed on her left called, 'No use shouting. They're all being briefed in Sister's room. Use your bell.'

She rang, and when a student nurse came running, demanded a phone. 'It's urgent,' she begged. 'Police business.'

Someone must have left special orders, because the girl brought the trolley at once and plugged it in, even offered the coins needed to place the call. Z rang 'C' Division and asked them to contact the Superintendent. Less than ten minutes later, the call came back and it was Yeadings himself.

'Sir,' she said, 'I've remembered. There was a note on my desk, unsigned and addressed to The Housekeeper. It said there had been another delivery and the stuff was in the cellar behind the claret bay. I think I...'

'Went down on your own, Z?'

'Just meant to take a look. Some of the staff weren't beyond pulling a hoax if they'd learned I was in the job. And one of them *had* recognized me. A Mattie Gray, on the game, well known to uniformed branch. But she's at Chardleigh Place as a waitress. Calls herself Hannah Minton.'

'So what happened in the cellar?'

'I'm not sure. I fetched the key. I remember unlocking the door, was groping for a light switch. Someone must have been in there, flat against the wall, waiting. There's only a small square landing. I think... It was the scent!—that was it! It was Mattie. She'd drenched herself in the stuff to go out on the town. But she must have come back and decided to—get rid of me before I could make trouble.'

'Good girl. We'll get right on to it. Leave it to us. Just concentrate on getting better.'

He hadn't sounded all that surprised, she thought, as the telephone trolley was wheeled away. She hadn't been asked to spell out Mattie's names. And now suddenly she understood why the WPC wasn't beside her bed any more.

Yeadings already knew what she had just told him. He and Beaumont and the others had broken through without her. She had remembered too late.

YEADINGS WENT BACK to the commandeered office at Chardleigh Place. A uniformed constable stood stolidly back against the door after he had entered. Seated at the table opposite 'Hannah Minton', DS Bunter watched him come in, shake a head at the offered chair and lean against the wall. 'I've just had a call from the hospital,' Yeadings said heavily and let the idea of bad news sink in.

The girl had been denying any knowledge of the attack on Z. She showed no flicker of nerves, but her eyes went harder.

'Oh my God!' said Bunter in shocked tones, picking up his cue from the Superintendent.

'So we'll be taking you in for questioning at the divisional station,' Yeadings warned the waitress.

'Why me? I've not done anything. Anyway I'm on duty, can't just drop me job like that. I'd get fired.'

Yeadings smiled in the direction of the recorder tape still turning on the desk. He leaned across it and picked up the notes Bunter had prepared for the girl's statement. 'What a lot of old Brothers Grimm,' he said, scanning the first paragraph. 'Don't even seem able to get your own name right, do you, Mattie? We'll have to get something more accurate than this before we go to court. Better go along with the constable now and pick up a few things you'll be needing overnight.

'And no lip, mind,' he cautioned as she started spitting fire. He let her rip for a second or two, then nodded at Bunter to kill the tape.

SEVENTEEN

'MY NAME'S BEAUMONT, Mr Gardner,' the voice on the phone said. 'I was the police officer called in at the time of your wife's—er, accident.'

'Oh yes?' He looked at himself in the silver-mounted mirror and turned his head to check the two sides of his moustache were even. The left half looked just a trifle out of true. The man on the other end of the line seemed to be waiting. Was some comment needed?

'That was—terrible,' Gardner offered huskily.

'Yes, and a lot of extra work all round because we couldn't get hold of you at the time. Sir.'

'I assure you it was unavoidable, Officer. Change of address. Pressure of business, and all that.'

'Really, sir? What business would that be?'

There was a short silence. 'Something new I'm working to set up. At the moment I'm not in employment, but I have a project in mind which needs looking into.'

'In what line would that be, sir?'

'Does it matter? Insurance, if you must know.'

'Indeed, sir. Interesting job, I should think. Well, what we need is for you to check over some details with us, if you would be so good. Shall we call on you or would it be more convenient for you to drop by?'

'I'll come to you. Less bother for you.' And no risk then of Janice overhearing anything unsavoury. She'd got the impression that Penny died some time back, as the result of a domestic accident, an awkward fall on some stairs.

'Right then, sir. Can you make it this evening?'

'That's a bit short notice.'

'Get the last details filled in and then the job's done. We don't like paperwork lying about.'

'I see. Well, if it isn't going to eat into my evening...'

'Thank you, sir. Six-thirty? You know how to get—?'

'I know where the local nick is. Who shall I ask for?'

'Detective-Sergeant Beaumont. I'll see that you get sent straight to me.' He put down the receiver.

Angus Mott smiled grimly. 'So he'll walk into our parlour?'

'No trouble. Hopes it won't take long and spoil his evening.'

'Could spoil the next few years of his life. I've had a word with the Boss, and he wants us to concentrate on the Anneke killing. We'll do it this way...'

'I THOUGHT PERHAPS we could go out somewhere for dinner,' Janice was telling Gardner. She felt too drained to be bothered with cooking. She had garaged the car and on entering the flat dropped into a deep armchair with a sigh. He forbore to ask how the afternoon with her father had gone. He could see, and he didn't need her moaning.

'Eat out, why not? Only my credit card's on the blink. Had a nick in the edge and the machine gobbled it.'

'We can use mine. Did you phone for a new one?'

'Couldn't get through. You know how it is; they put me on hold. Music while you wait. I'll write them a note tomorrow. Can I pour you something?'

'Not if we're going out, thanks. I'll just take a bath, be ready by seven. Is that all right?'

'Better make it later. More fun when the restaurants are full. Saturday night, they should have a good crowd in. Anyway I have to pop out and see a man first on business.

I'll ring and reserve a table for eight p.m., eh? Back in good time.'

She nodded, struggled out of the chair, undressed and put on a bathrobe, left the door ajar while the water ran. She heard the front door of the flat close after Ronald and felt an unaccountable rise in spirits that wasn't due to the perfumed bath gel.

It must be tiredness; she'd never before found Ronnie's company oppressive. Not that it was his fault. The real discomfort was in being positioned between two very different worlds, between her father and her lover. Secretiveness was exhausting.

'WHY DO I GET the feeling, Mr Gardner, that you're holding something back?' Beaumont asked innocently.

'Good God, I've told you everything short of when I last sat on the lavatory. What more could you want?' He was still rattled because this was the same puppet-faced man who had accompanied the Social Services girl earlier on.

'Let's see now.' Beaumont played the dumb Plod, even to licking his forefinger to turn the pages on his desk. 'Mrs Gardner—that is, Ms Winter as she preferred to be called— was found dead in the early morning of Wednesday, twenty-third June. Could you tell me where you were on that and the previous two days, Mr Gardner?'

The man looked outraged. 'What the hell are you implying?'

'Routine question for a spouse in a case of violent death, sir. Start with twenty-first June, a Monday.'

'How the hell would I know?'

'From your diary, sir?'

Gardner blew out his lips like a petulant child, but he reached inside his jacket, riffled through the pages of a small red book. 'Twenty-first June. There you are,' he said triumphantly. 'I was with my mother in Colchester, went there on the twenty-first, stayed two nights. Came back the afternoon of the twenty-third. Ask her. There'll be three witnesses, with her husband and my sister Freda.'

'How much of the twenty-first did you spend there?'

'All of it from midday on. Never budged out, except to go for a drink at the local with an old friend. Back by eleven, and the old girl had stayed up to see me in.'

'M'm. No trips out by car, say to Dedham, or Ipswich or Harwich?'

'I told you; in Colchester all the time. Anyway I had no wheels of my own then.'

'Have you now, sir?'

'Locally I use my girlfriend's car,' he said stiffly. 'What is this? It isn't tying up loose ends.'

'Would that be the only car you have driven since—say, the beginning of June?' Beaumont ploughed impassively on.

'Yes it is! What do you think I am—a kid that takes joy rides?'

'You're sure about that, Mr Gardner? The only car you have driven since you traded your BMW in a month back is the Toyota owned by Miss Janice Furnivall?'

There was a flicker of unease in the man's eyes now. He hadn't known they would go ferreting out details like that. After all, why should they?

'I'm perfectly sure. It's not the sort of thing I'm likely to forget.'

'No, it's not, seeing that you make a profession out of occasional chauffeuring and freelance car sales. Perhaps your diary would show appointments for that?'

'That is quite irrelevant. Damn it, I'm not standing for any more of this!' Gardner rose explosively and made for the door, almost colliding with a man who had just come quietly in, but he still faced the seated Detective-Sergeant. 'I don't know what you're talking about, and I refuse to stay and be badgered.'

'Did you get that, Guv?' Beaumont asked.

Mott blocked off the doorway. 'I did. Funny thing, Mr Gardner. Last time we met you were called Arnold Coleman. Fortunately the real Mr Coleman has put us right about that. Do you remember me, Mr Gardner? From that weekend at Chardleigh Place? My name's still Mott. Inspector Angus Mott, CID, Thames Valley Police.

'Nice car, the red Porsche you were driving for Mr Brightman. Perhaps you'd like to tell us about that little arrangement.'

SUPERINTENDENT YEADINGS had left them to get on with it. After all, you don't train Alsatians and then jump through the hoops yourself. On his way home he had a sudden urge to make a slight detour. Waiting in the convent parlour, he felt he should have telephoned in advance. Weekend and all, everyone might be at prayers, or whatever nuns did when they'd time off from teaching.

He was afraid too that the Mother Provincial would have forgotten him, or—even worse—have moved on elsewhere, then there would be a lot more explaining to be done.

But it was the same small, quiet lady in the black habit, although the skirts were shorter now and showed a trim pair of black tights from mid-calf down and shoes shining like wet blueberries. She came forward holding out her hand and looked genuinely pleased. 'Superintendent, how good to see you again.'

'You remember me, then.'

'And the sad case you were involved in. You're certainly remembered and sometimes prayed for, Mr Yeadings.'

'Well, I won't say I don't need it, Mother, especially over what I've come to see you about.'

She motioned him to a chair and sat listening, her head cocked as if to catch each slight cadence fully. 'Yes,' she said at the end of his explanation. 'It was young Felicitas you saw, a postulant then, now a novice. But you do understand that a *pupil* with Down's Syndrome would present quite a different situation?'

'I do. And then, we're not Catholics, any of us.'

She was watching him with bright, birdlike eyes. 'Has Sally been taught to say her prayers?'

'Yes. Nan or I hear her every night. I don't know about the mornings.'

Mother Provincial nodded, adopting a more down-to-earth expression. 'We do have—we make a point of taking—one or two spastic or crippled pupils. It's part of education as we see it to prepare our children to accept disablement and make the necessary allowances.'

'Yes. It was because I hoped for a more gentle attitude than...'

'We can all behave as barbarians, Superintendent. But children have native kindness as well as an understandable wish to outdo the less able. Have you considered that it might not be kind to your daughter to set her among children who accept a certain amount of competitiveness as the norm?'

'I understand that. She'd necessarily be slower than the others, but if—as a result of the recent assessment—she's offered a place at the Comprehensive school...'

'We give a test of capability before offering a place. Let me have some details of her age and interests.'

She made notes on a small pad which she produced from her skirt pocket, and seemed pleased that Sally was to help at the Garden Centre on Saturdays.

'She only started today,' he admitted. 'She won't be paid, of course, because she's under age, but at the end of each month the helpers choose goods up to a given value.'

'Has she decided what to ask for?'

'Oh yes. She spent days poring over the catalogue, then chose a damson tree. We've got a plot ready for it in the garden.'

'If she came,' said Mother, staring past him through the window, 'I imagine the present headmistress would place her a year behind her age group and in the slower division. She might appear larger physically than the others. Would that matter to her?'

'Not if they accepted her. She understands that she's different.'

Mother Provincial rose, indicating that the interview was over. She held out her hand. 'Tell your wife I'll ring her, Superintendent. We'll arrange a suitable time for her to come for afternoon tea and bring Sally. There will be a few day-girls staying on for prep, and we'll see how Sally takes to them.'

IF THE TWO DETECTIVES had hoped for Gardner's complete collapse when confronted by Mott, they were to be disappointed. Clearly it was a horrible shock to the man, but he had made an art of sliding out of sticky corners.

He didn't attempt to deny the previous meeting, but after an instant of gobbling panic showed his good white teeth in his charmer's smile.

He held out his wrists to Mott in mock surrender. 'I'll come quietly, Angus. How are you, you old rogue?—or undercover goody. Well, well, you had me completely fooled. Was the delightful Paula a WPC as well?'

'No. We were on holiday,' Mott said curtly. 'You gave a false name and address for the register.'

'Lord, I'd like to know how many names are the right ones in hotel registers these days. Don't be stuffy. As for the chauffeuring thing, you're surely not going to betray my little bit of black economy to the providers of my only solace and welfare.'

Mott felt a worm of loathing uncoil in his guts. He nodded coldly to the chair across the table. 'We have a few more questions for you, Mr Gardner, concerning a second sudden death.'

The slighter man's eyes narrowed and he waited. 'Second death? Whose, then?'

'Anneke Vroom. Don't tell me you never met her. I distinctly recall you introducing her at our table.'

'Anneke—*dead?* You're joking.'

'Would I be, Mr Gardner?'

'I mean—dash it all, she was good for another seventy years. No, that makes her sound like a used car. Sorry, old man. And you were fond of her, anyone could see that. What on earth did she die of?'

He sounded genuinely taken aback. Even the imputation of Mott's closer involvement with the girl might—*just* might—have been without intended malice.

'You don't read the daily press, Mr Gardner?'

'Only for the geegees, don't y'know.' Nervousness was making him overdo the phoney classiness.

'So how would you know if World War Three had broken out?'

'From TV. I usually catch one news bulletin per night. Didn't see anything about Anneke, though. What was it specifically that made her newsworthy?'

Mott turned away from the man's flip indifference. He nodded to Beaumont who baldly gave the details of the finding of her body.

Gardner started to ask something, thought better of it, stayed silent a moment and then said, 'When exactly would this be?'

'On twenty-eighth June the van was broken open and the body discovered, but it had been parked there for some days.' Deliberately Beaumont held back the twenty-fourth for the presumptive date of death. Let Gardner sweat out an alibi for another two or three days. They owed him nothing, and he was trying to put Angus down. People weren't allowed to do that to his Guv.

'Well, I was still at my mother's on the twenty-second, as I told you. Next afternoon I came back to Beaconsfield, dropped in on some old chums en route. They'll remember if you care to ask them. I'll make out a list. I've been drumming up some backing for a project I had in mind.'

'The twentieth, Sunday,' said Beaumont sententiously. 'Let's go back and start there.'

'The twentieth I was in Windsor with my girlfriend. Slept at the Beaconsfield flat. Caught the morning boat train on the twenty-first from Liverpool Street Station, dropped off at Colchester.'

'The boat train runs through to Harwich. Where the body was found.'

'Only I didn't go there. I didn't even know where Anneke was. Hadn't seen hide nor hair of her since I took the Porsche back to Coleman at Croydon. Done, finished! I didn't need a pair of wooden clogs parked under my bed.'

They let the words hang on, but he was too needled to feel shame.

'How long have you lived at your present address in Beaconsfield?' Angus asked at length.

'Oh, a month; more, probably. Say five weeks.'

'With Miss Furnivall?'

'It's her flat.' Sulkily. 'I'm thinking of getting a house somewhere in the neighbourhood.'

With subs from his mum? Beaumont wondered. The old doll hadn't sounded that flush with money. No; Gardner would be expecting the Furnivall girl to set them both up. If it lasted.

'So that at the time we met at Chardleigh Place, and you were accompanying Anneke Vroom, you were already co-habiting with Janice Furnivall?' Angus asked.

'Look, what is this—a bloody confessional? How about you, Mott? Shacking up with Anneke yourself on the Saturday night, and you'd gone there for a weekend with your fiancée!'

'That is untrue,' Mott said coldly.

'Who've you got to back your word? A copper who chucks his girl in for the first slag who comes along! And that's all she was. Anyone could have done in a tramp like that!' Gardner gave a harsh laugh.

Mott stared at him. Through a grainy film that seemed to slide over his eyes he saw him at their first meeting, seated on a bar stool, easy, confident, unconcerned; watched him—later that night—slip a familiar arm about Anneke's waist, the finger idly fondling her flesh.

Fingers that finally closed the chest lid on her?—having injected heroin, having crammed the heavy but inert body in, foetus-folded like the growing life that would also be extinguished? Gardner doing all that to the golden girl who'd sloughed off the restrictive past, survived abandonment by her lover, faced up to raising her coming child alone, gloried in her new-found assertiveness. Anneke, so vibrantly *alive*!

And then the shutter-flash images evoked by the glossy ten-by-eight death shots. Mott imagined her panic, desperately fighting for air, to force the lid back, feeling her body cease to respond, grow feebler at each second. His nostrils filled with the sweet, dank scent of mortality and putrefaction.

'You foul bastard!' His fists doubled, shoulders hunched. His own breath seemed to die in his chest. He found the man's eyes so close that they blurred together in a single blue stone. He reached out clawing hands to take him by the throat.

'Angus! Guv, that's it!' Beaumont was grasping his arm.

There came a heady moment when he knew he could do it—wade right in and tear the animal apart. A single moment suspended in time when he still had the choice. And he just didn't know, hadn't yet quite decided. But still had the power to decide, right up to the killing instant . . .

He leaned back stiffly, with difficulty drew breath, saw the man's face sweating fear, like a woman's in terror of a beating. A pathetic thing, puny, worthless.

'Don't you lay hands on me!' Gardner cried shrilly, desperate to capitalize on the momentary reprieve.

'I wouldn't soil them,' Mott hissed. Which was true now, whether the man was Anneke's killer or not. And how could he have been? It would surely have taken someone more than this manikin.

The two detectives kept on at Gardner until nearly nine-thirty p.m., when Mott signalled to Beaumont that overtime had taken all the bashing finances would run to. Gardner had retreated into dogged defiance, and only when he was on the point of leaving, in affected high dudgeon, did he suddenly lose colour and mutter, 'God, I said we'd go out to dinner!'

'Better move it then, Mr Gardner,' Beaumont suggested mildly, 'before the lady reports you missing.'

IT HAD BEEN a full weekend, and when DS Beaumont reached home there was to be no rest for him. Stuart met him at the door, dishevelled and in a pair of jeans that looked as if he'd been using them to clean his bike.

'Don't say you've left me the washing to do,' growled his father.

The boy was rolling his eyes and stabbing a finger towards the kitchen. 'She's *here*,' he ground out.

And not just 'here', but rather 'back', Beaumont saw, because alongside the staircase wall were her blue suitcases and the soft holdall he'd given her three Christmases ago.

God, *not now*, when he'd taken just about all he could, what with Angus on the point of GBH. And when he'd just had the good fortune to run into Alison, who was equally fancy free and might even get to be interested. Not when all he wanted, after a day of war by words, was a bath and bed. Bed to himself.

He threw open the kitchen door, stomped in and glared at its only occupant.

Small and miserable, hunched in his corduroy-covered armchair, sat Cathy, her face swollen with crying and the end of her nose red like a traffic light.

EIGHTEEN

ANGUS MOTT ARRIVED back at his flat to find Paula there. 'I began to think you would never come,' she said. 'Dreary Saturday. I've tomorrow and Monday free, but of course you'll be knee-high in murder and mayhem!'

'I'm free right now. And I'll prove it.'

'M'm,' she said, hugging him back. 'Fine, but leave me one hand loose to microwave our supper. You don't need to open the wine. I did it an hour ago, and I'm halfway down the first bottle.'

'Never mind the cooking. Cummalongamee. It's you I need, not food.' He towed her to the settee where they made love among the cushions.

'How about the Anneke case?' Paula asked eventually, when both lay relaxed, listening to *Scheherezade*.

Angus grunted. 'We pulled Gardner in. But let him go.'

'Who's Gardner?'

'Oh Lord, how far did you get in the story? Gardner's the one we met as Coleman. And you won't know about Z, will you? She's in Windsor General with concussion and fractures. Recovering well, though. I called in there before I came home. That's why I was late.'

'Poor Rosemary. What on earth happened?' They moved out to his kitchen. Paula listened fascinated, her hands busy with the salad, while Angus brought her up to date, simultaneously grilling steaks under buttered onion rings.

'So the attack on Z was nothing to do with the main case? Just a personal matter?'

'It seems so. This Mattie woman thought Z had caught her out in the badger game. There was big money to be screwed out of guests she was "entertaining" in her room at Chardleigh Place. One of the waiters used to rush in and claim to be her husband. You know how it's played.'

'I thought everybody was wise to it by now. But she must have been crazy to think she could get away with murder.'

'She swears she merely meant to frighten Z, didn't think it would do more than put her out of action for a while. But having locked Z in down there, injured, will damn her in court. She's a stupid woman, liable to act first and think afterwards, if at all. So far she's only been charged with GBH. What happens later rests with the Crown Prosecutor.'

'But Coleman really being Gardner,' she considered. 'Yes, I see: he was play-acting all the time. The sort who gets high on being one up on everyone else. Did he really kill both of them, his ex-wife and Anneke?'

Mott was cautious. 'He could have, if he posted the pâté in Harwich on the twenty-first. It's no distance from Colchester, where he admits to visiting his mother. He was certainly back in this area by twenty-fourth June, the date the pathologist gave for Anneke's killing. And the sticker in Anneke's pocket implied the van had been parked in High Wycombe then.'

'Which you said was the day after his ex-wife was poisoned and fell down the stairs. He sounds a pretty dangerous character.'

'If he lied about the time he left Colchester he might even have been on the stairs to give Penny Winter a push. There's still some checking to be done on his precise movements. And there's a small point I'd like cleared up about that weekend we were all at Chardleigh Place.'

'What's that?'

'You remember the crazy night I went walkabout because you weren't in our bed?'

'And found I'd taken refuge in the car, thinking you'd gone off with Anneke. I'm not likely to forget!'

'Well, if we thought at all, we assumed after that that Anneke was with Gardner.'

'And she wasn't?'

'Apparently not. He accused me of—er...'

'Is that so? She was in her own room, then.'

'I guess so. Paula, how about coming with me on Monday? You could drop in on Z. It seems she didn't turn up any leads on a drugs ring; just minor crimes and a certain amount of gossipy speculation about the manager's interest in the Dutch girl.'

'I'm game, but do you really think Denison might have had a hand in Anneke's murder?'

'I don't, but I get the feeling there's something there we've missed shaking out.' He hesitated, then admitted, 'Actually we do have an alternative suspect to Gardner for Anneke's killer. She'd taken two days off and flew across to Holland, returning next day. We haven't discovered yet what she did while she was there, but Johan Groeneveld, the probable father of the baby, was on the same flight as Anneke back to Heathrow, booked separately. There'd have been crowd enough even in the departure lounge for him to avoid her spotting him, if he was careful.'

'And he has an obvious motive to get rid of her, which Gardner hasn't? I see.'

'Groeneveld has a new woman, so he wouldn't have welcomed Anneke chasing him up with a baby. He also had access to heroin at work. At present we're waiting for fresh information on him from Amsterdam. They're checking where Anneke went on her quick trip home. It could be that she faced Groeneveld out and threatened to sue him for the coming child's maintenance. If he was desperate he might have decided to follow her and kill her here where he isn't known.'

'Groeneveld and Anneke; Gardner and Penny Winter.' Paula looked thoughtful. 'Weren't they rather the same situation: the men's rosier futures threatened by women and children surplus to requirement? It sounds as if you have two similar cases which simply overlapped.'

'First wife twice removed,' Angus said. 'Once by divorce and then by murder. Yes, except that the Dutch couple weren't actually married. But basically the story's the same.'

Abruptly he laid down his fork and pushed his half-eaten meal away.

'Angus, what is it? Would it help to tell me?'

He didn't answer immediately, and she waited.

'Today—I nearly—piled into a man. Gardner. He made me see red. I know he's a parasite, a nasty, hollow, narcissistic little wimp, but that doesn't excuse... Not even charged; just in for questioning. It was his attitude, his bloody indifference to the dead girl.'

'His wife or—'

'Anneke.' Angus sat with one hand shading his eyes.

She let the silence build up for a moment, then said gently, 'You know why, Angus. You're feeling bad about her yourself. Because you didn't see her as a real person while she was still alive.'

He rubbed his brow, grunted. 'Maybe. I certainly do now. In a way she haunts me. All the same, wanting to knock the tripes out of him ... And I would have, if Beaumont hadn't stopped me. And he's supposed to be the wild one.'

'And you so laid-back. It just goes to show. You balance each other. I guess he understood how it was getting to you.'

'I don't want my sergeant *understanding* me. Hell, he's there to do what I say!'

Paula threw back her head and laughed. 'Just as I am, O master!' She came round the table and took his face in her hands, kissed him gently on brow and tip of nose. 'Awful to be understood, isn't it?' she teased.

He looked uncertainly at her, then let the corners of his mouth turn up. 'You stinker, you won't let me have even a moment's sulk, will you?'

'Not while a good steak's going cold. Eat up, darling. I made a strawberry shortcake while I was awaiting my lord's return. I refuse to eat it on my own.'

RONALD GARDNER fiddled with his latchkey in the lock and when it wouldn't turn had recourse to ringing. There was a slight sound from somewhere inside the flat but no one came to let him in. He bent and hallooed through the letter-box. He could see the light was on and a dark shadow moved across his line of vision.

'Janice, open up, there's a good girl. We're late enough already!'

The shadows returned and there came a sudden snapping back of the deadlock. The door opened wide and she stood confronting him, pale with suppressed anger.

'You noticed! Well, *I*'m not holding anything up. Have you any idea what the time is? It's gone nine-fifty. The table was booked for *eight*! Where on earth have you been? I've been worried stiff. I thought you'd been in some accident.'

With narrowed eyes he took her in; sharp, strident, stringy. A harridan he hadn't seen before. She needn't think she could butter him up one moment and then turn vicious on him like this. As if he hadn't had enough to upset him tonight. 'Shut up,' he snarled. 'D'you want all your neighbours to hear?'

Hit her where it hurts, he thought, seeing he'd scored. So ruddy respectable!

She backed and he followed her in. As she collided with the telephone table he put out a hand and gripped her arm, brutally, but with the excuse that he was steadying her from falling. He watched her teeth bite into her lower lip and tears come to her eyes. God, now she was going to start crying.

'Look, if we're going, we'd best be on our way...' He emphasized the words with a shake.

'We aren't...going...anywhere. I rang them at nine. Cancelled the table.'

'Well, that's bloody silly! They're used to people turning up late. We'll not get in anywhere now and I'm starving.'

'Starve, then!' She actually stamped, pulling her arm free. He looked at her in disbelief.

'What's got into you? Look, I'm a bit late. All right, I admit it. But you haven't even asked why. Fine if I'm carried in on a stretcher, eh? You're a damned uncaring bitch and I bloody well won't put up with your tantrums. God, anyone would think we were married!'

She was visibly trembling. It made him want to shake her and shake her till her eyeballs rattled. He reached out for her again, and then went rigid.

The image of Angus Mott's accusing eyes overtook him, boring furiously into his own. The shock of the recent interview suddenly caught up with him; the forced bravado fled. He felt sweat start out again on his forehead. So soon after their accusations—no, just questions and suggestions so far—and here he was feeling murderous about this other stupid woman. And she wasn't worth it. None of them were. Why couldn't they all leave him alone?

'Ronnie, what is it?'

Now he had her worried. He had to think quickly. 'I— I've had a bit of a shock. Someone I knew...'

He'd been meaning Mott, who'd seemed just a gullible fool when they'd first met, but wasn't at all. And Anneke, murdered. But the real shock was Mott coming after him, finding out about the Porsche, his borrowing Coleman's identity, his not being an insurance man at all.

And then connecting him with Penny and the kids. With Penny's death. And Anneke's.

Only, had they actually gone that far, or were their suspicions only in his mind? Had they merely been doing their police inquisition thing, leaning on him for the sadistic delight of it all?

He'd have to go somewhere quiet and play it all back in his head, remember exactly what had been said and implied. Exactly what he'd said himself in reply.

'I—I'm going to lie down.'

Uncertain, she watched him move away, slightly alarmed for him but still not utterly convinced. First he'd complained that he was hungry, but now he was putting on a sick act.

She had sat there alternately worrying and steeling herself not to be fobbed off this time with excuses when he did return. Other instances of his indifference arose to haunt her, insisting she should at last admit to their existence, shoddily disguised under displays of affection.

What did she really know about him anyway? Why had it taken him so long to admit to her that he was a widower with two children? What was she to believe he actually saw her as?—older than him, and not attractive enough for anyone else ever to have been interested. His eyes when he made love were round and china-blue and innocent. Just now, as he'd gripped her arm . . . She shuddered.

He was going towards their bedroom. She knew she didn't want him there. After she'd phoned the restaurant to cancel dinner she had been so furious that she'd started to fill a suitcase with his things, ready to leave them out on the stairs. But that was too public, and she was such a coward about scandals. It mattered too much what other people thought. All the same she had tried to nurse her resentment, knowing that she always forgave too soon, never could stand her ground as she should with anyone who gave offence.

'Just give me a little while,' he said in a pathetic voice. 'I'll feel better soon.'

She ought to have locked the bedroom door to keep him out. Too late now. But she wouldn't be joining him there. There was always the guest room, only she wasn't sure she could trust herself even in the same flat with him tonight. Already a part of her was feeling sorry, admitting that it was such a small failure to be late for a dinner date; and surely there could be admissible reasons...

She sat down on the edge of the settee and was suddenly afraid. There came to her a hollow pain and the certainty that she didn't want to go on in this way. She couldn't bear feeling like this, doubting and miserable, seeing nothing ahead but repetitions of offences and uncertainties. It wasn't just this evening's fiasco; the realization had been creeping up on her. Things she'd tried not to notice were now openly visible. She knew she'd been a willing dupe, overeager for attention at any price. With her eyes opened she found her pride now on a precipice edge.

Before he came, life had been dully but enviably safe, with the outside world decently distanced and herself well able to view it with astringent detachment. It could not be the same ever again. True, that after Ronnie there might never be anyone else. But was that so awful? Perhaps having no one was better than this everlasting mistrust.

ON MONDAY MORNING Adjutant de Vries checked through his notes. He had deliberately broken off his questioning of Groeneveld at a critical point to give the boy something to stew about. And surely there was plenty. He knew now the case that was building against him; with motive, means and solid evidence of opportunity.

His only defence to date was flat denial: he had not known of Anneke's child and wasn't its father; they had parted amicably; he had not known she was in England; he had not seen her since she left his rooms to go to Mevrouw Henstra; he had never in his life visited England; he had once had a passport and used it in Germany and France, but it had been lost and would anyway be out of date.

It was when de Vries lingered over details of access to morphine derivatives at his place of work that the young man really turned green and the policeman had known he was cornered. Almost incidentally he had mentioned DNA identification. Specimens from the foetus could be matched with Groeneveld's own blood. If it was proved he'd lied over that, what trust could be placed on anything he said?

Then, instead of pushing on and booking the boy, he had broken off the interrogation, fixing an appointment for further questioning.

Yesterday morning he had received confirmation that the air passage booked by Groeneveld had certainly been taken up. The passenger list showed his name as well as Anneke's, the seats being distant from each other and on opposite sides of the aircraft. If necessary he would get someone from cabin staff to come and identify the lad. Those KLM stewardesses had sharp eyes and good memories.

Meanwhile heroin supplies were being scrupulously analysed and quantified at the Institute where Groeneveld was laboratory technician, to check whether additives had replaced measures removed. By tonight he would have proof enough to pass to Angus Mott in England and, if the lad saw sense, probably get a confession to tie the case up tight.

He would interview the boy at work. As a precaution he rang through to the Institute first to confirm that Groeneveld actually had come in. He hadn't.

Perhaps that was a favourable sign. He would be sitting at home, petrified, chewing over how he could retrieve his case. As he saw each of his denials proved false he would fall to pieces.

De Vries decided to send two uniformed officers to bring Groeneveld in, then get it all down on tape. He made a second call to Personnel at the Institute and requested a written list of Groeneveld's absences over the past month. Let him try to get round that next time he swore he hadn't flown to Heathrow.

Twenty minutes after the patrol car had been dispatched there was a phone call: Constable Jan Nederkoorn reporting in that the bird had flown the coop. De Vries swore economically and asked what luggage he'd taken.

There was a pause. He could almost see Nederkoorn scratching his head. 'Waaal, the place is a mess. Can't say for sure. Been hitting the bottle, looks like. Dirty dishes in the sink. Plenty more on the floor, broken.'

'What about the girl who lives with him?'

'No sign of her. Must have left too and taken all her stuff with her. Neighbours clammed up, all say they heard nothing, saw nothing. Like a lot of brass monkeys. One old lady on the ground floor thinks she heard a door slam about two a.m. and then a motor-scooter start up. Groeneveld had one, it seems, and there's nothing of the sort here.'

'Right. I'll get its registration and have an all-points call put out. Return to base. We'll let the experts go over the place.'

Megadamn! he thought. Have to admit to the Commisaris that the lad's slid away. Should have put someone on watching the house. Too confoundedly mindful of all those cautions about economy on overtime!

Bad news leaks fast in a police post. De Vries felt it as he slouched along the corridors. He was too old a hand not to pick up atmosphere when it centred on himself. Spears of silent accusation pointed in his direction.

A head came through the operations door. 'The Commisaris—'

'Wants to see me. I get it.'

And the Old Man was aquiver with it, like a neat little hamster in grim earnest.

'What's happened?' de Vries helped him out.

'Report first.'

De Vries complied and Commisaris Stuyvesant's cherubic façade went stony at the news, the once-merry eyes sparking with wrath. 'And what am I to inform Inspector Mott's superior officer? That we have only witless nincompoops here in the Netherlands? I spoke with Superintendent Yeadings only last night and he agrees that we have an almost certain case against Groeneveld. They may be pressing alternative charges against their English suspect for a separate killing.

'And while you wave adieu to this wretched youth on his motor-scooter, it is left to the German police to locate the antiques dealers. Which they have self-righteously done. Maes and Breitner have been arrested overnight in Düsseldorf. You had better go there and see what you can make of them, while we cover up for you over losing Groeneveld.'

His ears metaphorically stinging, de Vries faded from the room. The Commisaris requested a line to Yeadings's South Bucks number and within minutes was explaining that the missing owners of the death van found at Harwich had now been arrested in the Rhineland, were at present undergoing interrogation, and that until this had been satisfactorily concluded no charge would be brought against Anneke's ex-lover. He assured the superintendent that all progress made would be immediately passed to him, and he sent the good wishes of the department to the excellent Inspector Mott.

Yeadings replaced the receiver thoughtfully. 'Now what's got up his nose?' he demanded of his desktop. When Angus dropped in to say he was on his way to Chardleigh Place for a session with Denison, he relayed the message.

'Tulips from Amsterdam,' Mott commented wryly. 'I'd hoped to hear they'd already charged Groeneveld. On mature consideration I really don't fancy Gardner for the Anneke job. Not his kind of killing; he hasn't the guts, just as he hasn't any real motive. Do you think in Amsterdam they're having second thoughts on Groeneveld, sir?'

'Couldn't say. There's this diversion to questioning the two dealers, but I get a whiff of politics off it. Did you ever get the impression young Groeneveld might have powerful friends?'

Mott groaned. 'I'm pretty sure the police are straight, sir. It'll be a technical hitch of some sort.'

'It had better be a minor one. We badly need to score soon. The ACC's going on again about statistics. What's holding us back on Gardner for the other case?'

'There's nothing yet to tie him in with posting the pâté at Harwich. The Essex force are circulating photos, but to date nobody recognizes him. He could have disguised himself; it would make sense. And counter clerks seem notoriously oblivious of the general public. However, now Bunter's been returned to base, we may see some progress from that quarter.'

'M'm. Unfortunately Gardner's fingerprints in Penny Winter's flat can easily be explained away because he helped her move in. We've rather run out of steam on this one, Angus. I hope to God we aren't waiting for him to do the same thing again with the new girl, Janice Whatsit. Have you assigned anyone to keep an eye on her?'

'Beaumont will follow her to work and sit outside for a while. But if she doesn't stir from home at all this morning he'll be donning overalls and climbing a telegraph pole, then going in to check on her phone.'

NINETEEN

DESPITE UNDISPUTED and undivided occupancy of his own room all night, Beaumont had met the dawn in a sorry state. It was his conscience, almost threadbare as he admitted, that had kept him tossing, not Cathy's physical proximity, because on Saturday night Stuart, surprisingly perceptive, had offered her his bed.

'I can kip on the settee, Dad,' he'd said. 'I want to see the late film anyway.' He then dragged his duvet into the lounge and set himself up with a four-pack of cola and the TV sound turned high.

Left with the kitchen as battlefield, Beaumont and his wife had sat stiffly opposite each other at the formica-topped table and balked at opening hostilities. He declared his territorial rights by filling the kettle and making tea.

'Mother's getting very difficult,' Cathy started off, still suppressing a tendency to sniff.

'Oh yes?' Meaning, well, she's a woman.

'Of course, she's never had to hold a job down and run a home and bring up kids all at the same time. It stands to reason she wouldn't understand the strain.'

'How many of those have you just been doing?' he asked, po-faced.

'What d'you mean?'

'Well, job you may have, but no bloody body's been running *this* home, and it's months since Stuart left you and came back here. Not that he'd care to be called a kid.'

'No? Well, he's not old enough to be sitting up late watching movies either, when he's got homework and school on Monday,' she came back tartly.

'He's putting up a sound barrier,' Beaumont retorted. 'Even you should see that. We embarrass him. And you smother him. Why d'you think he prefers to live here in manly squalor instead of nibbling triangular cucumber sandwiches with you at his Granny's? He thinks you've been behaving like a kid yourself, running off and doing this being-your-own-woman thing. I wonder you didn't set up camp at Greenham Common while you were at it.'

'Who's being childish now? You know I went because I wanted a better kind of life, not just to be looked on as furniture or some kind of food-vending machine.'

'Grew out of marriage,' Beaumont said damningly. 'We both did. Nothing wrong in splitting up, to my mind. Only you don't seem able to make yours up what you want.'

She sat nervously pleating her skirt between her fingers, head down as she asked in a small voice, 'Does that mean you don't want me back?'

'How the hell would I know that, with you dropping it on me like this. Do *you* actually want to come back, or have you just reached a point where everything else has gone sour on you too?'

That had hit the mark, and that was when she started shouting. Apparently even the job had fallen through. On Friday she'd been given a month's wages in lieu of notice.

In the next room Stuart turned the sound even higher.

On Sunday both Beaumont and his son ate out. They returned to a tidier house. Cathy was tired, subdued and apprehensive. She had made up a bed for herself in the boxroom. Now, in the unwelcoming light of Monday morning, Beaumont decided to let things run their course. There were pros and cons in her staying or going. There were certainly faults on both sides. What mattered to him now was that he'd made a better job than she had of their months of separation. It left him in the stronger bargaining position, although if Cathy opted out of her bid for freedom and moved permanently back, how free would that leave him?

The answer rushed at him as he shaved, resulting in blood spurting from a gash on his jaw. He saw himself in the same dilemma as Gardner and Groeneveld: tied to the past and to a woman he felt nothing for. And look where it had got them. God, he could see why marriage required a licence: it was the most lethal weapon in the armoury!

He tore off a strip of toilet paper and stuck it on the cut. It promptly reddened and fell off. Somewhere in the bathroom cabinet there ought to be a styptic pencil. He rummaged and just caught himself in time from shouting to Cathy demanding where the hell she'd put it.

Status quo, he thought. But this morning I'm off out, nannying Janice Furnivall, in case Gardner takes his troubles out on her.

PAULA DROPPED ANGUS off at Chardleigh Place and drove on to Windsor to call on Rosemary Zyczynski. Her frequent strings of visitors had persuaded Sister to put her in a small side ward. A young medic was seated on the foot of her bed but the call was obviously a social one and he rose at once to be on his way.

As he passed, Paula peeked at the plastic card pinned to his white coat. 'What do you need with a psychiatrist? You, of all people,' she demanded after he had left.

'He was telling me his hang-ups,' Z claimed blandly.

'Trouble with his libido?'

'With his senior consultant, actually. How are you, Miss Musto? Is Angus in the offing?'

'Paula,' she insisted, said she was thriving, returned the inquiry and was told what she could clearly see: that Rosemary had been bounced around some, but was now getting back in form. She then explained what Angus was up to at Chardleigh Place, shaking Denison out about his personal links with Anneke. 'Did you feel there might have been something there?' she asked the WDC.

The girl eased her weight gently from one buttock to the other, winced, then admitted, 'You never really know about other people's intimacies, do you? I'd have thought he'd be more like Father Bear with Goldilocks myself, but maybe that's a satisfactory basis for a sexual affair. Afraid I'm not all that well up in these matters.'

She sounded gruff and Paula remembered there was some story about a bad experience in Rosemary's past; that she hadn't much use for men. Funny, because the young doctor had seemed . . . Ah, well.

They chatted generally until a nurse rattled in with the telephone trolley and announced there'd be an incoming call on the half-hour. Prompt to the minute it came, and it was Angus Mott.

'Is this for me, or. . .' Zyczynski asked.

'You first, Z. I thought you'd want to hear what the Denison-Anneke link was. It seems he has a brother over in High Wycombe. When Paula's through with you I'd like her to pick me up and we'll go to see him. Want to guess what his job is?'

'Er, not another hotelier?'

'An obstetrician.'

'Of course! Anneke went to him about her abortion! But she never had one.'

'According to our Denison at Chardleigh, his brother managed to dissuade her. Healthy mother, healthy foetus. The only drawback was little money and no job. So when

Anneke was on the point of finally deciding, he tipped the scales by asking his brother to take her on as temporary staff at the hotel, at least until the baby arrived. Meanwhile Anneke should get in touch with the putative father and see what future support was forthcoming.'

'Which presumably she did, when she flew back to Amsterdam. And that must have been when Groeneveld decided to get rid of her, picked up an air ticket and followed her back. It all fits. Will the Boss be applying for extradition?'

'Have to eventually, but Groeneveld hasn't been pulled in yet. Some doubt over evidence from the two antiques dealers, though I don't see how it could let him out. I'll be ringing de Vries myself later to see what's holding things up.'

'That's great, though. I'll pass you to Paula now.'

'Right,' Paula said, springing up and taking over 'I got the gist of it. If you're ready to move off, Angus, I'm on my way.'

LESTER DENISON was a big man, but without the theatrical aura many surgeons assume. He had a comfortable, crumpled look despite the starched white coat. His hands were almost childlike, the backs touched with a soft, sandy down. His voice was as soothing as the rest of him, but his blue eyes missed nothing. He looked thoughtfully at Paula as she took out a notebook and balanced it on her knee.

'You're not a policewoman, I think.'

'Miss Musto is a barrister,' Angus said quickly.

The surgeon was looking at her left hand. 'And we're engaged,' Paula confirmed for him.

Denison nodded, now completely at his ease. 'And this is the young lady who was with you, Inspector, when you met Miss Vroom at Chardleigh Place. It's all right; my brother has wised me up. Now, how can I help you?'

He had heard, of course, that Anneke was dead, but only in the last two days, having been abroad until then. Normally all clinical details he had made on her case would be confidential, but if he could provide anything likely to lead to her killer, then he was willing to open up. 'I suppose there's no doubt that it was murder?' he asked.

Mott explained about the chest she was found in, how it had an external catch which had to be pushed home.

'I had hoped...' said the surgeon. 'The story of the mistletoe bough, you know. Not that that would have been any less horrendous for the poor young woman once she had realized she was trapped. No sign of any drug-taking showed in the tests made here. I am convinced myself that anything like that would have been totally abhorrent to her. Especially in her pregnant state. A delightful youngster. I was impressed with her courage. It can't have been easy finding herself abandoned and pregnant after such a restrictive upbringing. Only a faint sense of personal guilt, and we managed to talk that out.'

He provided them with a list of dates. She had visited him on three successive days, having first learned of his clinic from an English girl she had met in Amsterdam, and the same girl had lent her her studio flat nearby while she was studying art in the Netherlands.

'Such a good life wasted,' he said. 'It had been hard for her up till now. We talked about her leaving home, her first attempts to take over control for herself. I was able to persuade her that this was the turning point, for two lives. The real challenge.'

He looked down at his hands. His voice dropped a tone. 'She was reborn. A free spirit emerging.'

'She really got to you.'

He almost bridled then. 'A lovely youngster. Abortion can leave more than physical scars. Don't mistake compassion for passion, Inspector.'

Whichever, it would be an uncomfortable emotion for a man with his job, Mott thought. No, I'll not diminish him in my mind, the way I did Anneke at first.

'So she opted for life,' the doctor continued sadly, 'and was killed. For that very reason, do you think? Or from some chance encounter? I'm sure she knew no one else here until I sent her by taxi to my brother, after he'd agreed by phone to keep an eye on her. He would naturally have informed me earlier, once he knew of her terrible end, but I was giving a paper at the Stuttgart conference and arrived back only on Saturday.'

'And when were you expecting to see Anneke again?' Mott inquired.

Mr Denison looked through his desk diary. 'She was due to see me on twenty-fourth June at four-thirty, but I see it's crossed through. Certainly she didn't turn up. I seem to remember my secretary said someone phoned in to cancel and a second appointment was made for this coming week.'

The secretary was summoned and cast her mind back. Yes, she did recall the message. It was a man who had phoned in to cancel, although she wasn't sure now what the excuse had been. Perhaps something about being delayed somewhere. Amsterdam? Yes, it might have been that. She had insisted on giving him an alternative date for when Mr Denison would have returned from Germany, and then she had marked up the clinic diary provisionally for two-fifteen p.m. this coming Thursday.

Beyond that, the woman was of little help. If she had noticed anything special about the voice at the time, it had slipped her memory since. There were so many foreign accents she heard every day that as long as she got the sense of what was said she took no note of the voice any more. High Wycombe was a multi-ethnic mix, after all.

ANGUS MADE TWO CALLS from a public telephone at the clinic. The first was to de Vries in Amsterdam who, being away from his desk, was asked to ring Mott back at the Falcon's number. Then he reported to Yeadings on his morning's conversations and, on foot, followed Paula to the hotel where he found her scanning the table d'hôte menu.

'I'll treat you,' she offered. 'I've just received a small bonus from old Wheatman.'

'It's nice to be a rich woman's plaything,' grinned Angus. 'I accept. Once you're away from your Temple Chambers and become a provincial Crown Prosecutor, you won't be able to afford me.'

'Did you tell Mr Yeadings I was shadowing you?'

'Not in precisely those words, but he gathered it.'

'He didn't object?'

'Regards you in this case as a valuable witness.'

'So may I know if he reported any progress?'

'There isn't any. He wants me to let him know if de Vries comes up with anything on the quiet. Commisaris Stuyvesant believes in passing on only the good news, and at present there's none.'

Paula nodded and they turned their attention to the meal. Between cheeseboard and coffee the call came through from Amsterdam.

In the background Angus could hear the clatter of dishes and a Dutch television show turned low, then Eva's high heels tapping across the kitchen's ceramic tiles. Which meant that de Vries was at home, and the call came out of his own pocket. Keep it brief, then.

'You want to know why the delay?' asked the Dutchman (surely from the side of the cheroot?). 'Well, I cocked it up, if that's not as rude an expression as it sounds. Gave the lad time to weigh his chances. So he flitted. I'm supposed to be in Düsseldorf, but I wanted to hang around here where the action's likely to be. Luckily the Rhineland police are keen to co-operate, so the lines have been kept busy. I'll drive down straight after lunch and see the statements signed by Breitner and Maes.

'Both give the same story, in satisfactorily individual wording. They were picking up a set of inlaid caskets (possibly of dodgy provenance!) and the dowry chest was thrown in. They also picked up Anneke. She was taking a short-cut across the car park at High Wycombe where they were sitting eating their midday sandwiches and she noticed the Netherlands registration on the van. She approached them, seemed friendly, had bought some confectionery which she shared with them, all crowded together in the cab.

'She told them she had an appointment locally for four-thirty and volunteered to look after the van and contents while they called on a jeweller they'd had correspondence with. (Something faintly fishy in that bit of business too, it seems.) However, they arrived back at three-forty and everything seemed in order, except that the girl had gone, taking her overnight grip with her. They'd held on to the car's keys, and the rear was still locked. They looked in to check, and it all seemed the way they'd left it. Trusting souls, I tell myself.'

'Anneke was the sort you would trust. Fellow-countrywoman in a foreign land: why not take her at her word? It sounds as if she was overtrusting herself.'

'From then on they didn't attempt to keep their journey low key; stopped for petrol en route and chatted with the garage man, returned to the same lodgings in Dedham, near Colchester. Continued buying locally until almost their time of departure. All very innocent. Went to pack the last load of small stuff inside the empty chest, and—'

'Found it occupied. I see. It could well have been like that, except it meant Groeneveld risked killing her in broad daylight and carting her round to the van's rear in a public car park.'

'They found on the way to Harwich that the screen between cab and rear had come loose, but thought little of it since the stuff was still safe inside. Anneke must have been unconscious after the injection and bundled through that way, Groeneveld following to hide the body. When the dealers found her they ditched the van and bolted home in sheer panic, convinced they'd been framed, and nobody in a strange country would believe their version of what had happened. Must have had spare licence plates among their gear.'

'Abandoned their valuables? Do you go for that?'

'With Breitner, yes. But Maes, the major shareholder, he's something else. Filled his luggage with small, portable stuff—snuff-boxes, jewellery, George III silverware. He had the necessary paperwork to back it, and he bargained on getting lost on the Continent before anyone discovered the body. At one point they half hoped they could make a claim that the van had been stolen and get insurance on the lost stock, but then they realized they'd hesitated too long.

'Look, Angus, I'm taking it they're clean—of the murder, anyway. Small-time traders making the fast buck and pushing their luck a bit. Maybe a bit of faking, but drugs?—no. Your chief will get all this faxed through tonight at latest. Meanwhile, for your ears only, eh?'

'Thanks, Jan-Willi. It still leaves us with Groeneveld as prime suspect for the murder, then.'

There was a significant pause. 'It would, but for one thing. You see, his alibi stands. At least three senior members of the Institute have witnessed to being with him and speaking to him on the day when he was thought to have followed Anneke over to England. He may have meant to kill her, and could have supplied the heroin, but someone else would have had to do the job.'

MOTT RANG THE BOSS again and gave his news in the same order. 'Are you there, sir?' he asked in the ensuing silence.

'I was counting to ten. Where does this leave us, Angus? A proxy for Groeneveld? Or has he been set up all along and the plan fell down over the alibi? Must we put Gardner back in the frame for Anneke? Have to find out where he was between, say, noon and three-thirty on the twenty-fourth. But how would he know where she'd be then? Did they just happen on each other by chance?'

His voice lightened. 'Who else is a possible? This gynae-cologist—he knew she'd be coming in for her appointment. Find out if he had a full book that afternoon and if he made any cancellations apart from Anneke's. It sounds fantastic, I know, and it doesn't appear he could possibly have a mo-tive. On the other hand, his brother might have. They could be in collusion, either or both of them with something to hide. Is it beyond reason that Anneke had some hold over them, which could explain their readiness to help her out over the baby?'

Mott took that question as rhetorical. 'Maybe our best chance is Anneke's missing overnight grip. Unless Breitner and Maes were lying, it disappeared at the same time as the girl. I'll get a description circulated, have all left-luggage lockers scoured in the area, and that includes inside the clinic and at Chardleigh Place. Unless it's been moved on since, it should have something to tell the scientific boys. Fingerprints don't rub off as easily as film fiction would have one think.'

BEAUMONT HADN'T NEEDED to resort to any Telecom disguise, because Janice Furnivall was only too eager to get out of the flat that morning and immerse herself in work. As instructed, he lingered outside her office block long enough to ensure she didn't depart again after arrival, then the DS flipped a coin for surveillance on Gardner (heads) or a thorough further read-through of his notes on the Penny Winter death. It came up tails. He drove up to the Mausoleum at West Wycombe, turned the car to get the best sunshine and dived into his briefcase.

It helped to relax and close his eyes at intervals and reconstruct the scene. It wasn't long before he found himself walking down an unfamiliar street with an infant version of Stuart toddling at his side, pulling at his hand and howling for his Mummy who was lost. He bent to wipe a yellow candle of snot from the unhappy child's face and suddenly it lit up. Stuart was staring past his father, lifted a plump little finger to point, and shouted, 'Mummy's coming!'

But the woman who rushed up and lifted him high, twirling him in her arms, laughing at the child, at both of them, wasn't Cathy at all. She was big and bosomy and black. Sister Barbour.

I wouldn't mind being married to her, thought the dreaming Beaumont, and the prospect woke him.

Now why, in the name of all that was sanguinary, should that one forgotten figure rear itself again in his subconscious? Was he at some deep level lusting after her ample virtues?—while his everyday self felt randy at the skinny delights of near-punk Alison?

More likely that something he had just read before nodding off required a second perusal. He gathered from the floor some scattered sheets which had escaped from their folder, cracking his head on the steering wheel.

Nothing remarkable sprang to notice on a further reading, and he sat contemplating the inconsequential nature of dreams. All the same, the Penny Winter case had begun for him with Sister Barbour ringing 999, and his having been in the neighbourhood, and gone sniffing for suspicious circumstances in a simple fall downstairs.

And the intuition—serendipity, whatever—had proved bang on. The fall had been subsequent to bacterial poisoning, and the poison had most likely been sent through the post. Death occasioned as the result of a criminal act—which was murder. *If* there had been malicious intent.

And no outbreak of salmonella poisoning had followed in the Harwich area. That was the significant thing. Gardner, the ex-husband—still liable for maintenance arrears, and without official earnings but with expectations tied to a lady in comfortable circumstances—was a devious and unfeeling con-merchant. He might well have picked on this cold-blooded way of dissolving his embarrassments. He couldn't be certain the pâté would kill, but it would upset the eater long enough for him to take advantage of her helplessness.

Oh, it had to be Gardner. So why was part of his brain bothered over Sister Barbour? Maybe he should just check up on things, see if there wasn't some way she'd benefited by Ms Winter's removal. To his knowledge nobody had seen fit to find out whether Sister Barbour had connections with Harwich or been away from her duties on the day the pâté was put in the mail.

TWENTY

COMMISARIS STUYVESANT was white to the gills. So it struck de Vries, sleepless on his return from Düsseldorf and now lounging to attention. Never had his senior officer looked so unSanta-Claus like and bloodless. It boded ill.

Something to do with his own handling of Groeneveld, almost certainly. Given that lapse of time, the lad had got right away. Or even done the final thing.

Holed in one, Jan-Willi, he told himself, as the Commisaris lashed at him with the new-found facts. Piddling himself because there'd be an almighty inquiry and the department would collect everything flying off the fan.

Regrettable, of course, as suicide always was; but Groeneveld had judged himself and chosen his own sentence. It saved the state a lot of expense. And guaranteed no further killing: death was inarguably a thorough deterrent.

But even an adjutant has remnants of conscience. He suppressed a sigh, blinked world-weary eyes, fixed his gaze a foot above the speaker's head.

'And this now,' Stuyvesant said with deadly venom, 'what are we to make of this?'

It was an oblong sheet of paper torn from a writing block. At the top were two holes where something sharp like a pin had penetrated through from the front and then back again. The second hole was lacerated as if clumsy hands, or the wind, or both, had partly torn it free from its attachment. Only five words scrawled on it, the last one underlined. 'For you, my beloved. *Understand.*'

'Odd sort of suicide note,' de Vries commented. 'Is the handwriting authenticated as Groeneveld's?'

'As far as a non-expert such as myself can tell.'

'And the message?—not addressed to me, seemingly.'

There was a shocked silence. Twice Stuyvesant seemed on the point of speaking, but remained mute. At last he twisted himself from his seat and strode towards the window. 'Even for you, de Vries, that is in unbelievably bad taste,' he ground out over his shoulder.

'Sir. Nevertheless it was intended for someone.'

Stuyvesant turned back. 'The girl, surely,' he said testily.

'Anneke? What good would his suicide do her? She's past either reading or exacting revenge. She may have started life believing in life after death, but I'll bet Groeneveld never has done. Anti-clerical, atheist politico, according to the posters in his rooms. Progressive, they like to call it. Note apart, are we sure he did this to himself?'

The Commisaris frowned at him. 'Dietrich has had a look at the knot. It was tied by a left-hander, which Groeneveld was. The forest floor is damp and peaty there. No prints of shoes other than his own. He stood on the motor-scooter to put the noose round his neck, then kicked it off its bracket. He'd slightly misjudged the drop. The toes of his shoes kept scraping...'

De Vries turned sickly away. Not the instant job intended, then. No broken hyoid bone. Slow, struggling strangulation.

'Adjutant, are you...?'

'All right, sir. Quite all right. Well, that message, then—if it was genuinely a suicide note—was for somebody left behind. Someone alive who would benefit from what he did... once it was understood.'

'Ye—es.'

'So we look for the new "beloved". Did Groeneveld do this to save her from facing his lengthy trial and imprisonment? Funny sort of consideration. Leaves her alone and undefended. Certainly takes some understanding, as the note implies.'

Stuyvesant bristled. 'Perhaps to save her from what he saw as police harassment? That will certainly be suggested by some, including our more rabid newspapers. I am taking you off the case, de Vries. In fact, I have no choice but to suspend you from duty indefinitely until we have a clearer view of what the young man was about.'

De Vries gave a stiff little bow. He waited for Stuyvesant to add more, but nothing came. From behind his chair the Commisaris bent forward over his desk and started shuffling papers, his head lowered. De Vries shrugged, more to relax shoulder tension than from disrespect, turned and quietly left the room.

He threaded his way between the moving figures in the building as though they were strangers. Outside, a tricky breeze had blown up. There were little wisps of cloud streaking the sky, patterned like cream stirred into coffee. Sun blinds flapped brightly; here and there the canal water's surface flipped like shuffled cards. The street odours were stronger, warmly familiar. And Groeneveld wouldn't share all this any more, wouldn't pad off to work in his worn trainers, *putt-putt* off on country jaunts with his scooter, a girl on the bracket. How the young wasted themselves! It was stupid, unnecessary, corrupting to those left behind. All because—

Why? Why had he needed to kill Anneke at all—or *have her killed* (since it seemed now that he'd an alibi at work for the day of her death)?

And apart from Groeneveld's fate, how about himself? Suspended until they had a clearer view of what Groeneveld was about. Yes, that was where everything stood still. The case suspended as much as himself.

On impulse he set out for the cobbled street where the boy had lived, from which Anneke had been sent packing, having no rights except the claim in her belly. And according to Groeneveld, that claim undeclared, presumably because she was too proud to use it as argument against her supplanter.

He climbed the narrow stairway to the paint-blistered door. It stood ajar. So had the forensic experts beaten him to it? He listened, expecting familiar voices as they searched. There was only a low arrhythmic strumming. He pushed the door open and walked in. Someone was lying face down on Groeneveld's bed, curled tight with the coverlet grasped close and the irregular pulsing sound was from a human throat, a soul in torment.

The policeman's eyes travelled from the naked feet up the tight jeans to the thin shoulders over which the black hair tumbled, and at once he understood all there was to know about Anneke's lover, her being supplanted, her acceptance of dismissal as final, her early despair, her murder and finally Groeneveld's need to kill himself.

The dark, tormented face which stared up at the policeman now made it clear why no trace of Groeneveld's new woman had been found in these rooms.

De Vries tried to remember the man's name, but it had never been important. Until now.

He was the uncle of the Indonesian girls who served alongside Anneke at the restaurant. It was her sometime boss who had taken away what home and family she had, as well as her means of earning a living. *Ari*, that was it.

The man had recognized him.

'You know, then,' de Vries said heavily, 'that your lover is dead; that he left a note for you?'

'Is it true? The woman in the room downstairs, she said the police had been; that Johan...'

'Hanged himself. For what you did.'

'I did nothing. Nothing! I don't know what you are talking about.'

'Oh yes, man, you do! And you're going to tell me. It may take a little time, but in the end you are going to tell me everything. You will be glad to, because I have learned a lot about Anneke Vroom. She never deserved to die like that, shot full of the heroin you stole from Groeneveld's place of work, and crammed into a dowry chest. And he, for all his failings, never deserved to give his life to save your miserable skin. But once he'd heard about the missing heroin, and that someone had used his name to book a flight to England, he knew who.

'He hadn't a passport. Did you know that? But you had, and you used it to hunt Anneke to her death. There should be checks at ticket control that the booked name's the same as the one on the passport. You thought it would be safe, and you knew where she would go to see her doctor. In all innocence she had told you, when she came back to say why she didn't need your money after all: she wasn't having the abortion you'd tried to persuade her into. Her child would be brought up on what she earned decently herself.

'And still you were afraid of her—afraid that if Groeneveld ever got to know about a baby coming—his child—he would want her back and you'd lose him forever.

'Well, now he's gone too. And you're left to face the havoc you caused. It's a devious story, but I've outlined it for you, so now you can find the words yourself to fill in the details.

'You will put on your shoes and we shall walk together back to my office and you will sit there, in the quiet, and think what to write down. When that is done, then, perhaps, you will have begun to repay your debt to the dead.'

YEADINGS WAS BRIEFING his team on the Penny Winter case. They seemed to have come to a dead end. It had to be because they weren't angling in from the right direction.

'We've still a whole lot of unanswered questions,' he told them. 'Where did the pâté come from? Why did no one else eat it? How much can the little girls remember of that evening before their mother died?

'I'm afraid there's no escaping taking them through it thoroughly this time. I'll tackle that follow-up myself. DS Beaumont, I had the impression there were gossipy things the next-door neighbour would have coughed up if encouraged. So encourage her, also any other people in the same street, and whoever's garden backs on to the dead woman's.

'That leaves the ex-husband's end to be covered by DI Mott and DC Silver. New faces for the girl he's living with now. Check how her version of his moves at the relevant times ties in with what his family say in Colchester. I'll be contacting the Essex force again, and with any luck we may get DS Bunter on the case at that end. A pity we haven't Z back on the job, because she'd already been in touch with the sister and it seems there's no love lost between Freda Gardner and Ronald. We'd likely get the facts straighter from her than from the over-protective mother.

'Well, on your way then. One more concerted shove and we may get the ball rolling.'

FROM THE PAPERS in his bundle Beaumont found out the address of the crèche where the Barbour baby was cared for while her mother was at work. Funny, that after his dream about the black nurse last night, Yeadings should have picked on him to contact her again. He drove over and parked outside. It was a very ordinary corner semi with a garden on three sides. He could see three prams parked with raised sun canopies. Two small children were taking turns on a slide. One little girl had worn her pants right through.

From under the wall which he was craning to peer over there rose up a severe young woman with a shovel in her hands. 'Are you looking for someone?' she demanded fiercely.

He pulled out his warrant card. 'Is the Barbour baby here?' he asked when the young woman's hackles had settled slightly. 'I know her mother works shifts, but I wasn't sure which one she's on at present.'

It was still morning. Beaumont said he'd call back with Mrs Barbour to pick up Marigold that afternoon. The young woman was still suspicious. A good thing she was. It looked as though the children were in safe enough hands.

He had paperwork to occupy him until a snatched lunch. When he arrived for the end of the early shift at the old folks' home he rang the doorbell and announced he was to give Mrs Barbour a lift home. This was to ensure that she was still there, and equally that she would be prompt on her time of departure. He then returned to his car, parked outside the front door and was rewarded some minutes later by being observed from an upstairs window where the curtain was momentarily twitched aside.

He waved up at the movement and saw a gleam of white teeth in the dark beyond. In no time at all Sister Barbour was with him, tripping down the steps with a self-conscious swagger and clipping on her seat belt as if a male escort with car was the least she was entitled to.

'Well, Sergeant,' she greeted him cheerfully, 'how is your case going?'

'It has to take its place in the queue,' he said dourly. 'We've made some progress though.'

'I haven't seen anything in the local paper about you treating Ms Winter's death as suspicious. But if you're still around, it must be. 'Less you're fancyun me, eh?' She nudged him suggestively, rolled her eyes, then shouted with laughter.

'Would I stand a chance?' he demanded, giving in to her good humour.

'You know what you jes' said about queues . . . However, I'm real glad to see you for another reason. I've been feelun bad about it ever since. Still got Ginny 'n' Miranda's sack of toys. Well, your young police lady wasn't to know they didn't belong my house, I s'pose. Like to pick them up after I collect my Marigold?'

So it was that Beaumont, plied with tea and gingernuts but without acquiring any further useful information on the family next door, made his arranged rendezvous with his chief toting a multi-coloured sack crammed with fluffy toy animals, building blocks and scraps of bright fabric intended to entertain the two small daughters of the late Penny Winter.

WHICH WAS THE MOMENT that a call came through for the superintendent from Commisaris Stuyvesant. Anneke Vroom's killer—Groeneveld's homosexual lover—had been charged, had confessed and a full report was on its way, together with photographs of the man for corroborative evidence from possible witnesses at Heathrow and High Wycombe.

He had booked his flight in Groeneveld's name, used his own passport, hidden from Anneke in the departure lounge and on the plane and followed her to High Wycombe. There he found his opportunity when she sat alone in the van's cab. Mid-afternoon on a very hot day. She'd been dozing. No one about and he'd had the hypodermic ready and a knife to threaten her.

Beaumont had his doubts. 'One man carted her round to the rear and crammed her in the chest. A big, healthy girl like that?'

'Pushed her through the loosened screen, and followed her in. Then scarpered, thought he'd got away with it.'

'Until de Vries went after Groeneveld?'

'Until Groeneveld learned of the diamorphine. Maybe he recalled Ari had gone missing about that time. He put it all together and arrived at the truth. Basically he was a decent lad, couldn't face his own part in it, passive as it had been. Grief—and a wild attempt to save his lover—drove him to take his own life. More wasted youth, but at least it broke Ari so that he admitted the killing.'

Yeadings sighed. 'I'm going across to St Nick's now to talk to the Gardner children. You can come with me. Tote the toy-sack and do a Santa act.'

THE RECOVERY of their treasures helped loosen the little girls' tongues. They seemed to have settled in, but arrangements were already under way for their fostering.

While Yeadings manipulated a Roland Rat hand puppet he elicited that Ginny was adverse to food 'with lumps in', (which could cover Ardennes pâté). Beaumont squatted alongside the younger child and watched her pull toy after toy from the bag of surprises. 'I think this one's got eczema,' he told the Superintendent, and the matron agreed.

'Very fussy about her food,' she confided. 'I've kept her on bland things without additives, and it's starting to clear. She turns her nose up at any kind of meat.'

Which is what Yeadings had come to find out. Neither child would have wanted any part of the poisoned pâté. So

Gardner could have been certain that his ex-wife, with an empty larder, would have scoffed the lot herself.

They made preparations to go, although Ginny had taken a liking to the big man with waggly black eyebrows and held fast to his hand. Miranda, searching for ever smaller items in the toy-sack, was stuffing them into a crumpled Jiffy bag, unconcerned with what the others were about.

While she struggled with an old plastic teething-ring, Beaumont held the Jiffy bag steady. And suddenly swore.

Both adults glowered at him.

'Oops, sorry! But look, sir,' he commanded eagerly, unceremoniously emptying out the tiny treasures and thrusting the padded brown bag under his chief's nose. *The corner with the stamps has been torn off!'*

Yeadings examined the bag. It had certainly gone through the post, and been addressed to Ms Penny Winter. The block capitals appeared to have been written with a blue ballpoint pen.

'If you could find some other bag for Miranda,' Yeadings suggested, 'I'd like to hang on to it. There's a chance we may have the piece that was torn off, in which case it's of vital importance to our case.' He felt a surge of hope. There'd probably be minute traces of pâté inside the bag, however carefully the inner wrappings had been sealed. All taken together.

MOTT AND DC SILVER HAD spoken to Janice Furnivall at her office. Throughout the interview she had been coldly distant and made it clear she considered their approach at her place of work little short of offensive. At first disinclined to give any information about Gardner's movements, she relented when Mott offered an alternative meeting, in the man's presence, at Janice's flat.

'No,' she said shortly. 'I shall be staying with my father for a few days and the flat will be closed. Mr Gardner will be looking for accommodation elsewhere.'

'I see.' Mott did, and he hoped she'd have a locksmith standing by, ready for Gardner's first sally from the building.

'There are only a couple of details we'd like you to confirm for us,' he said. 'They concern Ronald Gardner's movements on the day of his wife's death and the previous day. He tells us—Miss Furnivall, are you all right?'

'SHE HADN'T KNOWN the police were interested in Penny Winter's death,' Mott told Yeadings when they all met up. 'Gardner had first given her the impression that he was a bachelor, then admitted recently that he'd had a wife but she'd had a fatal accident some time back which he was still too upset to discuss. If she'd seen the local newspapers, the name Winter wouldn't have meant anything to her, and the first she knew of his children was last week when the Social Services called to see him. He implied then that they'd been in care for a matter of years because he couldn't give them a settled home.'

'And now she's sending him packing?'

'Not because of these new suspicions about the killing. She'd already decided before we got to her. Our arrival just served to strengthen the opinion of the man she'd at last come round to. Too many deceptions unmasked plus some unmanly bursts of spleen, is my guess.

'By way of washing her hands of him, she opened up, told us he'd come and gone without her knowledge while she was at work, but he'd certainly been away during the Chardleigh Place period and also when he claimed to have stayed with his mother overnight in Colchester. Not that that gets us any farther.'

'Maybe a Jiffy bag closer to nailing him,' Beaumont purred, tilting the Pinocchio face as if twitched on puppet strings. He left it to Yeadings to explain.

'And it matched the torn bit the stamps were on?' Mott breathed in delight.

'Perfectly. We've had the torn edges photographed up to a hundred magnifications, and there's no doubt.'

'So—'

'So a lot rests with the handwriting experts, because the saliva result is negative,' Yeadings warned him. 'We already have a sample of Gardner's block capitals in the address which he added below his statement regarding the Coleman impersonation. If we get a positive on that, we'll have him in and face him out with the analyst's final report on the salmonella, which I understand Angus has here.'

Mott frowned. 'Let's see how good a case we have, to get Gardner on a murder charge. His ex-wife—Penny Winter—died from food poisoning. Self-administered, but unknowingly. And at last we have the analysis through.

'As we had learned in general, the poison source was processed cold meat; in this case certainly Adrennes pâté. The really significant fact is that the level of salmonella present was above any previously found in retail goods by the food science eggheads. *Cultured*, the report says.'

He looked around at them, all alerted for the final throw. 'Gardner's not made of heroic stuff. Faced with all this, he shouldn't hold out long.'

TWENTY-ONE

GARDNER HAD BEEN questioned steadily for over three hours with a break for a meal which he'd made a poor show of eating. Mott and Beaumont had directed the interview in turns, the one patiently, the other with periods of brooding silence broken by sudden shifts of angle. The man was unnerved but sticking to his original story.

Mott went to report to Superintendent Yeadings and found a surprise visitor with him: Rosemary Zyczynski, en route between hospital and home.

'You're not going back to Auntie's, I hope,' he said severely.

'No need. She's learnt to manage without me while I was laid up. It's back to my old digs and my own things, thank heavens.'

'And two weeks' sick leave before you see the MO again,' Yeadings added. 'You should have gone straight back to bed, not dropped off here.'

Her face was thinner and the soft brown eyes seemed even more enormous. She turned them on him, looking so frail that a puff of wind might blow her away. But tough as old boots at the centre, he thought, and that was what mattered in the job.

'I had to know how things were going,' she said.

Mott took a chair across the desk from his chief. 'Gardner still denies handling the package, claims he doesn't know what it contained but is guessing there's something sinister about it. All the same, he can't get out of admitting he was in Colchester, quite close to Harwich and he could have posted it.'

Yeadings grunted. 'It doesn't seem the right time to drop bad news on anybody, but Bunter's been through to say Gardner's mother's been rushed into Colchester General Hospital. Renal failure. Went into fluctuating coma during the night and her husband didn't realize the seriousness until this morning. I don't want some future defence brief saying we threw shock at him, to break him down, but he has to be told. He hasn't been charged yet, so he has every right to insist on going to her bedside. If he does, I'd like you to drive him over, Angus.'

IT WAS ONE OF THE MOST painful scenes Mott had been a party to in years. They arrived in late afternoon. Too late. The screens were round Mrs Boulter's bed and the family had assembled in a waiting-room off Sister's office. Recriminations had already begun as he followed Ronald Gardner in.

Boulter looked like death himself, head lowered, cheeks sucked in, while Freda lambasted him for usurping her place as the dead woman's nearest of kin; and Mother wouldn't have died if she'd been at her side last night.

'I did what I could,' the man insisted. 'I didn't know how bad she was. She just said she was tired. She wasn't due for dialysis for another three days. I sat and held her hand, like she asked, till she went to sleep. You were there downstairs. You could have done it, if she'd asked for you.'

'Only she didn't, did she? Though we've only your word for that! Oh my God, look what's just come in!'

Gardner had entered and stood there helpless, hands hanging down, regarding them. 'Mum's gone?'

'I'm sorry, lad.' Boulter made a clumsy gesture of sympathy, but the younger man stalked past him and deliberately slapped his sister's face. In a split second there was a free-for-all, with fists and handbag flying and magazines sliding to the floor from an upturned table. A nurse came running in, shouting for them to have regard to where they were. 'Or I'll call the police,' she threatened.

Gardner had his face in his hands. Blood ran between his fingers from where Freda had scratched him. He gave a choking sound between sob and laughter. 'He *is* the police,' he said bitterly. 'Go on, Inspector, sort this one out.'

MOTT'S PHONE CALL was held until Yeadings's line could come free. Normally Nan tried not to ring him at work but this had been something she couldn't keep to herself. 'I had a call from the convent this morning,' she said, 'inviting Sally and me to tea at five. We're just back.'

'That was a quick response. How did it go?'

Nan paused, and he could sense her reluctance to claim too much. 'It's a lovely place,' she said cautiously.

'What did Sally think?'

'She was a bit overcome, but the one they called Mother gave her a job to do, counting out plant labels and writing up names for the herbaceous border. Quite a lot of plants Sally knew already. They were soon chatting away like old friends.

'Mike, they're so clever with handling children. I don't want them getting too much influence over her!'

Afraid that the child would get pulled into the community: a secular mother's nightmare. But when all was said and done, communities could outlive the most protective parents. 'It sounds as if you think they'll accept her.'

'I don't see how they could do otherwise after being so encouraging. They're going to write to you.'

'We'll talk about it tonight.'

'Of course. Try not to be too late. 'Bye, love.'

Yeadings put down one phone and lifted the other. Mott brought him up to date on the Gardner end of things. 'Is he staying on to make the funeral arrangements?' the Superintendent asked finally.

'No. Seems to be slipping out of this one too. There's a widower, you know. Boulter's coping, as far as the venomous daughter lets him. God, what a pair of washouts that woman had for offspring.'

'Right; best bring him back, then. I'm knocking off now. You can ring me at home if I'm needed.'

AT COLCHESTER Bertie Boulter stood in the doorway of the undertaker's and tried to make up his mind.

Whatever Freda and Ronald said, he owed them nothing. The old dear had had little of her own to bring to him; just the house and some furniture they'd mostly replaced since. Two years back he'd paid off the last of her mortgage. From the money point of view she'd benefited more than him, not that either of them had been much bothered about it, because they liked to share things.

And Freda had continued to live with them. Whatever she'd paid towards her keep, that had been between her and her mother; but, knowing the old dear, it wouldn't have been anywhere near what the girl got back in home comforts.

He supposed there'd have to be some new arrangement made now, if Freda meant to stay on. Whatever they decided between them, it wouldn't be comfortable.

But it was doing the right thing by Ronald that caused the terrible struggle in his mind. Because to be fair all round he'd have to betray someone. The old dear hadn't known the awful mess Ronald was in. Better she'd passed on before the storm broke, like. Trouble was that it left him, Bertie, to decide what must be done.

He'd seen Ronald off again with the detective after giving them tea and sandwiches at the house. That was when he'd heard the full story. That poor young wife of Ronald's, Penny. Everyone here thought it had been an accident. Shocking, of course, but by the time news had reached them she was in her coffin and the little girls taken into care. He himself hadn't believed what the old dear said about Ronald going to make a new home for the kiddies. He couldn't anyway if he got taken to court for murder, found guilty and sentenced to life. He was desperately denying he'd had anything to do with her death.

There was right and there was wrong. But when you'd got two wrongs to choose between, what could you do? Take it to someone who understood these things, someone discreet. That seemed the only thing. He was responsible, and it was asking for more trouble, but in the end there was really no choice. He moved off into the street, making for George Bunter's house.

GEORGE'S MOTHER OFFERED him more tea and he was full of it already, but the lad saw the need for something stronger, shooed the old lady out and took him upstairs where he kept a bottle of single malt.

They'd got ever such a little bit tiddly, Bertie thought, by the end of the story. At least he supposed young George must be feeling much the same as himself. He had this lightheaded idea that if he closed his eyes he could go back in time and none of it would have happened.

But then something odd took over, like one of those old films when the timing went wrong and everything rushed frantically forward until it stopped on a single frame. And there he was in the old dear's room again, sitting holding her hand. And he didn't even know she was going to leave him.

SHE HUNG ON TO HIS HAND, and her weak blue eyes beseeched him to be kind. 'Bertie, I've not been a *disagreeable* wife, have I? I don't want to go knowing you think badly of me. I've done everything for the best, always. Only, sometimes . . . well, it doesn't always work out the way I've wanted.'

'You've been a great old chum to me these last years, one of the best. And don't you go talking like that, about going. You want to keep cheerful, old duck. Enjoy every day as it comes. Doesn't do to let things get you down.'

'It's the children, see, Bertie. All along I've tried really hard to give them a good life. Only they don't seem . . . contented, like.'

'That Freda's a sour, ungrateful cow, if you want the truth. It isn't anything you or I've done makes her like that. It's her nature.'

'Oh, don't say that, dear. It was me having Ronnie upset her. She was such a nice little girl until he came along. A bit jealous, see. Because her little brother needed so much more looking after, being delicate, and he was such a dear little chap with his winning ways.'

Bertie had his own ideas about that, but he'd been this way before and he knew better than to disagree. The poor old doll was besotted with the boy. She'd go to the grave thinking he was God's gift to mankind, whatever shifty little tricks he played on her. Do anything for her Ronnie, Ma would.

'Bertie, would you do something for me? Something special?'

'What's that, then?'

'No; promise first.'

'All right. Got to please me old chum, haven't I? What'm I to do?'

'You remember that package I asked you to post? If any-one asks about it, just forget you ever saw it, will you?'

'What package is that, then?'

'Doesn't matter, dear... if you've forgotten already.'

Her voice faltered. She went on staring past him up at the ceiling. She really did look rotten, he thought, eventually drawing his hand free as her own relaxed with sleep. There was sweat on her forehead and her breath had a slightly sweet, autumny smell. But she was well under now, should have a good night. He'd tuck himself up on the sofa down-stairs, give her more room. And not have to hear that raspy snoring in her throat...

'ALL DONE FOR THE SAKE of dear Ronald,' said Mott bit-terly when the news came through. 'She wanted to be sure he'd be free to make a new beginning, with the nice, re-spectable girl he'd found. Take over the children, live happy ever after. Fairy tale stuff.'

Yeadings grunted. He was still hearing Bunter's soft Essex voice—'Poor woman—slowly dying over a matter of months, years maybe—she had to have a dream, had to be-lieve she could influence his future, leave the world a little better, as she saw it. And her world was Ronald, always had been. Spent herself at the end as she'd done all along, mak-ing things so easy for him that he never grew a backbone, believed there would always be an easy way out.'

'Whatever she did,' Yeadings said, 'she's beyond human justice now. It leaves us nothing to do but write up our re-ports, put in the statements from her husband and daugh-ter, and close the file. Two parallel files now, both complete: Penny Winter's and Anneke Vroom's.'

'And Gardner goes scot-free!' This was Beaumont, wanting all the ends tied up. 'He's a skunk of the lowest or-der, and we're left nothing we can pin on him. What a worthless shit! Not even much good as a con-man, fools himself more than the should-be suckers. The most his sort get clobbered with is arrears of maintenance. But his wife's conveniently killed and most of the debt's wiped out.' Beaumont jabbed a finger roofwards. 'If there's anyone up there, he's not on the side of Laura Norder.'

'Cool it, Skip,' Mott ordered.

'But how did the old woman do it?' Silver demanded.

Yeadings shook his head. 'She came out of coma long enough to answer questions her husband insisted on asking. He worked out the rest for himself.

'It seems that a fortnight or so earlier there were three mild cases of salmonella food poisoning around Colchester, quickly diagnosed and traced to source. All stocks of a single recipe of homemade pâté were removed from a small delicatessen store and the public warned.' He remembered that himself.

'Mrs Boulter had bought some and didn't declare it. She had meant at first to hand it in as instructed, but it lay for a while in the larder. She said she had no intention of using it, but I think it must have fascinated her, this small, ordinary packet with dangerous potential, a delicacy which she knew her ex-daughter-in-law couldn't resist. And she knew too that neither of the little girls would touch the stuff, even if they were given the chance.

'Eventually Ronald called in, and on an impulse to protect him, she wrapped it, using her rubber gloves, addressed it in block capitals, and asked her husband to drop it in the post. I don't suppose he even inquired what was in it, maybe thought it was some small article of Penny's or the children's that they'd left behind at their old house. He took it to work, and it went out with the plumbing catalogues and estimates, weighed and with the appropriate stamps on. They don't lick them, but use a damping pad, which is why the saliva test was negative. One of the office girls who comes from Harwich took all the mail back home with her on her free afternoon. That's how it came to be posted from there.

'Mrs Boulter didn't see herself as a killer. Obsessed by what she saw as her son's misfortunes, she "did it for the best", and having set the thing in motion left it to fate to decide the outcome. By the time it reached Penny the pâté was a time bomb. She noticed nothing amiss because of the preservatives and, feeling down, the girl had already been stuffing herself with mint chocolates. The dry biscuits must have helped it all stay down for a while, but in the early hours she awoke feeling ill, ran for the bathroom, vomited on the way, choked, fell, broke her neck. And that's where we came in, after little Ginny found her on the stairs and ran out into the road screaming for help.'

There was a short silence. A WPC looked round the door, said, 'Sir, for you,' and came across with a sheet of paper.

'So the case is closed,' Mott said quietly. 'Accidental death, they'll probably find at the resumed inquest. We don't have to exact revenge, do we?' His eyes were on Beaumont, challenging him. The DS said nothing, hunched and frowning at the floor.

'There's never any question of revenge,' Yeadings cautioned, looking up from his reading. 'But it's out of our hands now, once the reports are completed.'

He glanced back at Beaumont and felt a flicker of sympathy. The man's perky crust was pierced. This case had left its mark on him. Some personal frustration seemed to make him respond unusually to what the victims had suffered. But private, whatever it was.

Mott, too, had been affected by the other case: at present less the eager rugger forward. He had fallen short of his own standards of fair judgment. His first reaction to Paula's career needs and then his failure to see the Dutch girl as an equal human being had induced a new sense of inadequacy.

In his head Yeadings heard verses from Wordsworth's *She Was a Phantom of Delight*—

'A lovely apparition, sent

To be a moment's ornament...'—Mott had seen Anneke that far, but the deeper appreciation came too late—

'A being breathing thoughtful breath.
A traveller betwixt life and death.'

Well, the lad would be the better for the experience. They all mature with time, he told himself. And Rosemary Z, poor lass, picks up more honourable scars. Only I stay untouched, shuffling the papers. And now there's another to pass on to them.

He cleared his throat. 'You'll need to get your reports in sharpish. We've had a telex from Herts County force about a blue Ford Granada. Stopped for speeding, and the driver downed a Traffic man with what looked like an AK-47. Heading south, and licence details passed to us.

'It's just been spotted in a Datchet hotel car park. Datchet again, and linked with firearms. Maybe the schoolboys' homemade fireworks weren't the only cache there after all. The Support Unit's standing by. I want a stake-out set up...'